SONG OF THE SEA

DUCKIE MACK

ISBN: 9798356695025

Illustrations by Sheilkuroi

Cover Design, Interior Formatted, Chapter Headers
By Luke Parkes

CONTENT WARNING

Please note *Song of the Sea* depicts a character processing grief and the loss of a parent. I hope readers will find that I've handled this with sensitivity. However, I wished to include a note for anyone who may find this content triggering.

CHAPTER 1

CALDER

A whistle cut through the water. The distinctive cant was a signature meant for one being and one being only. Me. I was being summoned and everyone knew it. There was no way to hide or ignore the call. Even though I was the target, the sea carried it for all to hear.

I made a hole in the back of a plastic dog and filled it with sand to weigh it down, setting it on the shelf that jutted out of the rock between a winged horse and a soldier doll with moveable limbs. It was an odd collection for a twenty-three-year-old but they weirdly brought me comfort. Once I was certain the objects would stay where I left them, I darted out of my private haven before someone was sent to look for me.

Heads dipped in respect as I made my way quickly past others. *Fuck!* What did they want? Why did they call me in such a way? I would have seen them in a short time anyway, supper wasn't far off and we usually ate together. It must be official business. I racked through my memories as I tried to recall if there was anything pressing.

When I came to the threshold of the throne room, my arrival was announced. I rolled my eyes at the formality of it, but straightened my shoulders as I glided in. My parents weren't alone. I tried to read their expressions as I closed the distance to them. My father had the look he got when he was set on something and nothing would change his mind.

My mother was stoic, firm, and confident when it came to governing those under her. She was a strong female who was respected and admired, my father's equal in many ways, but in some she even surpassed him. My mother was tough on us. Turning wild children into respectable young royals was no easy feat, though we all felt her love carry through her actions. Currently, her chin was raised high, her lips pressed together in a thin line, the fidgeting of the large pearl ring on her finger the only sign that something was bothering her. This didn't bode well.

My father dismissed the others in the room and I felt a chill swirl around me. His long white-streaked salmon hair danced over his shoulders as he lifted his head while somehow looking down at me at the same time. He bore his pearl-encrusted crown that was woven into the threads of his hair. I bowed partially, understanding that the male before me wasn't currently my father; the one that taught us how to sneak around the palace or who played pranks on us, but my king.

His cant resonated deep and strong and without any doubt of the power that came with it. *Son*. The single note vibrated through me, making me feel like the fry I'd once been. I tried not to cower under it, but instead faced him eye to eye, or nearly. He had a few inches on me, but he carried himself higher than any other. As kings did.

Your duty has always been to serve our kingdom in whatever way is needed for the good of those in our care.

I stiffened, wishing to bite back a response, but managed to force a calm tone as I hummed back, *I understand, Your Majesty. It is my honor to serve.*

For just a moment, my father's eyes crinkled with pride, before his face shifted back to the stony one that the king wore. *Our worlds grow ever smaller, our resources fewer. We cannot continue on in the same way that things have been. But we don't have to face these changes alone. Other kingdoms are weak where we are strong, and the opposite is true as well. I grow weary of fighting for what we need. Lives are too precious to be wasted in war. I've met with King Katal who has proposed an arrangement. One that would help build trust where there hasn't been in the past.*

My mother worried her ring to the point where it looked as if she would twist her finger right from her hand.

What...what kind of arrangement? My heart beat wildly in my chest.

The arrangement is well...a union between our people.

My father rarely bumbled. Each cant, hum, click, or whistle was done with precision and certainty. Fear squeezed my chest at what he was holding back.

My mother looked between us. She stroked her hand down my father's arm, drawing his attention. Her gaze flicked up to which he indicated his agreement. He swam quickly out of the throne room, my mother charging after him. When I didn't immediately follow, she snapped out my name, before pushing upwards. Right. To the surface. Whatever they wanted to discuss, they wished to do so without anyone overhearing it. The sea held few secrets, instead, they flowed with the currents.

The pressure changed and shifted as we drew ever higher though it had little effect, our bodies were designed to adjust with ease. When I broke through the surface, I saw my father helping my mother sit upon an algae-covered rock.

Since we were no longer in the throne room, I pushed the expected formalities aside. "What aren't you telling me?" My voice always sounded so strange to my ears after not using it for some time.

My father cleared his throat as if needing to recall how to form the words to speak instead of through cantonation as under the water. When he started, he spoke slowly, "We discussed many options before landing on this one, I just want you to know. It was not my first choice, but King Katal was set on the idea and will not be appeased with anything else."

I turned my attention to my mother. "The more you don't tell me, the worse my imagination creates. Please tell me what is happening."

"Oh, Calder. My sweet boy. I hope you'll understand." She reached out and brushed her hand against my cheek. An action that felt strange with the air whispering around my skin.

"Calder, the king has asked for a marriage between our families." My father spoke, finding his voice once more. The words sounded caustic, harsh, the meaning struck me across the face.

"What? You can't be serious? He expects me to marry one of his daughters? I can't. You both know I could never be with a female. It is not in my nature. It wouldn't be fair to either of us."

My father had the nerve to look angry. I was the one who should be angry, had every right to be. "You think so little of me that I would see you in a marriage not fit for you?"

"I...what do you mean?"

"The king has daughters, it's true. But he has a son as well. One who holds interest in males as you do. That is the reason he sought us out for this. There are few choices for an equal match within the seas. The king wishes you to take his son's hand."

My jaw clenched. I shook my head in disbelief. They wanted me to marry this son. "Do I not get a choice in the matter? For all your stories and crooning of the love you two feel, I don't get a chance to find that?"

A tear formed in the corner of my mother's eye. Had we been underwater, she might have been able to hide it as saltwater met saltwater, but above the surface, there was no masking the drop on her otherwise dry face. It was strange to see such emotion from her. "You could grow to love him."

"And if I don't? You'll see me trapped in a loveless marriage...for what?"

"To protect our kingdom." My father's voice warbled, a mix between wordspeak and cantonation. Whether above or below, the message would have felt the same. This was done. It was already in motion.

It was all too much. My head throbbed. Whether from the brightness of the sun gleaming on the water or my fate that had been sealed, perhaps both. I couldn't stay there a second longer. I dove into the water, letting it cocoon around me, flicking my tail as hard as I could to put as much distance between myself and the decision made for me.

I went to my haven. The sea cave was the one place that was all my own. I had a room in the palace. But there were always others around, including my siblings who didn't seem to understand the concept of privacy. I swam in tight circles within the cave. And when that didn't work, I switched directions to go the other way. Back and forth as I replayed everything in my head. Hours passed as I stewed over it.

It wasn't fair. Why did it have to be me? I knew the answer, though. Of all the royal families among the seven kingdoms of the sea, it was only known that Katal's son and myself were attracted to males. Any other options would mean marrying someone who didn't bring the same kind of name or power with them. I curled my fingers into a fist and slammed it against the rock. The water cushioned most of the blow, but a wave cast out from the action, knocking over the items that had been on my shelf. I groaned as I swam to collect the sinking toys.

It wasn't my fault I was the eldest. I didn't choose that lot, it had been chosen for me. Sometimes, it felt as if my younger siblings thought that I could do whatever I wanted, but that was the furthest thing from the truth. What did I care for position and power? I loved my kingdom and I took my role seriously, but I didn't see the harm in finding a match for love and not for diplomacy. I looked down at the winged horse in my hand. How I wish I could mount the horse and let it fly me away.

With great care, I returned it to its spot. To some, these things would be trash or refuse. Either thrown away intentionally or lost to the ones that cared for these items, I couldn't know for sure. Many things found their way into the ocean. Most of them unpleasant and a big part of the problem that our kingdoms were currently facing. Poisons, pollution, waste, litter, all corrupting the pristine beauty that once covered most of the earth. With the human population growing and spreading across the surface, it left fewer and fewer untouched safe places for the beings that were housed within the seven seas.

It was no longer neighboring kingdoms that held the greatest threat, but the people who didn't even know of our existence. But an alliance? I hated to admit there was some merit, but I also didn't see how it could fix the problem at hand. How could my marriage stop the sands of time and human advancement?

I looked over the toys, picking up the soldier. I'd found it tangled in strings of plastic and seaweed and nearly bypassed it. But the legs of the figure had been sticking out and I had been so fascinated by them. I had legs of my own when I commanded them and took to the surface of a nearby island. But still, the legs on the doll called to me. No toy or statue below the surface ever depicted a bipedal form. Strength was seen in our tails and flukes, human forms were a weakness. I stroked a finger down the full length of the soldier's legs. Legs! A spark of an idea. Maybe...just maybe.

CHAPTER 2

DENVER

I woke to loud rapping on the door. Bolting upright, I swiped at my scruffy cheek to clear any drool that might have collected and flattened my hands over my black hair to make sure it wasn't too wild. The sides were trimmed short, but it was a little longer on top and had a tendency to flop the wrong way when I slept on it. There was looking purposefully messy and then there was fell-asleep-at-my-desk messy.

"Come in," I shouted, hoping it wouldn't be obvious just how out I had been.

"Sorry, Dennie, uh...Mr. Greene, a customer is asking to speak to the manager."

"Okay, thanks, Ella. I'll be right out." It was still

weird to be addressed as Mr. Greene. That had always been my father's name. Not mine. And Ella was my friend but she was trying to be careful to call me that in front of customers. I didn't like it. I stood and patted down my clothes to clear away any wrinkles that might have formed. Sliding the desk drawer open, I found a package of breath strips and popped one in my mouth. It melted on my tongue and the pop of peppermint helped wake me fully, making me feel a little fresher. I didn't normally have a habit of falling asleep at work, but I was doing the best I could.

I walked out to meet a little elderly woman. A flowered hat sat crooked on her head and she held a plastic box in her hands. She and her husband had been to our store off and on for years. I tried to recall her name, something like a chia pet. Ah, right. "Good afternoon, Mrs. Chibalsky. How can I help you today?"

"Oh, Denver, dear. Look at how grown you are. You're quite the handsome young man. Why...I have a granddaughter about your age."

I had to shut that down before it went any further, "Thank you, Mrs. Chibalsky. That's very kind. Tell me, what brings you to the store today?"

"I was hoping to talk to your father, dear. Is he

in?"

That pang in my chest that never fully went away flared up. I discreetly sucked in a deep breath, bolstering myself. "I'm sorry to inform you, but he passed away a few weeks ago. The shop is mine now."

She placed the box full of screws and washers on the counter and rested her hand on my arm. "Oh dear, I am so very sorry to hear that. He was a good man and he will be missed."

The platitudes. They were always well-meant and I appreciated the sentiment but they were still hard to receive. "Thank you. I appreciate that. Now, why don't you tell me what's going on and I'll see if I can help."

The old woman twiddled her thumbs. "Oh. Well, it seems rather unimportant now."

Everything did after the mention of a loss. But business was business and each customer was important to my dad. I pointed to the box that she brought in. "Were you looking for a set of washers to go with those?"

She grabbed the box and held it gingerly in her hands as if the bits and bobs it held within were precious. "These were my Earl's. He was a collector of sorts. He's passed too. And it's taken me some time to even be able to look at his workshop. It is filled with an assortment of tools and hardware from ages past. I cannot bear to simply throw it all out and I don't have the energy to do a garage sale. Earl often spoke of his conversations with your father and their shared interest in aged tools. I thought he might be interested in buying the whole lot of it. At least then I would know it would be shown the same appreciation that Earl held for it."

My dad *did* love old things. The more life they had seen, the better. He loved to imagine the stories attached to them, the hands that had held them, or the things that were constructed with them. I could see it was a difficult thing for her to ask. I hadn't touched my dad's stuff yet either. There were still papers stacked on the desk in the hardware shop's office that had been there before he died. I knew I had to go through it all. But it was too hard to think of touching papers that he had touched. Notes in his writing. If they stayed where they were I could almost pretend that he was still here. That he would walk through the door at any moment, the last month would all be a horrible nightmare that I would wake from.

I reached out and held her trembling hand in my own not entirely steady one. "It would be an honor."

I didn't know what I would do with it all, but I knew Dad would have taken them in a heartbeat. We made arrangements for me to come to her house and take as much as I could from her late husband's workshop. After she left, I slumped against the counter. Ella put her arm over my shoulder.

"Are you doing alright?" Her voice was soft, full of sympathy.

"Yeah. Some days are harder than others. And moments like that...bring it all back to the surface."

"You did the right thing, though. It's what Mr. Greene would have done. He'd be proud of you, you know." She squeezed my shoulder.

"Thanks," I murmured before pushing myself off of the counter. I retreated to the office once more. The sign my dad made and surprised me with a year ago sat in the back covered up. The "& Son" part of the Greene & Son Family Hardware Store sign peeked out beneath the cloth. We'd gone round and round that day.

He told me he had a surprise for me and his eyes sparkled with glee and anticipation. After we'd closed the shop that night, he pulled me into his office for the unveiling. So full of hope and joy and I met him with nothing but anger. It had always been his dream to run the shop together and eventually pass it down to me. But that had never been part of my plan. I had big dreams for my future. Dreams that included music and seeing the world. I'd lived every single day of my twenty-four years in the city of Bayview Park. I wanted to see what lay beyond it. To play my guitar and sing and do so much more than stay here and run the shop.

At the time I was too young and selfish to care that it hurt him when I told him I didn't want anything to do with the shop. That as soon as I could I was going to get out of town. Except...he got sick and I stayed. He died and I was trapped. Trapped with a shop that had been his child as much as I was. Beholden to run a business I didn't want. All while facing the very real lack of him within these walls each and every day. There wasn't a single spot in the building that he hadn't touched. And now it was all in my hands. My head dropped to my desk...*his* desk.

Each hour that passed seemed like three. Ella knew her stuff and Jimmy came on for the evening shift to help close up. With sympathetic looks and well wishes, I was able to leave the shop and draw a breath for the first time all day. It would get easier. It *had* to get easier.

When I got home I threw a frozen pasta dish in

the microwave. It was all the effort I could muster for food. There had been several times since my dad passed that I hadn't even thought about it, couldn't bring myself to care. But Ella noticed me looking sallow and made me promise to eat whatever I could manage. Little by little, I started eating more. But frozen meals were my max for the time being.

After I picked my way through the bowl, I pulled my guitar from its case. As soon as I felt the weight of it on my lap and my hand curled round the neck, the heaviness that seemed to follow me home peeled away slightly. My guitar was my comfort. It grounded me in ways nothing else seemed to. With the first strum, the sound vibrated through me, a lifeboat to keep me from sinking into the dark depths.

A bump against my elbow let me know that my faithful music partner was ready for me to play too. I reached over and scratched the black cat's head. Shadow was the first pet I'd had as an independent adult living on my own. He was a discount cat. Big, overweight, black. That was all he needed to be to get overlooked by everyone else at the shelter. They lowered his price hoping someone would take him and they wouldn't have to put him down. I hated the stigma with black cats. They were beautiful, regal, precious. This big bargain baby was meant to be mine.

Shadow had taken a little time to adjust to his new home. I had been worried about him being afraid of my guitar but once I played it the first time, he came right over. His little whiskers brushed against my arm and he meowed to the music. Such a sweet, music-loving chonk.

He pawed at the acoustic guitar, urging me to continue. Shadow was the best companion, especially during the last month. With all the condolences and sad eyes I got from everyone else, he simply loved me and didn't ask any questions. If I had to hear someone ask how I was doing one more time I might lose it.

I plucked and strummed out a tune as I hummed along. It was a piece I'd been working on for a while. The music was there, but the lyrics hadn't come yet. I had so many things I wanted to say, that I *needed* to say, but they seemed to get stuck in the back of my throat and wouldn't form. Until the words came I continued to play and let the music speak for me.

CHAPTER 3

CALDER

You could do worse. He is *handsome.* My brother sat in my room watching me. His expression baffled me. It was a mixture of regret, sorrow, and something else I couldn't quite place. It almost looked like jealousy, but I didn't know what he could possibly be jealous of. My impending forced marriage to a male I've met a few times in my life? Unlikely.

Since when do you talk about how handsome males are?

Marin shot me a look. *I have eyes, I can observe beings around me. I'm just saying at least he would be nice to look at.*

Marin was barely a year younger than me. His

hair was more of a copper tone compared to the crab red of mine. His tail a shade lighter than my dark blue. We'd always been close and I could see the hurt in his green eyes as I packed the few things I could take with me. Leaving him behind was one of the hardest parts about this, but I couldn't stay here and simply await my fate.

Handsome has nothing to do with it. I want to be able to choose my path and not have someone thrust on me that I didn't get to pick. In the end, I might not be able to anyway, but I had to try.

But that's it? You're just going to leave me? Leave us?

I crossed the space to him and held his face in my hands. *I'm sorry, but I have to do this. I have to try to show Father that there's more than one way for me to serve our kingdom. I am more than a hand in marriage for some prince.*

Of course, you are! But even married, you can show the difference you can make and you can do that here.

I cut him an exasperated look. We'd gone back and forth and I wouldn't be changing my mind.

His eyes lowered. *Just promise you'll come back.*

I will, Marin, I swear. Besides, I was under a firm vow to do so, one that could not be broken. I had one year. I didn't know what I could accomplish in that time, it hardly seemed like any. But if nothing else, it prolonged my sentence. That Father even met with King Katal on my behalf to set the date for the engagement was a surprise. It was clear my father thought my little venture was pointless, but the Kings both seemed satisfied with the date.

Before I left, I went to my haven. I grabbed the three toys and shoved them into the sewn seaweed bag that Coral, our younger sister, made for me. With a last glance around the space, I sighed and pushed off. I'd already had my goodbyes with my parents. And while my father tried not to show it, his tone carried concern and well-wishing for my journey. My mother put a pouch in my hand and squeezed it tight. She told me she wasn't sure how far it would go but hoped it would help me get settled.

With the strap across my chest and the bag on my back, I swam. Farther than I had ever gone on my own. The nearest islands wouldn't suffice for what I hoped to do. They were too small and disconnected from the world, which worked nicely for the beings in our kingdoms. We had a friendship with the people. An understanding. They respected the sea and everything in it and kept our secrets. And in return, we helped drive fish to their nets. It was symbiotic and should have been all the proof we needed that we could work *with* humans.

The world beyond those isolated isles carried a lot more to fear for merfolk. And I was heading straight into the unknown. Was going as far away as possible to get away from an arranged marriage a touch melodramatic? Perhaps. But it felt like the only way I could escape.

As time and fathoms passed by me, the sounds and scents changed. The vast sea around me a reminder of how very alone I was on this journey. Besides the few trinkets and coins from my mother, I carried a note written in my father's hand. It granted me permission and safe passage through any waters I would travel through. With contentious relationships between kingdoms in the past, a prince would be seen as an arm of the throne. Entering waters without permission could raise eyebrows and defenses. At the bottom was also a declaration that I was promised to Taneesh, son of Katal. I despised feeling like I was owned by someone, that I was not my own. I wished that I could tear that section off and cast it to the depths of the abyss.

But it was done for my protection. A promise

that two kingdoms would retaliate should anything happen to me. I kept it tucked away and hoped that no eyes would ever have to look upon it. The anger I felt only strengthened each swish of my fluke, propelling me closer to land and further from the politics of the sea.

Navigation became trickier as the water thickened with oils and fumes from ships. It grew harder and harder to breathe. I'd never been this close to heavily populated areas. We always kept a wide berth. Uncertainty swirled with the murky water around me. Seeing the pollution up close, perhaps my father was right. It was worse than I thought. Parasites, spreading and destroying all they touched. How could one year be enough to make a difference?

If a year was all I had left of freedom, I would do everything I could. I could spend this year back home under the weight of the impending engagement or I could use the time I had been gifted and make it matter. The deadline would come either way.

I surveyed my surroundings carefully. I knew I had to keep away from any boats as we had been told they had technology that lets them read the water for fish. When I was certain I wasn't near anything or anyone, I surfaced. Cautiously, I peeked up, my eyes barely above the water so as not to draw attention. When it seemed as if there was no one close enough to notice me, I raised myself higher so I could draw air into my lungs through my mouth. Normally, I could breathe underwater, but it was growing harder to do so with the filth that reached out as dark fingers stretching into the water.

I stayed as low to the surface as possible, trying to see what I could. It was difficult to focus my sight above water. There was something far away. Something big. It was hard to tell exactly but I could feel the vibrations churning and stirring beneath the water. A rhythmic pulse and churn that made everything tingle. A loud booming honk sounded and I covered my hands over my ears and ducked back under the water. My eyes slammed shut as I tried to recover from the overwhelming noise.

I swam deeper, as deep as I could, letting the whorl and whoosh of the tide comfort me. A lullaby that I had heard in my young fry days when we stayed nearer the shore as we learned how to control our shifts. I tried to let it envelop me. I drew in another deep breath, filtering the oxygen from the water, but it wasn't as satisfying or calming as it should have been. Not with the bite of pollution it was laced with. I needed to get to the shore and out of this corrupted zone of the sea.

With the greatest of caution, I wove my way to the least congested side of the shore. Far fewer boats to navigate around. Before I allowed myself to touch the dry sand, I closed my eyes and called within myself to pull my legs that remained tucked away. It had gotten easier over the years, though shifting while still in the water was quite difficult. There was a connection between our tails and the sea. The water called to us, drew the tail forward. When we were small, we were too weak to be able to keep it back. Any drop on our skin and the tail would come forth, even if we were ashore.

The battle waged within. What my body needed, what it craved, versus what I willed it to do. It always came with a singe of pain as legs pushed forth and separated, the tail subsiding. It felt so strange to feel the water flow between my legs, reaching places that it couldn't normally. Tickling, itching followed the shift, and...sinking. I kicked each foot separately in an awkward manner, working much harder than I had to with my fluke. But I only had to get a short distance before I could touch the seafloor as it ascended to the beach. I collapsed in the shallows under the immense effort. How humans managed to swim miles with these sticks attached was beyond me.

The sun bore down on my naked cock that was now revealed when it normally was protected within the sheath of my tail. I covered myself with my hands, feeling exposed to the elements. I lay there fully nude except for the strap across my chest, the hard plastic digging into my back. Sitting up, I twisted the bag around to open it.

Within it, I had a small bit of clothing made of a material that wasn't bogged down by water. I'd caught glimpses of men and women on the islands wearing something similar. I stuck my legs through the two smaller holes and managed to wiggle the slurpy material up and pulled them on over my soft ass. I patted the bouncy cheeks, enjoying how different they felt from my firm, hard tail. The black material reached just to the top of the crack that split them and covered everything in the front. Humans were shy with nudity. While my full legs were revealed to the crease in my thighs, I felt that at least I wouldn't get too strange of looks.

I stood and wobbled for only a moment but took in my surroundings. The waves crashed powerfully over the rocky shore, the reason why boats stayed away. I tried to judge the time of day by the position of the sun in the sky. It was almost directly overhead, blaring and blazing, much hotter than I was used to beneath the surface. A seagull cried out, the sound piercing my sensitive ears.

Further down the beach, I saw my first group of people. They had sticks and seemed to be stabbing into the sand. Curiosity got the better of me and I had to see what they were doing. Were they hunting for sand crabs? Or collecting kelp that washed ashore? I squinted, trying to focus, but looking through lenses that were designed to cut through water made it difficult. Everything was distorted and blurry.

I walked closer with my bag slung on my back, my bare feet balancing on stones and hot, shifting sand. My hair hung heavy on my head. Normally it floated around me weightlessly, but now I felt it slump over my shoulders. I grabbed a fist of the red locks and squeezed out some of the water to lighten it.

When I neared enough to see what the humans were up to, I sucked in a gasp with surprise. They carried two different kinds of sticks, some had pointed ends and others had claws. They would jab the pointy ones into paper on the sand, picking it up and dropping it in a large shiny bag. The clawed ones would open and close around pieces of trash, removing them from the beach.

They were...cleaning the beach? I didn't know they did that. With all the muck and stew that I swam through, it made the task ahead of me seem all the more daunting. I didn't expect to find humans putting in an effort to reverse what had been done. It gave me hope. Maybe this year wouldn't be a waste after all.

"Remind me why we're doing this again," I mumbled as I stabbed a used condom and shoved it into the bag with a grimace.

"Because you needed to get out of your apartment, out of the shop, and out of your head," Ella said, grabbing a dented soda can with her pickers.

"And of all the things we could have done, you chose this? And in August? The hottest month of the year?"

She stood and waved her hand over the beach. "Fresh air, sun shining, the smell of the sea. It's not all bad. Besides, doing something for others is a good way to step out of yourself and your funk. And believe me...you were getting funky."

"There's a lot of stuff I have to do, though."

"And it will still be there when you get back. Jimmy's covering the shop and it's rare we have time available together anymore." She pulled a face as if she regretted her words.

It was true though. When I wasn't stumbling around in a fog, I was trying to figure out all the back office stuff that I didn't realize needed doing. My dad had trained me on some of it, but I'd been reluctant before he got sick and then we ran out of time. Time was a fleeting thing, it could go like the lover you hoped would stay or it could linger like the obnoxious uncle that you prayed would leave.

And she was right. The work would keep. It was a beautiful day and it felt nice to be doing...something. An hour later, I stopped and stretched my back, looking over the part of the beach we had cleared and the lack of trash behind us compared to the bounty of trash ahead of us. At least there was a noticeable difference. It was small in the grand scheme of things, but there was a little less debris that would make it out to the ocean.

The August sun was beaming down, heat radiating through me. I took off my shirt to sop up the sweat on my forehead and the beads running down my neck. My skin burned with more than the sun's rays kissing my skin. I felt a presence, like someone watching me. I turned around and spotted a tall man with long red hair, practically incendiary. He was toned with broad shoulders and his waist tapered in to meet the tiny black speedo he wore.

"Fuuuck," I whispered.

Ella snapped her head in the direction I was looking. "Well, damn! I don't even like guys but that is one pretty man right there."

"Yeah. Gorgeous." He looked like he had walked right out of the sea, glistening and wet. I had the sudden urge to catch the water trailing down his ripped chest with my tongue.

"You're welcome." Ella nudged me.

I forced myself to pull my gaze away from the beautiful creature to look sidelong at my friend. "And how do you get credit for that exactly?"

"If you stayed home, you wouldn't have that guy appearing in your dreams tonight. So you're welcome." She looked all too smug.

I flicked my eyes back up. He looked straight at me or it seemed as if he did. But he didn't smile or give any indication that we were staring at each other. My skin heated once more as I realized I stood there with my shirt balled up in my hand. I wanted to stand as bold and sure as he did wearing nearly nothing, but I quickly threw my shirt back on. My skinny yet soft frame couldn't possibly compare to his lean, chiseled body.

When my shirt was in place, I looked again and he was gone. "Was he a mirage? Bigfoot? A Beachy Bigfoot? Is that a thing? Maybe I've been in the sun too long."

"If he was a mirage, I saw him too. In which case, I think we call it a day and get a drink."

"That's the best idea you've had all day." Everyone was wrapping up anyway. We turned in our pickers and pokers. With a glance over my shoulder only to find a complete lack of magical men on the beach, I sighed and followed Ella to her car.

We opted to return to the city, instead of hanging out at a beach bar. Ella said if we stayed, she wouldn't have been able to have a conversation with me, that I'd be too distracted looking for my dream guy. Even twenty miles away and with no logical reasoning whatsoever, I still found myself checking the men with long hair that would pass by. Besides seeing the striking hair and that hot body, I hadn't been close enough to see his face. Shame that.

Ella eventually had enough of trying to entertain me and decided it was time to find some entertainment for herself. After making sure I was okay to leave, she left me for the dance floor. It wasn't long before she was grinding against a raven-haired beauty with big boobs and a tank top that barely contained them. There was plenty of eye candy for me to enjoy there too, but nothing was holding my attention. I left my tip at the bar and waved to Ella as I walked out, knowing she would find her way into that girl's bed before too long.

Back at my apartment, I played a quick song for Shadow and gave him some treats. But when my head hit the pillow I was anything but tired. It was nice to get out of my rut for a little while. Most days consisted of going to the shop and home, that was about it. Today was the first time in the two months since my dad passed that I felt even remotely normal. But that brought its own pain too. The bad days were hard because I missed him and felt the hole where he should be. The good days were sometimes harder because I felt bad for *not* missing him or thinking about him.

I knew he wouldn't want me to be thinking about him every minute of every day, not if it hindered me from living. But knowing something and feeling it were two entirely different things. Ella had been right, though. I'd been spending too much time in my head and it was wearing on me. What I needed was a distraction.

I flipped over on my stomach and tucked my pillow under my chest, holding my phone in front of me. I did a google search for men with red hair. A wide variety of pictures popped up, with various shades of red and different styles. Did I really think I would find him like that?

With that body though...he looked like an athlete, like an Olympic swimmer. On a whim, I searched for Olympians with red hair. No such luck, though I lingered a little longer on some of the pictures while I scrolled. Not him, but not bad.

I closed my eyes and pictured his tortilla chip-shaped body. Broad shoulders, tight pecs, trim waist. He seemed inhuman. It had to be the sun. No way a guy like that would be standing around without a bunch of followers or cameras around him.

I imagined the slow path of a water droplet rolling over that hard chest or his ripped abs. I put my phone on the other pillow as I thought of what the firm body would feel like beneath my tongue.

Mmmm. I rolled to my back and pulled my shorts down, freeing my hardening cock. Blindly, I reached into the nightstand drawer and pulled out a tube of lube. I didn't always use it on myself, but right now, I wanted to sink into the moment. I slicked myself, gripping and pumping.

I would lick my way down, exploring every inch that had been covered by that small speedo. Every...single...inch. I would swallow him as he tasted of saltwater and heaven. He would grab me in his strong arms, lifting me as though I weighed nothing. He would flip me over and I would feel his long hair draping over my back as he lowered himself down.

My knees widened and my hips lifted as I stroked faster. When I imagined his tongue tracing between my cheeks, circling, teasing, it was enough to push me over the edge. The spurts that hit my chest weren't my own. In my fantasy, they were his as I brought this god of a man to pleasure. That thought alone was enough to prolong the orgasm. I groaned loudly.

Shadow hopped up trying to stand on my chest. I batted him away with my clean hand. "Read the room, dude," I grumbled. He rarely wanted to cuddle, but when he did, it was always at the least convenient time.

I sighed loudly and reluctantly went to the

bathroom to clean myself up. It would have been much nicer to stay in bed and snuggle against a hard chest. When I returned, I landed with a flop. I needed to get laid, when I was actually in a state of mind to appreciate it. If a two-minute sighting of a possibly not real person was enough to make my toes curl, it might be time for me to find someone. A real, actual person that I could touch and who could touch me. In the meantime, Beachy Bigfoot served a purpose in redirecting my thoughts and knocking me out, so there was that.

I felt slightly renewed the next morning when I pulled in front of Mrs. Chibalsky's house. She had the garage open and even from here, I could see that it was full to nearly overflowing. I was grateful I'd managed to get some sleep because this was looking to be a long day.

The door opened and the old woman greeted me, "Good morning Denver. It's so good of you to come."

"Good morning, Mrs. Chibalsky. It's my pleasure, really." Maybe not how I would choose to spend my day off, but like the beach clean-up, it was better to be doing something than the nothing that consumed me for so long.

"Come in, come in. Would you like some tea or

lemonade?"

"Lemonade sounds great, thank you."

I followed her in and noticed the air carried a scent of mothballs. The living room had two recliner chairs, both with knit afghans folded over the backs. A yellow sofa sat across from them. Lots of bright colors in the array of furniture. Though everything looked and smelled old, it had a welcoming feel. Nostalgic in a way, which was strange since my grandparents' house was nothing like this.

Mrs. Chibalsky's hands shook as she poured the lemonade into a glass. I wanted to step in and do it for her, but she seemed rather pleased to do it. I thanked her when she handed it to me.

When I took a drink I had to school my expression to keep from showing how sweet it was. Cloyingly so. But I continued to sip as she led me to the garage. When she flicked on the light, shadows danced across her face. A glint of hope was followed immediately by sorrow.

"Sometimes, I think Earl will be standing there at his workbench, tinkering with a clock or faucet, or some old thing that didn't need fixing." She chuckled.

"I understand. There are times I walk into the store and expect my father to come out of his office listing off the deliveries that would be arriving that day."

She patted my hand, a simple action, but I was grateful for the lack of sympathetic words that accompanied it. "I should probably leave you to it. You know what you're looking at much more than I do."

"I know a little." I shrugged. "What exactly do you want me to go through?"

The old woman's eyes misted. "Can you take all of it? Only...can you leave me any keys you find? Earl had a particular fondness for them and I think I should like to keep those."

She left me in the garage with the door open, sunlight filtering in and the bulbs glowing above. Where did I even start? Though I wore a t-shirt with the store's logo on it, I rolled up my imaginary sleeves. "Time to get to work."

A couple of hours later, I had box after box loaded into my truck. It was a mixture of gently used tools that could be sold off—Mrs. Chibalsky had said as much—and the plethora of outdated and rusted bits, screws, nails, handles, drawer pulls, knobs. These were the things Dad would have loved. He would have oohed and awed over each drawer opened as they revealed more and more treasures.

I still didn't know what I would do with it all, but my taking them was a kindness to the old widow. I took the wooden box that I had filled with every key I found and brought it into the house. Mrs. Chibalsky was sitting in the recliner, knitting shakily. I presented the box to her and tears began to roll down her cheeks. She set her needles aside and took a handkerchief out of her sleeve, dabbing her cheeks. She patted the arm of the chair beside her, indicating for me to sit.

"Forgive me, I know it seems silly crying over keys that don't go to anything. But he was everything to me. And this is a reminder that he is still with me. Tell me, Denver. Do you have a special young lady in your life?"

I cleared my throat, debating whether to correct her or not. Mrs. Chibalsky wasn't family, the specifics didn't matter. "No, ma'am. There's no young lady."

She studied me, "A young man, perhaps?"

I felt one side of my lip tug up. "Not yet. But perhaps one day."

She smiled knowingly, "There are so few things that matter when you look back. At the end of the day having someone to share your life with, to give of yourself to, and to be loved wholly, that's all that matters. Not who they are or what kind of package they come in."

Her words surprised me as much as they touched me. So often the older generation was cast as people who were stuck in the past. Looking around her mothball-scented house and after hours of rifling through antique hardware, I would have agreed. But we didn't give them nearly enough credit for the experiences that shaped them.

"Thank you. That's nice to hear."

The widow's eyes crinkled. "Denver, dear, make me a promise."

I arched a brow, unsure of where she was going. "What's that?"

"Don't lose yourself to your grief and the responsibility you have placed on yourself. You're too young to miss out on living and loving. I'm old. I've lived a long and happy life. I grieve, but it is a comfort in a way too. I have a lifetime of memories with the man I love. He was with me through all of it. But you are only just starting out. You don't have those memories to wrap around you and rest in. Your father wouldn't want you to stop living. And he would want you to follow your passion and to find a partner who will cherish you. It's not good for a man to be alone. I want you to promise me right here and now, that you will follow your heart, wherever and to *whomever,* it leads you."

Ella tried to tell me the same thing many times, but I hadn't been ready to hear it. And it meant something different coming from a woman who knew the pain of loss. My chest ached and my throat tightened. I knew in my heart that she was right. Dad wouldn't want me drowning and hiding away. He would want every good thing life could offer me.

I drew a deep breath and with the greatest effort I said, "I promise." And I meant it. I didn't know what that would look like yet or what I would need to do but I wanted a life outside of the shop. And someone to share it with.

CHAPTER 5

CALDER

It had taken a few weeks to get myself situated, longer than I hoped. I was hyper-aware of every dawn. Each day that ended brought me closer to the deadline. I wished I had been granted more time. I had completely overestimated how easy it would be to find shelter and a path.

Clothes had been the first issue. The small suit I dressed in after shifting was fine while I was near the beach. Once I got further from the sea, I started hearing whispered comments about how inappropriately I was dressed. Comments they likely assumed I wouldn't hear. But I did. I heard a lot. Too much. Everything was so loud. The cars, the people, noise surrounded me and it was all I could do not to walk around with my hands clasped over my ears.

I had come a long way since that first day. The coins that had been salvaged from ancient shipwrecks my mother had given me held great value. With a little help, I'd been able to find clothes and a place to stay for the night. I spent days observing people in everything they did. How they walked, what they did, where they went, how they interacted. More and more I saw humans walking around with ear coverings. At first, I wondered if the noise of the city was too much for them too. But when I asked a young girl about them, she let me hear the music that was coming from them. Music unlike I'd ever heard.

"Is there always music in them?" I asked.

She looked at me strangely before showing me a phone that controlled it. "Some people use them for noise-cancelation too, which is good if you have a meeting or playing a game or something."

Noise-canceling. That sounded perfect. I needed to do something because I was having a hard time concentrating. Everything seemed to be made of sound and it drained me of energy. As soon as I got a pair of headphones and slipped them on, I breathed a sigh of relief. I could still hear, but it muffled a majority of the din. I wore them everywhere.

What came next were glasses. Everything was fuzzy. My eyes were adapted to the sea and the distortion that water caused. But on land, nothing was the same. If I was going to learn how to help my kingdom, I would need to be able to see clearly. Many humans wore lenses over their eyes and I'd overheard enough conversations to understand that those helped with vision. After inquiring about how to get them, I learned that a doctor would have to recommend them. That wasn't something I could risk. Under examination, they would be able to see how different my eyes were, quite distinctive compared to human eyes. Would it reveal who I was?

No. It was too dangerous. I couldn't let myself be known. That was the one thing my parents impressed upon me above all else. Humans were known for dissecting or destroying anything they thought was different. I would *not* become an experiment. As much as I didn't want to return to a life that wasn't my own, that would be a far worse fate.

Not risking a doctor, I did something I regretted even for a moment. A pair of glasses removed, sat beside a man on a bench while he was talking on the phone. He was distracted and I was desperate. I walked by and snagged them, leaving one of the ancient coins in its place as payment. I hoped he would forgive the exchange if he knew how much I needed them.

Once my vision and hearing were under control, I was able to focus on what I needed to do. I had been staying in a hotel for the first week or so, but that wouldn't work in the long run. I needed privacy and couldn't have people knowing my comings and goings. Besides it was maddeningly loud at night with people walking about, doors opening and closing at all hours.

For as loud as humans were and as destructive as they could be, I had met several nice ones too. Ones that seemed willing to help someone they didn't know. And before too long I managed to secure a small place of my own. It was much smaller than my room back at the palace, which now seemed worlds away, but it had enough to meet my needs. The owner apologized when he said there was no shower. I didn't care much for the concept anyway. Why would you want to only get a *little* wet? It would be torture, the worst tease. Making my tail cry with the need to be released, but not being able to stay upright if it did.

The bath worked well for sleeping too. I had hardly rested since coming on land. The headphones weren't comfortable and didn't stay in place when I laid down. The beds felt weird, hard, stagnant. I missed the water, the constant movement of it, the way it flowed over me. Each night I filled the tub and sank into it, my ears beneath the surface, letting my tail unfurl. It was strange hearing such quiet in the water without the sounds of the ocean and the creatures and beings that lived within. But the beat of my heart thrummed, a constant pulsing whirl. The repetitive sound and the vibration in the water were soothing compared to everything else in the human world.

I dipped even lower into the water, my face under entirely. I missed home. I wasn't ready to go back, but I missed it nonetheless. I canted softly, a song that my mother would sing for us when we were little. The sound bounced off the metal of the tub, echoing back to me. It was strange and jarring. In the ocean, the sound would be carried out far from where it began, not trapped and pinging around me. I gave up the cantonation since it wasn't relaxing like I hoped it would be. Instead, I tried to imagine it and hear it in my memories. I stayed in the tub all night, not caring that the water was cold. I was built for the temperatures of the depths, my most sensitive parts covered and protected by the thick skin of my tail.

I soon began my search for knowledge at a library. A building that seemed to house all the knowledge man had collected. It didn't seem all that big, considering how many centuries humans had been recording events through written word. I was most interested in books on the sea. I found myself shaking my head at some of the explanations they gave of animal communication and behavior. It was fascinating, though, to see them explain the movements of water and the distance it covered.

When I got to a book about the dangers of pollution, my chest ached. Each picture of a turtle's shell growing around the plastic that entangled it or the birds who were blackened with oil was horrifying. Humans were aware of the damage they caused and yet it continued to grow worse. How could that be? I took the book to show the librarian.

"I need to know more about this." I pointed hard at the page that showed a plastic ring around a penguin's neck. I tried but failed to hide the anger bubbling up in me.

The woman with a gray streak through her walrus brown hair looked at the page and then back at me. "More about what, precisely? The penguin, the pollution, plastics?"

"All of it."

"Listen, hun. If you pick one, I can point you to specific books. Otherwise, you're going to have a whole heap to look through."

"I don't mind, I have time." Well, not really, but the reading part was easy, despite the strain I felt in my eyes as I forced them to concentrate on the small letters. Each human language was derived from the same base roots as our ancient written one. With all the things the sea brought us, we had gained an understanding of many languages. What I didn't know, I learned easily, even though my eyes fought me over it.

"Have you tried looking online? That will be easier if you're not set on one thing in particular."

"On. Line?" I heard the term in passing, but I didn't understand what they were talking about.

The woman arched her brow and tilted her head, studying me. "Where did you come from?"

"I lived on a small island before I moved here." The lie came easier than it used to. It still sat sour on my tongue though. I knew enough of the islands and the people that lived on them that everyone I'd met so far believed my story readily.

"Okay. Right. Well, let's get you set up on a

computer and I'll show you what to do."

The woman led me to a desk that had a screen on it. She gave me a brief run-through of how to use it.

"And I can write anything I want in this box and it will find it for me?" I asked with awe.

"Yup, that's right. Why don't you give it a go?"

I typed *ocean*. The woman chuckled beside me. "You may want to be a little more specific than that. Look. See, it shows millions of results."

Millions of things about the ocean? It boggled my mind. I couldn't possibly read a million things in a year.

I added the word *trash* to the search and the number went down by half. Pictures and articles showed something called, "Trash Island?"

"Terrible, isn't it? Are you interested in environmental studies? We need some big brains working to figure out how to clean up our oceans."

"Environmental studies? What is that?"

She snickered and pointed at the computer. "Look it up."

I did just that. I stayed on the computer until the librarian told me it was time to close. I spent hours reading. Somehow it made me feel simultaneously closer to a solution *and* further away. Some humans acknowledged the problem and were working on it, but just as many seemed to fight against it. I couldn't understand why anyone would try to stop the healing of the earth and the oceans. A few big corporations appeared over and over again throughout my search, Cal Chem was one of them.

"Can I use the computer again?" I asked the woman as she escorted me to the exit.

"Of course, hun. You are welcome to use them anytime, as long as there's one available. Though if it's busy, we do have a time limit to make it fair for others. But if you're able to, some laptops are pretty inexpensive and then you could use it anywhere without waiting on someone."

I dipped my head, "Thank you, you have been most helpful."

The coins my mother had given me had lasted longer than I thought they would. Apparently, collectors went crazy for ancient monies. That they were rusted and corroded seemed to add to the interest in them. After three months on land with human responsibilities, a home and everything I needed, I'd used the last of the coins. It was time for me to figure out how to earn money, something I'd never had to think about before. Few options seemed tolerable.

Too noisy, too boring, too much sitting still. I already had enough sitting with my studies. I was used to moving constantly, slight flicks of my fluke, minute motions with my arms. Always adjusting to the flow of the water.

When I wasn't studying from home, I would take my laptop to either the library or if it was after hours, to a coffee shop. It was quiet, mostly. Some people conducted meetings there or get-togethers with friends or family. But more often it was others like myself, with a computer, keeping to themselves. They had music playing in the speakers, but they kept it more mellow and quiet, much less clangy and intrusive than other places. There was a sign in the window stating that they were hiring.

I didn't know much about a service job, or *any* job, for that matter. Things were much different above the surface. I doubted I could join hunting parties or scavenge or meet with diplomats, though that was something that I thought of doing. If I could reach the people making decisions and plead my case for saving the ocean, perhaps change could take place. But I had seen too many videos online of politicians and powerful people dismissing those who brought valid arguments. Protestors that waved signs outside of Cal Chem about toxic waste were rounded up and arrested instead of listened to. It was often said that they lined the pockets of those in charge to keep them out of trouble.

Brushing my hands over my pants, I straightened and walked up to the manager. I'd interacted with him a time or two and he seemed nice enough. His eyes met mine with a kind expression.

"Welcome back, Calder. How can I help you?"

"Mr. Robertson," I held out my hand and he took it. "I'm not really sure the right way to go about this, but I'm looking for a job and you have a sign saying that you're hiring."

He smiled. "I am, indeed. Why don't you come sit down with me and we'll talk."

He led me to a table far enough away from the other patrons to provide some privacy. Before we started, he pointed to my headphones. "Would you like to take those off?"

I'd never come in without them and wore them everywhere. It was cumbersome and I hated the weight of them on my head, but the noise without them was far worse. I once tried the smaller in-ear devices I saw people wear, but they hurt the sensitive cilia in my ears. "If it's alright, sir, I would much prefer to keep them on. I have auditory sensitivities and too much sound makes it difficult for me to focus. But I can hear you just fine with these on."

Mr. Robertson dipped his head in understanding and folded his hands in front of him. "Alright. Calder, why don't you tell me a little about yourself?"

"I come from a small island, the first of my family to travel to the mainland."

"Really? What brought you so far from home?" He seemed intrigued. I was sure it wasn't a story he heard too often.

"I've been pursuing environmental studies."

"Oh? And what sparked your interest in that area?"

"I am trying to make a difference in the health and safety of our oceans. As someone whose life and family's lives depend on the sea, it is important to me." It was the truth, though maybe to a different extreme than others might imagine.

The manager studied me, his fingers tapping together. "That's very commendable. It's not easy to step out of what you're used to, especially on your own. What kind of experience do you have?"

Hunting, leading, bargaining, politics. None of these things would matter and they would bring about more questions than I wanted to answer. "I'm afraid I don't really have any, sir. But I am willing to learn."

"You seem like a respectful young man and you're in here regularly, working on your studies, I assume?" I nodded in agreement and he continued, "Are you aware that we host open mic nights and have musicians play sometimes?"

I was aware and knew to avoid coming on those nights. "I am."

"Most of the time, it's pretty quiet here. Though we do have equipment that can be loud. And it can, on occasion, be noisy and crowded. I want to be respectful of your sensitivities, but I also need to know if you would be able to cope with the environment we have here. I need more help in the evenings but I don't want it to be uncomfortable for you, I only want to set you up for success. If that won't work for you, I can find something else that will."

In the three months that I had been walking among humans, I had gotten all sorts of different reactions to the headphones I wore. It had been life-changing when I first discovered that they would help cancel out a lot of the noise around me. Some people thought I was rude and gave me dirty looks, others seemed to think I was a fool and tried to take advantage of me. But this was the first time I had someone accept it for what it was and wanted to make things easier for me. I liked this Mr. Robertson, he seemed like a good human.

"That is very kind of you. If you don't have a problem with me wearing these, then I can tolerate it just fine."

"Okay. Great. I think we can give this a shot. Welcome aboard, Calder."

I shook his hand, "Thank you for the opportunity."

Ella was practically pushing me out of the store. "Go on. Go. Everything is fine here and you need to give yourself time for a mini panic before you collect yourself and be the badass I know you are."

Mini-panic? It might be a full-blown panic. Did I have time for *that*? I grabbed my jacket as she herded me to the door. "I don't know if I can do this."

"You can and you will. I'm sending spies and I'm anticipating a full blow by blow. No backing out, I will know. And if you do, I will kick your ass."

"You can be a little intense sometimes, you know that?"

Ella grinned wickedly. "Damn straight."

"You sure you're okay here?"

"I'm fiiine. Besides out of the two of us, which one is the scary bitch?"

I looked down at my five foot eight, one hundred forty-five pound frame and shrugged. "It's definitely not me. Okay. I'm going. For reals. Wait. Scarf or no scarf?" I held out the thick cashmere scarf I bought on a whim one day. It felt like something a musician might wear. A statement piece. Though I had my hat as well.

"No scarf. You'll get hot on stage and be miserable and fidget. Now, no more dawdling, get!" Ella yanked the scarf from my hand and closed the door after me, wiggling her fingers at me. Despite the cold, January night, she was right, it probably would bother me on stage. I used one in the past, but I was a baby musician and full of nerves. I fidgeted on stage, whether from stepping out of my comfort zone or from being too warm, I didn't know. But why add an extra problem I didn't need? I shook my head. Okay. I was doing this. When I got in my truck, my hands squeezed tight around the steering wheel as I tried to convince myself to go. I blew out a deep breath. I could do this.

The thirty-minute drive was enough time for me

to thoroughly warm up my voice and run through the set in my head. I knew it backwards and forwards. It wasn't the music I was nervous about. It was performing in front of a crowd again. I hadn't done it since my dad had gotten sick and then all focus shifted to him and after he passed, the store. He had been gone for five months now. It had gotten easier, but it did still sneak up sometimes. Like tonight. As excited as I was to sing again, the last time I was in front of an audience, my dad had been in it. I was currently channeling my grief into anxiety, not sure if that was better, but it drew my attention away from the hole in my chest.

What if I choked in front of a room full of people? What if I choked and it went viral and it ruined any future bookings? What if no one liked it? I knew with my style, I was never going to be a pop star or rock idol like Crow. Ella once insisted I go with her to see her favorite queer band, Crow's Nest. They were good, but too loud and rowdy for my taste. That wasn't me.

I glanced around, trying to decide if Ella had someone here watching. But whether she did or not, I needed to do this. For myself. I needed to know if I could or if it was time to let the dream go. Maybe I would only play for Shadow, he seemed pretty content with his concerts for one.

After grabbing my guitar case from the trunk, I made my way to the back door of the Beanwater Brew. It was one of the few places nearby that supported indie artists, poets, and musicians. I sent a recording to each one and Beanwater had been the first to respond, inviting me to play. It seemed like the perfect fit. It was a mellow environment. Customers didn't come expecting their faces to get melted off but for a relaxing evening out where they could enjoy some nice music and still be able to talk to each other. That was much more my speed.

My favorite black pork pie hat covered my brown hair. It had a brim that circled it and a round, flat crown instead of a pointed one like a fedora. A red ribbon wound around it and a folded piece of paper was tucked under the band. The paper had been there since the first time I played outside my house. I'd been so nervous that my dad told me to put something in my hat that would give me strength. When I didn't know what to put, he did it for me. A good luck charm of sorts, my magic feather.

That hat had seen me through a lot and was the most important article of clothing I owned. The rest of my outfit may have been a bit cliche but I hoped the loose v-neck and skinny black jeans made the audience feel like I'd been doing this for a while. I had a few gigs back when I was playing more in a very similar environment, but with the loss of time in between, it felt new all over again.

A single stool and a microphone sat on stage. I wouldn't be plugging in my guitar, it was an acoustic set and the place wasn't that big. As I adjusted the mic, all eyes were on me. I lowered my head, my hat tilting and shielding my face, giving me the illusion of privacy as I collected myself.

You can do this, Den. I positioned my fingers on the frets. My wrist was loose, the pick between thumb and forefinger held lightly so it could dance over the strings easily. One slow strum down and I lifted my head. I was ready.

My right hand started moving on its own; down, down, up, down, down. Over and over as I changed chords with my left hand. One more bar for the intro, I hummed along. Then I started singing.

The notes, the music, the words, they were my own. And hearing them come together and poured out to a room full of people lifted my heart with it. It was healing, cathartic. With each strum, I was reminded of how right this felt. The doubt fell away as every cell in my body settled as if I was made for exactly this.

Once I found my groove, my words were sure and strong. I looked around the Beanwater and was pleased to find most of the patrons had their eyes glued to me, their conversations stopped. I had been told that I might be nothing more than background music, but this was different. I held their attention. And when my song was done, claps rang out around the room.

I dipped my head in thanks and moved right into my second song. I had twelve total for the night. A variety of folk-style songs that ranged from light and cheery to a little sadder and more heartfelt.

A tall server carried a tray full of teas and coffees, delivering them to their owners. He wore thick glasses and headphones over his ears. With the lighting on me, it was hard to tell the color of his hair, an auburn perhaps. It must have been long as it was wrapped in a tight bun at the back of his head. Something about him drew my attention and occasionally, I would catch him staring at me.

I mean, I was on stage, *everyone* was staring at me. It was probably wishful thinking. Tall, lean, he moved with grace. It was hard to tell what he looked like from stage with the glasses he wore and his hair up. A sense of recognition rumbled in my gut, I wasn't sure why. I'd only been to the Beanwater a few times in the past and had never seen him here before. I would have noticed.

Internally, I smacked my head, trying to focus. Tonight was for me. But having someone interested in me, whether real or imagined, felt nice. I hadn't been with anyone since the quick fuck I'd had trying to escape reality when my dad died. It ended with me in a puddle of snot and tears and the guy patting me awkwardly before gathering his stuff and leaving. It was not a great moment.

But this...here, now, playing my music, feeling nearly whole again, it was a *really* great moment. Almost magical. I silently thanked Ella for giving me the push I needed, the old widow too. I might not have gotten here without her encouragement to keep working towards my dreams.

The final song was one I had gone back and forth on. I wrote it through the pain in my heart and the hole in my life. Words that had been stuck inside me with nowhere to go. They had been a cyclone, swirling and clanging around within me, needing release. The words were a wound, festering and seeping, until I finally managed to get them out. It was my hardest song to sing, but the one that meant the most to me. Maybe it was a bad idea to end my set with my most personal one, but I also didn't know if I would be able to continue after. So I either ended with it or didn't do it at all.

I bolstered myself and strummed. I had to do this, even if it was the only time I ever did. I needed to get it out. Through lyrical prose, I sang of a person holding a child's hand, of hanging ornaments, of learning to drive. A life lived and the love that had been there throughout. I thought of my magic feather, the folded note, and poured my heart into it.

The entire place had gone completely silent. Every person stopped moving, all leaning in a little closer, wanting to be nearer to every breath and syncopation. I took a quick glance and saw the slim, muscled server standing completely still. The headphones that he had worn through the entire set now circled his neck as he watched me with an intensity that made it feel as if we were the only two in the room. I had to pull my eyes away or I might not have been able to finish with the lump that was forming in the back of my throat.

When I was done, the quiet that had taken hold of the room remained for a minute before the bonds broke on the audience and they stood from their seats, clapping and cheering. My eyes welled, but I refused to let the tears fall. I rose from my stool and bowed. Another round of applause. It was incredible. I had forgotten exactly how this felt. Except, I had never had a response like the one I was now getting.

I chanced a glance sideways, watching the server who had his headphones back in place over his ears and was quickly making his way back to the counter. Strange. It felt like he was retreating or running away. Had I imagined that moment when it seemed time stood still between us?

"Thank you. Once again, I'm Denver Greene. You've been a wonderful audience." I bowed slightly once more and walked off the small stage.

The manager met me and shook my hand. "That was truly remarkable. I'm not ashamed to say you had me tearing up a little. Especially with that last song."

"That's very kind of you to say. Thank you for giving me the opportunity to play tonight." I wasn't quite sure what to say. Singing to a roomful of people was fine, receiving praise from an individual always felt awkward.

"I hope it's not a one-time thing. We'd love to have you come back if you're willing. It might not be much but I can work out something to give you a cut of the cover charge, which is something we would consider doing if there is enough interest."

I would play for free to have another night like tonight, but eventually being a paid musician was what I hoped for. It would be a start, at least. "Yes, we can work something out. I'd love to return."

Movement caught my eye over the manager's shoulder. I saw the server collecting empty glasses and mugs. The manager noticed my attention drift and turned around to see what I was looking at.

"Music is really powerful," he said.

I turned back to him, not sure where he was going with that statement. "Yes, I agree. It's gotten me through a lot."

"Yeah. But see him?" He indicated towards the server I'd been watching all night as if I could possibly miss the intriguing man.

"Yeah?"

"He's been working here for a couple months and a customer a little longer. But that last song...that was the first time I've ever seen him take his headphones off." He smiled with awe and patted my shoulder. "I'll be in touch and we'll work out a schedule. If you want anything, a drink or a dessert, it's on the house."

"Ok, sounds great. Thanks."

His words played back to me. What did that mean? Why did he wear headphones all the time? What about my song had him taking them off? Why did he flee after? How could I leave now, knowing that? Maybe I *did* need a dessert.

I had to busy myself or I wasn't sure what I might do. Any task I could do to keep my mind and my body in motion, I did. This wasn't the first time I'd worked during a performance. I usually tried to tune them out and focus on the job.

I tried time and again, but the vibrations coming out of the musician on stage hit me in a way I hadn't felt in a while, or ever. It was as if I were underwater and felt the cantonations, each song, hum, and chord filling my body and telling me the meaning. I felt *everything* from him. It was entrancing. Then he sang his last song and the waves of grief and love that rippled out of him slammed into my chest as if a spear had been thrust into me, knocking the wind from my lungs. I had to hear even the most minute sounds that came from him. It sang to me. *He* sang to me. For beings that communicated through sound and vibration, that felt as much as we heard, it was almost overwhelming.

I had the urge to run to him and hold him in my arms to give him comfort while equally wishing to hear him continue singing. Or playing guitar. Or whatever sound I could get him to make, just to feel him as deeply as I did now. In the stories my mother told me of her love for my father, a song was what had bound them together. A cant that aligned their hearts to sing as one. That was what I had always hoped for. A heartsong. I knew that it wasn't something that could be forced. If I married Taneesh, I might spend a lifetime with song never completed, only half the notes. It would be empty and unbalanced.

After Mr. Robertson finished speaking with him, the musician took a seat closer to the counter where I was trying to clean and keep busy. The Beanwater was clearing out and most of the people that had come for the show left shortly after he finished.

"Calder?"

"Yes, sir?"

"Get Mr. Greene whatever he wants, free of charge." Lee pointed at the musician I was trying to keep away from.

"Of course." My pulse kicked up and my palms sweated. There went my plan to keep distance between us.

With notepad in hand, I went to his table. I didn't usually need to write down orders. Living with great beasts and needing to hunt for our meals, I was able to process a lot of information quickly. It was vital. I might not hunt regularly, we had others that did that for the royal family. Though we often accompanied the hunters as a show of unity and to keep our own skills trained. Being able to note every swipe of a tail, every glint, every bubble, or change around you made keeping track of orders a breeze. My ancestors would cringe to know how my skills were being used now.

"Hi, what can I get for you?" I stared at the paper instead of looking at him, trying to keep my focus or I might lose it altogether.

"Your hair is red." Mr. Greene said with a strange tone, but hearing his voice so close and directed at me, even muffled, sent a shiver through me. That and the unexpected statement.

I flicked my eyes up to catch him studying me. The way he looked at me had me feeling something I wasn't sure what to do with. Wanted? Yes. Wanting? *Fuck, yes.* What did he say? Right, hair. "Yes. It is."

"I couldn't tell before, but now that we're closer, it's like *really* red."

"Uh. Yes. It's natural." I overheard people talking about hair color a lot and that was something they always seemed to want to know.

Mr. Greene gave me a crooked smile. "It's really nice."

"Thank you," I said casually, pretending those simple words didn't stir strange feelings within me. "Would you like something to drink? I recommend the hazelnut mocha. Though at this time of night, you may prefer the decaf version."

"Sure, that sounds perfect. And I think I'll get the double chocolate brownie to go with it."

"Alright, I'll have that out for you in a few minutes." I dipped my head and retreated.

With each word he spoke, no matter how asinine, it rang through me, making it hard for me to focus. I had debated and bargained with royals, fought enemies, wrestled Great White sharks, swam to the deepest depths, and yet a few words from this human and I couldn't collect myself. I'd managed better conversations with nearly every other customer that had come in. At first, I'd gotten weird looks when people noticed me wearing headphones while working, but once we started talking they grew more comfortable.

On occasion, a child or teen would come in with their family, wearing ear coverings like mine. When they saw me, they smiled broadly. It was like knowing I wore mine helped them feel better about wearing theirs. Perhaps, we were all just trying to filter the noise of the human world.

I turned my concentration to the drink, finding the process soothing. The motions that had become automatic. I tried to focus on that rather than how I felt around the musician. He made me feel unstable, in a good way. Like the waters shifting and swaying around me, instead of the stillness of the earth that normally felt so off. It felt both familiar and foreign at once.

With warmed brownie and the drink on a tray, I returned to the table. He was the last customer in the coffee shop. I felt his eyes follow my movements as I placed the items in front of him. When I was about to walk away he placed a hand on my arm. "Wait."

I sucked in a gasp. The light touch sent a surge through me. It was like the shock of an electric eel. Which was something you only felt once if you were smart enough to learn after the first time. It took me three times. But now, I felt that bolt of electricity flashing beneath the surface of my skin, branching out.

His hand fell immediately and I felt a tone of regret from him. “I’m sorry. I shouldn’t have touched you without asking.”

“It’s alright. You merely surprised me. I am fine. Is there something else you need?’

His face turned up to mine. I caught sight of a tuft of black hair on his forehead, peeking out beneath his hat, and had a need to know what it looked like underwater. What *he* looked like. “I was wondering if you might be able to sit with me for a minute.”

My body longed to move closer to him. I glanced back at my manager who was counting the drawer. He had been gracious with me, giving me an opportunity when I had no history or experience, or paperwork even. I didn’t want it to seem like I was taking advantage. “I’m sorry, Mr. Greene, but I need to finish my duties.”

“It’s Denver, please.”

"Very well, Denver." I liked the way his name felt in my mouth. I repeated it over and over in my head. *Denver. Den-ver. Dennverrr.*

He gave off vibrations of delight when I said his name, maybe he liked the way it sounded in my mouth too. "And you're Calder?"

I stepped back, my eyes widening, bumps rose on my skin, alerting me to danger. It was too good to be true. This human who sang to my heart, who seemed to have a strange hold on me. Was it a trap somehow? Had he been sent after me? "How did you know my name?"

Denver put his hands up showing innocence at the bite in my tone but pointed with one finger at my apron. The apron that had my name badge on it. *Fuck, what was wrong with me?* "Yes. That's me. I apologize. I'm a little out of sorts tonight."

He lowered his arms, resting them on the table. "It's all good. We all have off nights. I've had my share lately. Nice to meet you, though."

"Thank you. You as well. If you need anything else, please let me know." I left without giving him a chance to respond. I had to get away. Denver made me forget myself. Who I was, who I pretended to be. What was up or down. What was sea or earth.

I grabbed the broom and dustpan and meticulously swept the entire dining room, keeping as much distance between us as I could. I could feel him across the room, the buzz that was uniquely him. Even with the headphones, if I cleared my mind, ceased my breath, and focused, I could make out the faint beat of his heart.

He lingered for a bit and I wondered if he was hoping I would return to him. But after some time he seemed to realize that it wasn't going to happen. Denver finished up and said his goodbyes to Lee. As he passed me heading to the back entrance of the Beanwater, he said, "Goodnight, Calder. It was a pleasure meeting you. I hope to see you again."

I stopped, leaning on the broom handle, and tilted my head. I couldn't help the smile that started to tug at my lips at the thought of him wanting further interaction even after how stilted the first one had been. "I hope so too. Goodnight, Denver."

He tipped his hat and with guitar in hand, walked out. I sighed. I felt a weird twinge in my heart with the absence of him. I shook my head, trying to clear it. I needed to lay with someone. To sink my cock into them and release this tension that was building in me. In the months I had been ashore, I hadn't sought out anyone to fill that need. I'd been too busy acclimating, studying, and working. But maybe a good fuck would help break this strange grip the musician held on me.

The twinge in my chest plucked again, stronger this time. A stabbing pain. I yanked my headphones off and closed my eyes, trying to concentrate on the wave that was hitting me. The noise of nightlife beyond the Beanwater came roaring into my ears. When I removed them earlier, entranced by Denver's emotional song, the whole room quiet, it felt as if everything else had ceased and all I heard was him. It was the first time on land that I had actually escaped the constant din, instead of merely softening it.

That same focus called me, only this time it wasn't the beautiful notes that gripped my heart, it was fear. I took the broom with me and ran out the door that Denver had exited a few moments before. With each step I took, the vibrations grew stronger. Then I heard his voice, his tone laced with panic.

CHAPTER 8

CALDER

I took off running, imagining I was zipping through the water with each forceful stroke of my fluke driving me harder. When I rounded the corner, I saw three guys closing in on Denver as he clutched his guitar case against his chest.

"Hand it over!" A gruff voice shouted at Denver, the volume of it harsh to my uncovered ears. I could hear a sniffle and beneath that his racing heartbeat.

"Please, take whatever else you want. But I can't give you my guitar." Each word was filled with agony that ripped into me.

Anger with a trace of dread pulsed through me and I charged for them. They heard me coming and turned. One held up a gun and Denver shouted. I whipped the broom around, smacking the hand that held the gun, causing him to cry out and the gun to go flying. The other two dove for me. I twirled the broom around, bringing it to a resting position that would allow easy movement in either direction. I felt a current of air to my left, the motion of the man alerting me to his move, and swung out, catching him on the forearm. He yelped in pain. Next, on my right, I flung around, hitting him.

They all came at once. One grabbed me as I kicked and spun. They laughed when my glasses went flying. That was fine. I needed them for finer details, but I could see their general shapes. Even more so, their sounds and vibrations radiated from them, broadcasting every move. I fought each man, with broom, with fists, with feet. My body moved unhindered by the resistance of water that it was used to, giving me greater speed and strength. Before long, the three were winded and well beaten.

"Come on, let's go. It's not worth it." One man grumbled as he wiped blood from his nose that crunched when I hit it. The other two seemed all too eager to get out of this fight they knew they wouldn't win.

"Don't ever come back here again!" I yelled, before dropping the broom and facing Denver.

I could feel his stare boring into me, his guitar still clutched to his chest as he pressed himself back against the wall.

I stepped closer to him, his features fuzzy without my glasses. "Are you alright?"

"I...uh...yeah? I think so."

Not able to resist touching him any longer, I placed my hand over his where it gripped the case. That touch electrified me once more but also helped calm the adrenaline coursing through me.

"What the fuck was that?" His astonished whisper coated over me. Even at such a low level, I could feel every sound and breath from him.

"I heard something and had to come see what was happening. I just hope I got here in time. Are you certain you're okay?" I didn't smell any blood, besides what was scattered about from his attackers.

"Yes. You were right in time. I can't believe that happened. You, you saved me. But what's more, you saved my guitar. It's..." He didn't finish his thought as his body started to tremble.

I wrapped my arms around him, the guitar between us and he shivered uncontrollably. He drew in a sniffle.

"It's okay. You're okay." I whispered over and over in his ear. He was much shorter than me, maybe half a foot, his frame smaller than my own. The brim of his hat dropped against my collarbone.

"Thank you, Calder." He rasped.

With his voice so near me, the vibrations that came with it purred against my chest. My heart latched on to him. A new need arising. A rather inappropriate need considering the circumstances. But his presence, his sound, his smell, it made all my senses sing.

A different sort of shaking took hold of Denver. Was shock kicking in? But then his resonance changed. I could feel a shift in him as a chuckle snuck out of him. Before long the chuckle rose to a full laugh until he pushed away from me, needing space to catch his breath, as he howled.

I didn't know the cause, but I felt it rolling off of him and a smile stretched on my face. His laughing might be the greatest thing I had ever felt or heard, rivaling his emotion-filled song when he was on stage. I didn't want to ruin the moment but curiosity got the better of me. "What is so funny?"

"You...came...out...and..." Each word came hissed out between laughs. "Holy shit! That was so insane."

I snickered, enjoying his reaction. He lifted his eyes to mine and the laughter subsided, his energy turned serious. I couldn't see the intricate details of his facial expression but I could feel the intensity of his gaze and it warmed my body.

"That was so fucking hot." Denver inhaled slightly, I could feel the shift in him, the fear turned humor turned arousal. It was intoxicating and I couldn't hold back.

I cupped my hands on his cheeks, enjoying the way his dark, trimmed beard felt beneath them. Leaning down, I pressed my lips firmly against his. He gasped against my mouth. I began to pull away, scared of pushing too far, too fast. But Denver lowered his guitar case to the ground and grabbed my shirt, tugging me back and pulling me down again. Our mouths crashed together, his met mine with the same ferocity. Teeth nipped, tongues danced, breath shared. Every single part of my body felt alive and on fire. I had kissed plenty of males before, but not a single one compared to the way I felt with him. The way my heart reached for him as if it could twine together with his, attached and entangled.

I was full of want and need, my body ached with

it. My mind quieted until he became my whole world. Better noise-cancellation than anything that could be bought in a store. It was peace and it was agony.

Denver stiffened suddenly and I drew back, letting us catch our breath, letting the world come back in little by little. That's when I heard it, someone else was here. I should have noticed but I was consumed by the man before me.

"It's just your boss." Denver breathed out.

I relaxed, breathing a sigh of relief, but took another step back. With the space between us, everything else began seeping in. Every whoosh of the wind, every screech of tires, scuffling of feet, rats running, air conditioning units rattling. It was too much, And coming off the high that had been Denver, it all seemed to fold in on top of me.

"Calder, are you out here? Is everything okay?" Lee shouted and it echoed in my ears. I wanted to respond, but everything felt heavy and loud. I shook my head as if I could shake away a planet too loud.

Denver must have noticed the change in me, he carefully lifted his hands and cupped them over my ears. It wasn't as effective as the headphones, but it helped. Mostly it was helping me focus on him. I breathed in slowly.

"Is that better?" He asked softly.

I opened my eyes and stared at him, grateful for the connection and the buffer. "Yes. Thank you."

"Calder? Everything alright?" My manager came around the corner and found us standing close, though the lighting was poor. With Denver's hands on my ears, it must have looked like we were in an embrace. Which we were of sorts, but not the same as it had been a minute ago. "Oh. I see. I apologize for the intrusion, I was just worried. Um. Calder? We *do* need to close up though."

"Yes, sir. I'll be right there." I called back while keeping my attention on Denver.

"Take a minute to collect yourself." His footsteps retreated, the back door opening and closing once more. With him gone, I let my head drop against Denver's hat, the brim pushed back to reveal his dark hair beneath. Breathing him in deeply, I tried to calm myself. A moment ago, he was my whole world, now I clung to him as the real one pulled at me.

Denver slid one hand down to my cheek, brushing it lightly. He tilted my head and placed a light kiss on my lips. In a hushed tone, he said, "Stay here, I'll be right back."

He stepped around me and I leaned against the

wall, trying to concentrate on the sound of him, following every step, every breath, and vibration. He shuffled a few things around and a moment later he returned to me. I turned around and let my back fall against the wall. Denver held out my headphones that had gotten thrown when I charged after his attackers. As soon as they were in place, I sighed in relief. The effort it took to concentrate was exhausting.

He drew up my glasses and was about to put them on me, but he stopped. His head tilted, examining me. "Have we met somewhere? There's something about you that seems familiar, but I can't quite place it."

I shook my head. Whether I had seen him or not, I would have felt his frequency, the signature that was distinctly him. "No. I would have remembered you."

"Huh. I don't know." He put my glasses in place, his face less blurry. It still wasn't as clear as I would like to see him, but it was an improvement. "I guess it's just some sort of deja vu or something."

"Perhaps so."

Denver slid his hands in his pockets, shifting from foot to foot. "Thank you, Calder. Truly. I don't know what I would have done if you hadn't shown up."

"I'm just glad you're alright." I couldn't imagine what might have happened to him. And tried not to think too much about the way I had been called to him. "I need to get back inside. I don't hear anyone else nearby, do you think you can make it back to your vehicle? "

Denver picked up his guitar case. "Um, yeah. I suppose so. Well, goodnight, Calder and thank you again."

"Goodnight, Denver."

CHAPTER 9

DENVER

I was numb during the drive home. I didn't even remember most of it. Thankfully, some part of my brain was cognizant enough to get me there. My hand shook as I tried to open the door, my key slipped from the lock. When I walked in, I placed my guitar in its stand, grateful that it was still here to be able to do so. I didn't know what I would have done if something had happened to it.

Shadow meowed and followed after me as I slumped into my room. I flopped onto my bed, my arms and legs splayed out. I had my first set in almost a year and it had gone really well. It was amazing to be back in front of an audience. Normally, it would be playing itself out in my head over and over, but the whole performance got overshadowed by what came after.

Calder intrigued me from the start. From the way he froze and stared during my final song to the way he seemed almost uncomfortable to be around me. It was confusing as hell. And then the scariest moment of my life. The moments Dad always warned me about. A shiver coursed through my body at the memory of a gun pointed at me.

Everyone knew these things happened but you never expected that they would happen to you. I was an idiot and I should have let them take my guitar and leave me alone. But I couldn't. Not that one, it was too special. Then out of nowhere...Calder.

The way his body moved with power and grace even after he'd lost his glasses. I didn't know how poor his vision was but the lenses seemed fairly thick. Still, he didn't hesitate, it was as if he could anticipate every move they made.

And that kiss. *Holy fuck!* I'd never been kissed like that in my life. This person I had hardly spoken to yet he kissed me as if he had been waiting for me for an eternity. Two long-lost lovers reunited after centuries apart. I was certain I would never feel another kiss like it. One moment with a virtual stranger and I was ruined for any future guys.

Calder's eyes. The moment we locked onto one another, I was captivated. There was something about them. They were a deep blue color, deep as the ocean, but they had a strange filmy sheen to them. I hadn't noticed when we were inside in better lighting, because they were hidden behind his thick black-rimmed glasses. But I wanted nothing more than to be trapped in their gaze and dive into the oceans they held.

My phone buzzed and I fished it out of my pocket, secretly hoping it was the mysterious man from Beanwater. My excitement sank when I saw it was Ella. Which was stupid, I hadn't given him my information or gotten his. *Damn!*

Ella: How did it go, Dennie?

Me: I thought you had spies there, shouldn't you know already?

If she did have people there would they know about the encounter that happened? No. That was ridiculous, there was no one else in the alley with us.

Ella: You can go right ahead and fuck yourself, Den

I chuckled and pictured her giving me the middle

finger.

Me: I'll catch you up tomorrow, still processing it all.

Ella: Good? Bad? Give me a one-word summary.

One word to sum up everything that happened tonight? Amazing, terrifying, baffling, hot, arousing, magical.

Me: Intense

Ella: Well…shit. I am going to need all the deets. But I suppose I can wait until tomorrow. Get some rest boss man.

I tried, but it was near impossible with the number of images I had playing on repeat. Through it all, I couldn't shake that I recognized Calder from somewhere. Not his face, I knew I had never been close enough to notice his eyes or his high cheekbones. After a while, I searched on social media, trying to see if there were any friends or acquaintances that had pictures with him in them. Or that bright red hair that he claimed was natural. I grinned at that, it was a funny remark, but endearingly awkward. No pop of red anywhere in the people I followed.

I finally gave up on trying to rest around five in the morning and decided to simply shower and head to the shop early. If I wasn't sleeping I might as well do something productive. The office was slightly better than it had been after my dad passed. But there was a lot that still needed to be tackled. The back corner where the sign lay buried hadn't been touched yet. I stared at it, trying to muster up the strength to do it. It reminded me of the widow and how she felt about her husband's workshop in the garage. It hurt to look at, but it hurt even worse to imagine it all gone.

Nope. Not yet. I wasn't ready. Instead, I turned the computer on. After a few minutes, I had last month's inventory printed as well as the blank item list for me to do this month's. Inventory was tedious enough that I hoped it would keep my mind busy and not be stuck on the events of the night before.

It worked. Until Ella showed up. She came in an hour before the shop opened, as she usually did. When she found me counting a bin of loose hex nuts she tsked her tongue and put her hands on her hips.

"Okay, what gives? You started inventory early? Was it really that bad?"

I ignored her while I finished counting or I would lose my spot and have to do it all over again. Seventy-six, seventy-seven, seventy-eight. Done. I marked the paper and looked up at her.

"It wasn't bad. Not at all. It was probably the best, worst, best night I've ever had." I tucked the clipboard under my arm.

Ella's face knotted in confusion. "What does that even mean? I need details. Did they like your music or not?"

The crowd entranced by my final song, the standing applause afterwards, the misty response from the manager. A smile stretched across my face. "They loved it. It was incredible. The manager even asked if I could come back. It sounds like it might eventually turn into a paying gig."

"What?! That's amazing! I knew you'd be great. I'm so proud of you. And hey...you didn't die." She punched my arm as she laughed.

I rubbed the spot she hit as the vision of the three guys surrounding me took place. I *could* have died. I could have died in an alley without my guitar. I was too exhausted from lack of sleep to hide the impact that thought had on me.

"Woah. What was that? Wait. You said best and worst night. What happened, Den? Did someone...do something to you?" I caught the concerned look she wore, it was clear the direction her mind had gone. I wasn't a big guy, and besides being able to wield a hammer and a guitar equally, I was not intimidating. Ella had taken over the job of worrying about me with my dad gone. Though, she had done a decent job of it before he passed too.

"Uh...yes, but no. Not like that."

Ella gently grabbed my arm and pulled me to the office where she pushed me into the wheeled desk chair and sat across from me. "Are you okay?"

Calder's eyes boring into mine, his lips blazing against my own. I shifted in my seat as the memory of him redirected the blood flow. "Yes. I'm fine."

"Seriously, my mind is providing several situations that might have occurred. I'm gonna need you to start filling in the blanks before I go full-on mad-libs here and create a series of events that has me ready to grab my pitchfork."

I set the clipboard on the desk and rubbed my hands over my face before turning my attention back to her. "Promise me you won't freak out."

"That is exactly the kind of thing that is going to make me freak the fuck out. So I reserve the right to react how I see fit."

"Okay. Just listen first, please."

Ella waved her hand at me to continue and crossed her arms over her chest.

I blew out a breath, here goes, "I was mugged."

She shot out of her chair and stood over me. "Oh my God! Are you serious? What the hell? Why didn't you call me? Did you go to the police? Are you hurt? What did they take?"

"Ella, I'm fine. Not a scratch. Can you just sit down and let me explain?"

Her eyes roamed over me as if checking for any injury. I had been slammed against the wall, that was all. Calder had gotten there before anything else could have happened. She harrumphed and plopped back down in the chair, but her anger was mixed with concern as she waited for me to say more.

"I met a guy." Her brow arched to record heights as if it were trying to touch her hairline, but to her credit, she remained quiet. I told her everything that happened, from the coffee shop to the fight between Calder and the three muggers.

"That must have been some serious flirting for the guy to go all Bruce Lee on your attackers."

I shook my head, "No, it was bizarre at best. But..."

Ella leaned forward, "But what?"

"We kissed."

Ella let out a loud honk of a laugh and clapped her

hands over her mouth. "Wait, wait, wait. So you're telling me, you have this totally weird encounter with this guy, then suddenly he's your one-man superhero and then you kissed him? Unbelievable."

"Right?! Half of me is still trying to decide if all of that actually happened or if it was some weird fever dream. I blame the decaf."

"You *never* drink decaf."

"I know!" But it had been what Calder suggested and I would have agreed to any concoction he said.

"Fucking decaf," Ella said with a grin and we busted up. I might have been reaching the point of exhaustion that crossed into delirium but it felt good to laugh.

Once we settled down, she asked, "So what happened after?"

"After? Like with the muggers, or with Calder?"

"Um...all of it."

"I don't know. It was weird. Calder scared the guys away. I highly doubt they'll come back. I'm telling you, if you saw him move the way he did, it was incredible. But then we had this whole big epic moment and suddenly it was just over. He went back to work and I went home." At least it felt like a big epic moment to me. For all I knew, he was some sort of vigilante who went around kicking ass and kissing victims.

"Well, you know where the guy works right? You could always go talk to him."

"Yeah. I'm not sure about that. It was weird when we were talking, he didn't seem like he wanted me until he had me pinned against the wall."

"One; that's hot. And two; nothing wrong with someone who uses a little...*body language.*" The last two words came out like Ursula from the Little Mermaid.

"Ha. Yeah, I wouldn't mind learning the language of his body." Most of him was covered, but the way he moved and the defined muscles in his arms as he held me, I would *really* like to know what lay beneath.

"Well, at least you can see him again when you perform there next, right? Oh, and I am totally going with you. I need to see this guy for myself."

Did I want her tagging along if I got another chance at kissing Calder, not really. But maybe she could help me get a better read on the aloof man. "Fine."

CHAPTER 10

CALDER

Lee gave me a knowing look when I walked back in from the alley. As hard as it was to tear myself away from Denver, I was glad for the excuse to leave. The pull I felt to him was too strong and could easily get me in trouble. My job was the least of my worries though it was a real one.

"I apologize for my actions. I wasn't thinking." I lowered my head as I would in front of my parents or other authorities.

The manager pursed his lips. "Clearly. I have to admit, it's nice to see you do something human."

I stiffened and jerked my head up. How did he know? Was he in the alley when I fought off the attackers? Would I have to find somewhere new and start all over again? "Human?"

He laughed and patted my shoulder. "It's nothing, just glad to see you enjoy yourself for once. You are always working and when you're not working, you have your head buried in your computer with your studies. I appreciate how determined and dependable you are, it's admirable. But it's okay to take a break sometimes too. It's often better if you do. Let yourself blow off a little steam before you burn out."

I let myself relax a little when I realized he didn't mean anything *non-human* by his human comment. He was wrong, though. I couldn't take a break. I had so little time and I was already four months into my allotted year. I was cramming as many courses as I could, trying to understand what realistic steps I could take and how to have the most influence.

What I didn't need was a man who could make me forget who I was or risk exposing myself over. The scene in the alley flashed before me, how I had revealed moves that I knew humans shouldn't be capable of. He might have been seriously injured or worse and for that, I was glad I could help. That was as far as it could go though.

"So, you like him, huh?"

"Who's that?"

"The musician, Denver Greene. He's agreed to come back and play for us again." Lee winked at me.

"He's quite talented. I think that's a smart choice for the Beanwater."

"Just for the Beanwater?"

I opened my mouth to respond but wasn't quite sure what to say without betraying the thoughts I had. That I would listen to his music day and night, that I wanted to hear his gasp, that I wanted to feel his body pressed against mine.

"Relax. I'm just giving you a hard time. And...I'll let it slide this time. But in the future, please try to keep your romantic encounters outside of work hours and if possible, out of the alley."

"Yes, sir. It won't happen again."

As hard as I tried to focus on the paper I'd been working on when I got home, I couldn't. This research assignment seemed ridiculous with the time I had, but if it helped me to articulate myself and my arguments, it could help me present myself better and hold up against any rebuttal. Even carefully crafted words could be fileted with precision if they weren't strong enough to hold up against probing.

I should have been thinking about sources of renewable energy. Humanity had created many amazing things, but the power to run them was creating as many or more problems than the good it brought. We had no electricity beneath the water, but we had no quick way to communicate between kingdoms either. It took messengers and several days of swimming, and sometimes that made it too late to take action as quickly as it was needed.

When I tried to think of the way electricity could be harnessed, my thoughts drifted to the sparks beneath my skin, zapping and striking. The way his smaller form fit in my arms, his head resting on my shoulder, the sound of him; every note and syncopation that bled from him. I could feel it as if it were a part of me. I closed my laptop and cursed. Anxious and tense, I paced the one room of my house. I was on edge and needed a release. What I wanted to do was find Denver and learn every note he could make as I studied his body.

Fuck! I needed to swim. I was starting to lose control. The nights spent sleeping in the bathtub weren't enough. Letting my tail out helped, but it didn't satisfy the need that ran through the core of my being. It had been too long. And staying on two legs was only going to make this tension grow until I did something I regretted.

One of the first times I used the computer at the library before I'd gotten myself a laptop, I looked for a map of water sources near me. The closest thing was a stream hardly big enough to stomp around in. That wouldn't do. The beach I had first come ashore at was too far away to get to easily. Houses. There were a lot of houses within walking distance, some were bound to have pools. I couldn't simply invite myself over to someone's place and shift in their pool though. An empty house, perhaps? I found another website that showed houses for sale and tucked that information into the back of my head.

With a few neighborhoods in mind, I grabbed my keys and started running. I tried to slow my pace so it looked like I was a recreational runner, not as if I was racing the explosion building up within me.

Despite Summer Hills Community being relatively new, a few of their houses had *For Sale* signs in front. When I found one that conveniently advertised a pool, I looked around. It had a small sign on a stake in the yard and a sticker on the window saying it was protected by security.

I'd learned a lot about the flow of electricity and

how things functioned. That was one of the benefits of my studies on power. Maybe I could find the frequency of the security cameras and tap into it, cutting off the signal. I steadied myself and drew a deep breath, removing my ear gear. Dogs barking, televisions, radios, people arguing, breathy moans of passion. I needed to get around all of that. I tried to block out one sound at a time. I focused on the camera at the front of the house, putting all of my attention on that. One by one, the clamor quieted, and I closed my eyes trying to feel the vibrations of the frequency. It was there, barely, but I grasped onto it. After a few painstaking moments, I managed to find the trace I needed.

I couldn't cant as I did underwater, but I still had the same control over vocalization. I gritted my teeth and blew a thin stream of air between them, creating a whistle. It was too high a note above water for humans to be able to hear it, but the dogs nearby stopped barking as they listened. I changed the shape of my mouth, manipulating the sound until I could feel it grow nearer the frequency I needed. An extra push, a slight shift, and I could sense the two align. A moment later a faint click sounded. It was off. While I couldn't detect any other cameras with my eyes, I knew the signature to look for now. There were two more, one on the side of the house where the gate led to the backyard and one above the back door.

I stopped the one on the side, glanced around, and hopped over the fence before blocking the camera at the rear. I waited—listening for any other disruptions or cries of alarm—and relaxed when I heard nothing. The fence seemed to provide decent privacy, with no windows overlooking the yard. The water of the pool stung my nose with the scent of chemicals, but I was desperate. I'd never gone this long without swimming before. Mostly a day or two on occasion. Certainly not months.

I stripped out of my clothes, not feeling the cold winter air, and set them on the side of the pool along with my glasses and headphones. Next, my hair was set free from the binding that held it, brushing against my shoulders. I didn't like the way it felt when it moved in the breeze, it itched and whispered against my skin. Underwater though, I loved the slinky way it wrapped around me, the way it came alive.

Free of human confines, I dove into the shallow pool, releasing my tail at the same time. The release of pressure was immense, a blast of energy that rippled out of me. I sighed deeply at the relief, staring at my tail and flicking my fluke. Now that I was in the water, my vision righted and everything was clearer than it had been in a long time. Right. This was so right.

My body had been cramped, my muscles tight, everything had been closing in on itself. Now...I felt free, every part of me unfurled with my tail, tension rolling out of me. My skin felt itchy, my nose and eyes burned with the chemicals, and I couldn't breathe underwater because of it. But even with all of that, I still felt a hundred times better.

It wasn't a big enough body of water to let me fully stretch and push myself to my limits, but it was enough that I could swim in lazy ovals around the pool. Enough to feel like I wouldn't lose control of myself if a cup of water spilled on me. Enough to feel like I wouldn't attack Denver the next time I saw him. Though I had to admit the idea was rather appealing.

Twenty minutes passed in glorious silence. The pool was a larger version of the tub in my house. Sound bounced off the walls, instead of casting out into the sea beyond. It wasn't right, but it was more comforting than how quickly it pinged around me in the bath. I canted low and soft, trying to imagine that it was someone else singing through the water. I could almost convince myself that I wasn't utterly alone when water was meant to be filled with life. But it was merely my own voice wrapping around me, drowning out the choices I'd made, the future I sought to escape, transporting me away from the present. Until a different sound reached my ears.

I froze and shifted, calling my tail back despite the inner protest to keep it free. I stood on two legs in the shallow end, my wet hair draped around my shoulders. The sounds that had been muffled by the water, now blaring and pushing in around me and through it all, I could hear footsteps approaching.

Panic fueled my instincts. I couldn't be caught here. Not wanting to waste time dressing, I grabbed my clothing pile, put my glasses and headphones on to help me concentrate, and took off. With my free arm, I swung my body over the side of the fence, away from the nearing steps. I froze, standing there naked. My clothes were clutched in front of me when lights turned on, flooding the backyard. *Get your ass out of here!* I yelled at myself, trying to get my feet moving.

I scaled another fence and another, crossing yard after yard, security lights following my path until I finally reached the end of the block and turned the corner. I ran as swiftly as I could, listening to the neighborhood waking as I did. Mentally tracking my location, I envisioned a path that would get me somewhere safe. Bobbed through an alley, scurried around hedges, dashed through parks. The sounds of the neighborhood around me changed from alert to slumber with the distance I put between myself and the track of homes that I had been in.

I came to a copse of trees that provided enough shield from the streets that I allowed myself to stop. Leaning my bare ass against a tree trunk, I slipped my feet into my shorts and pulled them up. Throwing my shirt over my head, I casually strolled as if I had been doing so all along. A few police cars passed me but didn't seem to give any pause. I couldn't believe how close that had been. Though the thrill of it, the adrenaline pumping and making everything come alive felt amazing. Not as good as slicing through the water with my body but the tension that had been built up in me waned considerably.

When I got home, I was anxious to get the chemicals off me. I felt like I might shrivel up like a salted slug. My skin felt dry and ashen. Clearly, the pool wasn't the best option and I doubted I could return there again after setting the entire neighborhood on alert. From one too-small body of water to another, I sank into the tub as the water filled around me. With my face under, my ears submerged, I found myself relaxing fully and drifted off with an amused smile on my face.

CHAPTER 11

DENVER

I was pretty much useless after the high of telling everything to Ella, my exhaustion catching up to me. She ended up sending me home before noon. Some days it felt as if *she* were the manager at Greene Hardware. She was a lifesaver though. Ella knew her shit and she cared about the store which made it easy to trust her with it.

I was ready to crash and sleep for three days. Though Shadow insisted I feed him first, lest he die, even though his bowl was full of partially eaten niblets. For some reason, he only liked the first bite of every piece of kibble. After that, it was tainted by...himself. If you saw him, you would swear he ate everything he could get his little paws on. Once he was temporarily appeased, I made it as far as my couch. I kicked off my shoes, turned the news on for some background noise, and collapsed on the sofa.

When I woke, it was in that suspended reality where time and days all blended together. My throat was parched, I had dried drool on my cheek and my eyelids weighed fifty pounds. Had I slept for days, weeks, had the world around me been turned to thorns, guarded by a dragon? Was a prince going to come and wake me with the kiss of life? If he did, should I pretend to still be asleep and let him work his magic?

In my haze, the prince became the red-haired, glasses-wearing ninja who swooped in and saved me. He'd kissed me too. Maybe I wasn't cursed with the sleeping death, but those lips were enough to break any spell. Or cast one. Damn, that had been one hell of a kiss. I touched my lips, the ghost of him lingering.

"Next at the top of the hour, we'll bring you the latest on the incident in the Summer Hills Community." The news was still on?

I blinked my eyes hard, trying to get them to stay open. At the top of what hour, exactly? What time was it? I scrubbed my hands over my face and forced myself to sit up. Coffee. I needed coffee. The real stuff this time. I had a partial pot in the coffeemaker, the remainder of yesterday's coffee. I poured it into a mug and zapped it in the microwave, which blinked twelve o'clock repeatedly, not helpful. I kept forgetting to set it after the power had gone out a while back.

While my coffee heated up, the newscaster continued to ramble in the background. "Trespassing." "Footage." "Unidentified." I yawned and stretched, trying to clear the fog. It had been a while since I passed out that hard during the day. Not since I'd been drinking and sleeping my way through grief.

A ding and I retrieved my mug from the microwave. I grabbed the caramel creamer and started pouring it when I flicked my gaze up to the TV. "Nude man terrorized the neighborhood. No one was harmed, though he did trespass through several homes in his escape. It isn't known if he was targeting a particular house or canvassing for weaknesses."

"Really? Nude? What a sicko." I mumbled and took a sip. With mug in hand, I returned to the living room, about to change the channel when grainy footage revealed the very naked backside of a man as he leapt over a tall wooden fence with ease. It was fast and blurry, the camera only catching the last second of him before he was gone. But there was something odd about it. Besides the fact that the guy was hurdling in the buff. I rewound it and let it play again, my finger on the button. As soon as he was in the frame, I paused it.

I let out a loud gasp, my mug slipped from my hand and shattered against the tiled floor. I frowned at the tragedy of the perfectly-colored coffee puddled on the ground amidst the shards of one of my favorite mugs that read "It might look like I'm listening, but in my head I'm playing guitar." A double tragedy.

Before I moved to clean it, I had to know. I had to confirm what I thought I saw. I rewound the clip and paused it once more. I knew those headphones. While I hadn't seen his hair down before and the video had poor lighting, I was certain it was him. My gaze drifted down over his pixelated ass and I found myself wishing I could remove the censor.

"Not the priority right now, you perv." I lectured myself. But then maybe I wasn't the one who was the perv. I was staring at the very naked yet distorted image of a guy I'd made out with only last night, the same guy who was practically ding-dong-ditching with his ding-dong out.

I had my phone out and took a minute to figure out what time it was before I dialed. *Damn, I slept almost all day*. It was a little after four in the afternoon, which meant Ella was still at the store. I called the office phone knowing there would be a better chance of her answering that instead of her cell phone.

"Greene Hardware, this is Ella, how can I help you?"

"Ella! Turn on the news!"

"Why, hello, Dennie, nice to hear from you too." Sarcasm dripped through the phone.

"Yeah, hi, whatever. Just turn on something local."

I heard her typing on the computer. "What's going on? What am I looking for, exactly?"

"Is there anything about a naked man?"

"You know you could just go to Porn Hub, right?"

I sighed with exasperation. "Come on, just take a look for me."

"Hmm...fight at the high school, three-legged dog finds a home, neighborhood watch gets an eyeful."

"Wait...that last one, click on that."

"Okay, let's see. It says a call was made after

suspicious behavior in Summer Hills. Blah, blah, blah. Security was called, pursuit happened. Suspect fled on foot, yada, yada. Reports say that the suspect was completely nude." I heard her shuffle the phone around. "Seriously? Okay, so a streaker creeper freaked out a bunch of people. What's this all about?"

"It was him," I said.

"Him, who? Oh, shit! Is he one of the guys that attacked you? You gotta call that in Dennie? What if he and his gang are out there assaulting other people?" Concern sharpened her tone.

I had a feeling my muggers would be nursing their wounds for a while, they'd taken quite a beating. "No...not the guys that attacked me. It was *him.* Body language guy."

"Shut the front door! Are you serious? The dude who had his tongue down your throat is naked leaping guy?"

"Yes, that's what I'm trying to tell you."

"Bah ha ha!" Ella laughed so loud, I had to pull the phone away from my ear. She was heaving and gasping for air with how hard she bellowed.

"Ella, what do I do?"

She tried to settle herself down, "I'm sorry, Den. But that is fucking hilarious. The first time you see any kind of action in way too long and your Romeo ends up on the news buck ass naked." Snorts and giggles continued to come from the other end of the phone.

There had to be some reason for it. He had been nice, brave, okay, a little odd, but so very hot. Maybe he was helping someone else like he helped me. And somehow ended up in his birthday suit? I shook my head. There wasn't a good reason for that.

"Listen. As far as I can tell, nothing really happened besides some people getting a little shaken up. I have no idea why or how a person finds himself in a follow-the-bouncing-balls kind of position, but I think you have a pretty good instinct about people. So what does your gut say?"

Seeing him stand utterly still, entranced by my music, feeling his body pressed against mine, the way he looked at me. I might not know him, but it felt like my soul did. And even with all the crazy stuff that happened, there had been a moment when it was only us in all of the universe and I was drawn to him. No red flags, no warning bells. He felt safe. Of course, compared to the situation I would have been in had he not shown up, anything would have felt safe.

"I think I need to talk to him."

She hummed, "Sounds like a good first step."

"Uh...don't tell anyone about this, okay? I don't want him getting in trouble, at least not until I know what's going on."

"I won't say a word but I expect updates."

"Sure. I'll fill you in once I know more."

We hung up and my attention returned to the disaster on the floor. *Shit!* My mind roamed while I swept up the shards and sopped up the coffee. How had I managed to find myself entangled in such a bizarre situation? I needed to go see Calder. The thought made me nervous, but underneath it all, I was buzzing with excitement at seeing him again.

After the mess was cleaned up, I scrolled through my phone to find the contact info for the Beanwater Brew. My thumb hesitated over the call button. What if he answered the phone? What was I going to say? I blew out a breath. I owed it to myself to figure out what was going on. *You also owe it to yourself to see if he tastes as good as you remember.* The thought had me semi-hard which would make it even more uncomfortable if he answered. My dick twitched at the thought of hearing my name let out on a breath from his mouth.

He could be a criminal for fuck's sake. That did nothing to stop the growing excitement in my pants. I hit the call button and was equally relieved and disappointed to hear the manager answer the phone.

"Hi, Mr. Robertson, this is Denver Greene. I performed at the Beanwater last night."

"Oh good. I'm glad you called. I actually had a note to get in touch with you soon. I'd love for you to come back, we've had rave reviews on social media about the up-and-comer that played. I'd love to book you for another date."

Up-and-comer had a nice ring to it, made it sound like I was going somewhere. And who was I to turn down a gig? A gig where a sexy, mysterious, naked ninja might be.

Play it cool. "Sure, you have a great café. I'd be interested in playing the Beanwater again."

"Perfect. I'm thinking, depending on how it goes, maybe we can get you in here once or twice a month. That is, if you are available? I'm sure you're booked all over, so I'll be happy to get you whenever I can."

I wasn't booked anywhere else, not yet. But I didn't want to sound *too* available. "I'll review my schedule and we can discuss it soon."

"Okay, great. Thanks for reaching out."

"Uh, actually." I interrupted. "That wasn't my only reason for calling." It wasn't the reason at all, but

I'd gladly take the opportunity that was offered. I should have had my priorities straight; music first, then men. But Calder filled my every thought.

"Oh. Sure. What else can I help you with? Wait! Are you looking for Calder?" I could practically hear the smirk in his tone.

I cleared my throat, surprised that he was so blunt. "Well, as it turns out, yes. Yes, I am."

He tried to cover a laugh with a cough. My cheeks flamed as I remembered the intense moment he'd caught us in. "He's not in yet. Calder is scheduled for the closing shift. But he should be here in about an hour. Sometimes, he comes in early, but there's no guarantee."

"Okay. Right. What time do you close?" I tried not to sound too eager, but there was no hiding it.

"We lock the doors at ten and Calder's off at ten-thirty."

Another late night for me, but I *had* to see him and at least I knew where he would be. If he still showed up to work after his midnight romp, that is.

Anticipation trilled under my skin. I had five hours to kill before I would see him again. In the shower, envisioning the red-haired beauty had me giving extra attention to certain areas, just in case.

Once I was dressed, I had way too much anxious energy to simply stay home and wait. I grabbed my song journal and left.

It was only six o'clock when I stood outside of the Beanwater. I stared at my reflection, assessing my outfit, wishing I had gone dressier. I wore a pair of dark blue skinny jeans and a loose white v-neck tee with a light jacket. I had convinced myself at my apartment that this was nothing, merely a casual interrogation. But now, standing in front of the shop and seeing him bustling about inside, I wanted to impress him somehow.

My heart thundered, palms were sweaty. *Who's the creeper now?* I mocked myself as I watched Calder from outside. His back was to me but his head snapped up. He turned sharply, gaze locking with mine as if he knew I was there. Even with the layers of glass between us—the windows and the lenses he wore—I could see the shock of surprise. Was it a good surprise? A bad surprise? Was he about to pole vault his way out of there to escape me like he did in the neighborhood?

After a probably too-long staredown, I straightened my back and willed my feet to move. One step at a time until I was inside. Calder seemed to pull himself out of his stupor and met me.

"Denver? What are you doing here?" His voice was hushed, panicked almost.

I held up my journal, "I'm going to sit and write a bit. The environment was so lovely last night, I thought it might be a nice change of pace." The overly rehearsed line wasn't a total lie.

A shadow swept over his face. "Of course. Feel free to sit anywhere."

I couldn't decide if his filmy, ocean eyes looked heated or icy. Was he upset at seeing me? Nerves churned in my stomach as I sat at a small table towards the back. Calder floated around the room, checking on customers, taking and filling orders, and generally keeping his distance from me until I lifted my hand indicating I wanted to order. His hesitation was noticeable as he glanced around to see if anyone else was near enough to take care of me. There was only one other person besides him and the manager and she had gone to clean the bathrooms.

Calder seemed to resolve himself, straightening his back and holding his head up. Was it that much to ask of him to talk to me? It was *his* lips that first crashed into mine last night. I felt my heart bounce around in my stomach with nerves.

"What can I get for you?" Calder said abruptly, not even looking at me.

I gave him my drink order, full caffeine, and he started to turn away. Remembering how he reacted the last time I grabbed his arm, I said his name instead, "Calder?"

His eyes met mine for the first time since I walked in, a strange tightness in them. "Yes, Denver?"

I lowered my voice, hoping he could still hear me with the headphones, but not wanting others to listen in. "Did I do something wrong?"

His eyes immediately softened. Calder stretched out a hand and placed it over mine, squeezing gently. "No. You did nothing wrong."

That was a slight relief but it left me even more confused. "Does it bother you that I'm here?"

Calder shifted and looked around before leaning down, his mouth close to my ear. His hot breath ghosted over my skin. "It's just that your presence affects me. I have a hard time focusing when all I want is to kiss you again and the nearer I am to you, the harder it is."

My face heated, my groin heated, every part of me went hot at the mere suggestion. I gulped, "Oh. I'm sorry?" How did one respond to the intense wanting from someone like him?

He stood back up, a crooked smile on his face. "Don't be sorry. But if I'm distant, it's because I'm barely in control right now."

"Should I go then?"

"Don't go." That crooked smile stretched wider.

Fuck me! That look was enough to make me want to push him into the bathroom and see what would happen if he lost control. I shook my head, trying to free myself from the binds of his fierce attention.

"Can we...talk after you're done working?" I tried to force myself to remember that I had a reason for coming, besides losing control with him, no matter how desperately I wanted that. There was that whole naked marathon thing to consider. Curse those pixelated videos.

"Yes. I'd like that."

His tone dripped with sex and left me feeling like I was seconds away from coming right there. What kind of voodoo did he have that with so few words he shook me to my core? The next few hours were complete torture. Calder worked, attending to the duties of his job, all while there were heat waves that seemed to connect us. I was constantly aware of his presence. I knew exactly where he was in the room even if I had my head buried in my journal.

I tried to write, but all that ended up on the page were short nonsensical descriptions of fire and passion. I had never been so turned on for so long and it was driving me insane. If this was how Calder felt, I understood needing distance between us. What I didn't understand was how he felt so much for *me*. And why did I feel the same? It had been a while, sure, but this level of horniness was all new and all I had to go off of was one hot kiss and his whispered words in my ear.

The caffeine that was finally coursing through me for the first time since yesterday morning did nothing to help the jitters. When the last customer left, I could have busted out in hymns, singing of glories and hallelujahs. It wouldn't be much longer until I could finally be alone with him. As I got up to leave, not sure if I was allowed to be in the dining room after it was closed, Calder came over and put his hand on my chest.

"Stay. Please. After what happened last night, I don't want you waiting outside by yourself."

Shit. Had that only been last night? I almost forgot about the muggers, something that shouldn't be easily forgotten. And yet it seemed like a lifetime ago. I simply nodded and stayed in my seat. I watched as Mr. Robertson talked to Calder, pointing his head in my direction. Calder responded with a smile and a dip of his head. At least the manager didn't seem to have a problem with me being here. But the torture only ramped up. I watched him sweep and mop the floor as if I were watching porn with extreme interest in every move he made. God, I was hopeless.

After an endless amount of time, Calder went to the back and came out without his apron. He might as well have been back to his naked antics with how excited I was to see that one article of clothing removed.

He held his hand out to me as if it were perfectly normal for us. I took it, reveling in the way his fingers felt in mine. Without a word, he led me out as Lee locked the door behind us. "Have a goodnight, you two." He called out with a grin.

Calder pulled me around the corner and as soon as we were out of view, he crashed into me. His chest was to my chest, his hips pressed against mine. Hands went to the sides of my face and he smashed his mouth against mine. It was desperate and needy and I couldn't get enough of it. I grabbed his sides and pulled, drawing him as close to me as I could. I was hard as a rock. He was too, I felt him pressing against me. The hardness of him, the friction of my jeans, the fucking longest hours of my life, and I was nearly there already. With herculean effort, I put slight pressure on his shoulders to stop him. Calder immediately drew back.

His milky eyes looked over me like I was his feast after a famine. Holy shit, I'd never had anyone look at me like he did. "Fuck, Calder. I...wow. I think we need to cool it for a minute, or I might explode right here and that's not how I want it to happen."

Calder stared at my mouth and ran his tongue over his lower lip. "Yes. I suppose you're right. We should leave."

CHAPTER 12

CALDER

Denver nodded enthusiastically, his green eyes glowing. I didn't want to have any space between us, but it wasn't the same here as it was on the islands. You couldn't simply find a secluded place on a beach or behind the trees. Humans in the city were much more particular about privacy.

"Do you want to follow me? Are we going to your place or mine, or do you have somewhere else in mind?"

"I don't have a car."

"Okay, so you'll ride with me. You sure you trust me enough to get in the car with me?" There was a tease in his voice but with it a hint of uncertainty. Was he worried he would scare me off?

I slid my hand over his heart, the racing beat of it sent ripples of vibrations into me. I didn't have wordspeak to explain the way it felt, but if I could, I would cant the way my heart hummed in response to him. "I trust you, Denver."

He ran his hand through his short black hair, every motion and breath whispering to me. "Alright, I'm about thirty minutes from here, but could probably make it in twenty."

Twenty minutes might as well have been infinity. "That's too long. We'll go to my place, I'm about a fifteen-minute walk from here." With a car, it would be even faster.

"Right. Let's go then." This time it was Denver who grabbed my hand, twined his fingers with mine, and led me to his truck. Every touch was electric, I couldn't wait until I could roam over the entirety of him. I needed so much more than his hand in mine, but it was a nice start. I liked that it made me feel bound together with him as if nothing would be able to separate us.

The ride there was quick, which was good because I was nearly ready to burst. He followed me to the door of the old house. It stood by itself, or barely stood. The place had certainly seen better days. It was small and simple, much more so than my room in the palace or even the cave I had claimed for myself, but it suited me fine while I was on land. Denver followed me in, his gaze casting around the one room. It had a kitchenette, a two-burner stove, a round table big enough for two chairs, a small couch, a dresser with a fish tank on top that housed the bag my sister wove for me, a wardrobe, the bed, and the bathroom. I didn't need anything else.

Denver's eyes landed on the perfectly kept bed. "Are you sure this is your place? This bed looks like it's never been slept in."

"Once, but I prefer to sleep in the tub." Was that weird? I probably shouldn't have confessed that especially with the strange look he gave me.

"About that talk?"

I wanted to indulge him, but all I could focus on was his lips, his lips and everything below them. I let my eyes slide over him, wishing we were underwater and I could see him clearly, but I got enough of an idea. My gaze landed on the swollen outline in his pants. I could hear his heart pump faster, hear him swallow, his breath hitch.

"Right...we can talk later." The words came out

husky and the sound sent shivers through me. I grinned and a second later we were pressed together once more. Hands roamed, as we made our way to the bed, everywhere he touched me, even over my clothes, left a wake of lightning. Denver fell back on the bed. I paused long enough to take my glasses off, they were getting in the way, my frames bumping against his cheeks. When I reached to take my headphones off, Denver sat up, holding his hand out to stop me.

"They don't bother me. If you need to keep them on, I don't mind. Or I have earbuds if you want something less cumbersome."

I slid them off. "Denver, your body, it sings to me. It sings loud enough to block out the whole world as if we could slip away into the quiet of space, nothing beyond you and me."

Denver gaped and ran his hand through his hair. "Well, damn! That has got to be the most beautiful thing anyone has ever said to me. Even still, if you need me to be quieter, let me know. No guarantees, but I'll try my hardest."

I pushed Denver into the bed and settled myself between his legs. "Don't you fucking dare. I want to wring every sound out of you that I can."

My hands went under his shirt and he lifted his

back enough to let me draw it over his head. I ran my fingers over his chest, loving the way his soft skin felt. He had a little hair on his chest and I ran my fingers through it. He purred beneath my touch, his hips bucking under me. His vibration changed, it was sharper, more defined, and it hummed through my whole body.

"Calder, you are driving me crazy. I need to see you, to touch you. *Please.*" The begging tone was nearly enough to undo me completely. Denver was as lost in this as I was and that fact pleased me to no end. I pushed off him, standing at the edge of the bed. My shirt came off first. I could hear the breath lodged within him as he waited for the rest. I unzipped and rolled my pants down, toeing my shoes off and stepping out of them. I stood before him completely nude, enjoying the way his rapid pulse resounded in my ears. His arousal perfumed the air around us. I needed him with a ferocity greater than ever before.

I returned to that wonderful place between his legs, freeing him of his tight jeans, briefs, and boots as quickly as possible. When I leaned over him, his hands went to my smooth chest, sending bolts through me. He reached up to the back of my head, his fingers bumping the binding that held my hair.

"Can I take this out? I've been dying to see your hair."

"Yes." It bothered me loose and dry, but I would do anything he wanted at that moment.

He fumbled with it for a minute, before he managed to free it, my hair falling and sweeping against my shoulders. He inhaled sharply and my cock leaked with the sound.

"Holy shit! It can't be. You're the Beachy Bigfoot."

I pushed up, putting some space in between us, concerned by the change in him. He was still aroused, but I didn't understand. "What do you mean?"

Denver reached up, grabbing my lower back and pulling me back down. "I've fantasized about this, I can't believe it's actually you."

His lips were pressed against my neck, sucking and nipping and as much as I wanted to know more, all thoughts left my head. I kissed him hard, his tongue swept into my mouth, dancing with my own. I pushed my hips against his, our cocks rubbing against each other. It was thrilling and not enough at the same time. I wanted to be inside him, but at this rate, I wouldn't make it long enough to do so.

Denver must have had the same thought, he reached between us, wrapping his hand around both of us, sliding up and down. Feeling him touch me, the friction of his soft skin hard against my own had me moaning. Each pull, each rub, maddening and exciting.

His breaths were coming out fast and I lived for every second of it. With my weight on one hand, my other joined Denver's, stroking us together. We sped up, tightening our grips, his body sending off waves of vibrations that were strong enough to be felt through the center of the earth. This was how the plates shifted and lands spread apart, this was what shaped the planet. Denver's moans quickened and I felt his body tense, "Oh, God, Calder. I'm right there."

He arched his back and let out a loud groan as wet warmth coated our hands. The sound he made echoed within me and had me coming right after. We didn't let go, our hands clasped together around our dicks as we both tried to catch our breath. The release sent shockwaves through me.

Reluctantly, I slid off of him and got out of bed to grab a towel from the bathroom. When I came back, I stared down at Denver. I couldn't quite make out his facial expression, but the contented sigh that left his lips and the peace that rolled out of him were exquisite. I saw enough of him to know that we made a beautiful mess, I almost hated to clean it up, but I did. I tossed the towel aside and laid down next to him. The bed was still uncomfortable, but with Denver naked beside me, I could be happy sleeping on shards of glass.

Denver turned on his side to face me, his hand trailing over my chest. He leaned across and kissed me. Not the hard, rough kisses that were driven by urgency, but softer, tender ones. "Wow. That was incredible."

"Mmm. I want to do so much more with you, but that was a great way to start."

Denver's hand trailed down my side, over my hip. His electric touch had me hardening, ready for another bout. He traced a finger over my tip, eliciting a groan from me.

"I think we should have that talk before things go any further," Denver said, finger circling the head.

I bucked my hips, longing for more than the teasing touch. I bit out, "I'm not the one starting things."

Denver sighed and slid his hand back up my chest. "Yeah. Sorry. I just can't believe I'm lying here with you. I keep telling myself it's not real, that I'm having the best dream I've ever had, but you...you're here."

His finger danced around my nipple and I sucked in a breath. I wanted him to keep going, I wanted to feel his touch everywhere, but he had been wanting to have a conversation since the moment he walked into the Beanwater. Now that I was slightly relieved from the need that had been building up since we met the night before, it was probably for the best if we got to it. With the strength of ancient kings and warriors, I placed my hand on his, stopping his feathery exploration that I wanted so desperately to continue. I pushed myself up until I was leaning against the wall, hoping the upright position would help me concentrate better.

"What's a Beachy Bigfoot?"

Denver let out a laugh and sat up beside me, turning to face me. "A few months ago, my friend, Ella, dragged me out to help with a beach clean-up." I tensed. The humans on the beach picking up trash when I first came on land.

"Okay?" I wasn't sure what to say about it yet. What had he seen?

"So, we were there, working in the sun, tired, hot,

and out of nowhere, the most beautiful man I've ever seen is just standing there watching us. He was soaking wet wearing a sinfully small speedo. And then before I knew it, he was gone. I started to wonder if my imagination and the heat had gotten the best of me and I made up the whole thing."

"Beautiful?" I asked, latching onto that single word.

Denver reached over and lifted strands of my hair, letting them slink through his fingers. As much as I disliked the way it tickled my skin, his playing with it was almost as alluring as him touching my body.

"Breathtakingly so." His words were laced with wonder.

"You didn't imagine it. I was there that day." What were the odds? Out of all the beaches and all the times that I could have walked ashore, the naked man beside me who sang to my heart was there at that same moment. It felt too perfect to merely be a coincidence.

"What were you doing? Where did you come from?"

"I was swimming. Isn't that what most humans do at the beach?"

Denver sat up straight, facing me. "Humans?"

Fuck. I didn't mean to say that. "People," I

corrected, though I doubted it did any good.

His expression turned serious. "Okay. I have some questions for you and I want real answers, not just what you think I want to hear. Can you do that for me?"

I blew out a breath. I'd already revealed to him more than I should. But we were connected, I could feel it with every fiber of my being. His vibrations, his singing, his music, I felt it all within me. A heartsong that rang out between us. There was a force that bound us, that had brought us together to that spot on the beach, and again at the coffee shop. I didn't smell any ill intent or feel his frequency change to alarm. Curiosity filled him, but nothing set off alerts.

"I told you earlier that I trust you, Denver. And I do. But what you might ask or what I might answer is not something I can easily share. There are things about me that I can't have people knowing. And I have important tasks that I must attend to. I don't want to waste the precious time I have or get set back on the work I'm doing if I need to relocate to protect myself."

"Important work? The work at the Beanwater?" Denver asked, relieving some of the tension.

I chuckled. "Yes, urgent brew development.

Purely confidential. I can't say any more about it."

"I knew it. You were trying to throw me off the scent with that whole decaf ordeal."

"Decaf? You mean the drink you ordered last night?"

"No. The drink *you* suggested. It was all a ruse."

"If you don't like decaf, you could have said something."

Denver shoved my shoulder. "Are you kidding? When someone as hot as you recommends something, you don't ask any questions. Cup of poison? Why, yes, please. Make it a double."

I pulled him in for a kiss with a smile on my lips. He was amusing, such a delight. My tongue swept over his lower lip and he opened, letting me in. What was meant to be a quick peck, lingered and heated. Denver placed his hand on my chest and pushed back, breaking us apart.

"Not fair. You can't just kiss me into submission and force me to forget our conversation." His tone belied the message he tried to convey.

"Are you sure about that?" I teased.

"You know, I think I liked it better when we weren't talking."

"That can be arranged." One side of my mouth

tugged up.

Denver reached behind him, grabbing a pillow and shoving it between us. "There. No touching until I get some answers."

He wasn't angry or stern, but I could hear a trace of determination as well. I sighed. "Alright."

"Why were you running through a neighborhood naked?"

I coughed in surprise. "What? How do you know about that?"

"That's not a denial."

"No. It's not."

"You were on the news. Well...your ass was on the news. Your perfectly pixelated ass."

I sat up straighter. "What do you mean?"

"There was a video of a man leaping over a fence. It wasn't much, it only caught a second of you. But I recognized your headphones and I've only seen one person move the way you do."

"Shit. I thought I got them all." I dragged a hand over my face. This was a problem. If Denver recognized me, who else might?

"Got all of what?"

I slid my eyes sideways to him. "The cameras. But then I was running and couldn't concentrate as much as I needed to."

"I have so many questions, but can we start with why you were naked in the first place? Were you caught with someone's husband? Were you peeping in a window? Are you a predator?"

"Yes."

Denver put some space between us, worry tainting his scent, changing his vibrations. "To which one?"

"I'm a predator."

Denver launched himself off the bed. "Are you fucking serious? Please tell me you haven't touched a child. Because if you have, so help me, I am driving you straight to the police myself."

I was out of the bed next, holding my hands out. "A child? What? I would never, that's despicable!"

"Okay. You need to give me a straight answer right now." His words punched through the air and I felt the blow as if it were physical.

"I am a predator. You asked. I answered. But not in the way you are thinking. There is a food chain, yes?"

"Don't you give me any alpha, king of the jungle bullshit."

"It's more like...prince of the sea."

CHAPTER 13

DENVER

"What? What the hell is that supposed to mean?" The question boomed out of me, louder than I intended. I saw him wince and recoil. Calder said my body sang to him, but I wasn't singing at the moment. I was mad and confused and scared that I had the hottest, frottiest moment of my life with a pedophile.

Calder squinted and shook his head as though he were getting overwhelmed, the calm we had been in before shattered. "Just. Give. Me. A. Moment."

It tugged on my heart even though the logical part of my brain said I shouldn't feel any way at all about it. Exasperated, I grabbed his headphones, crossing the room to give them to him. "Here, put these on so you can hear me."

Calder took them, gratitude reflecting in those strange eyes of his. Gratitude and then something else, sorrow perhaps. "Thank you. You don't have to be afraid of me. I won't hurt you. I haven't hurt anyone and I don't intend to."

"Yeah? What about those guys in the alley? You sure did a number on them."

"That was different. You were in trouble. I was defending you, that's all."

I really couldn't fault him for that. He saved my life. But I'd seen what he was capable of. He could easily overpower someone if he wanted to. "What do you mean by *prince of the sea*? Is that like a cult or something?"

"I'm exactly what I said. This land is not my home. I come from far away."

"Where exactly? Why the song and dance? Just come out with it."

Calder seemed to consider his words carefully and I let my gaze drop for a moment. He was still gloriously nude. As was I. This was the strangest, most disconcerting thing to ever happen while naked. I forced my attention back up, away from his beautifully sculpted body. It would be much easier if he weren't so stunning.

"I'm not sure how else to tell you that won't seem far-fetched. I think it's best I show you."

I had to admit I was intrigued, while also slightly worried that he would take me somewhere to silence me permanently. "What are you going to show me?"

Calder appeared nervous, apprehensive. Whatever it was, it must be huge. "I need a minute. But can you cover your eyes or turn around? I'm not sure I can do it with you looking at me."

"Fine," I huffed out and turned around. "Please don't stab me in the back."

"I won't touch you, though I can't say I don't appreciate the view. Your ass is perfect."

"Calder!" I bit out. My dick betrayed me. I should not let one little compliment from a madman get me so excited, but damn I liked him appreciating my ass.

I heard him shuffle on the bed and almost turned around to see what he was getting up to. I imagined him laying there flayed out, cock standing ready, giving me a *come hither* look. Which I would absolutely *not* fall for.

A strange pulse of energy filled the room and a thwap sounded, coinciding with a loud release of breath from Calder. Curiosity got the better of me and

I turned to face the bed. What I saw had me stumbling back until I hit the door.

"Holy shit!"

Calder was propped up on his elbows, bright red hair flowing over one shoulder, headphones covering his ears still. He would have been gorgeous enough just like that. I let my eyes roam down his body, everything waist up was the same as I had seen it a moment ago, but his tan, hardened abs tapered down to blue scales. They started at his hips and cut in a V right above his groin. Midnight blue, iridescent scales that linked and overlapped and covered his entire lower half. Gone were his long and strong legs and in their place...a tail. There was no other way to describe it. Calder had a *tail.* A stunningly beautiful tail with silky translucent fins on the sides and a rather large fluke hanging over the edge of the bed, resting on the ground. The fluke hitting the floor must have been the thwap I heard.

"What? How? Who are you? Explain." Questions tumbled from me as I took in the sight. My hands itched to touch him to see if it was real. How would it feel? If I wasn't dreaming before, I certainly was now. Maybe Calder knocked me unconscious and I was laying on the floor, disassociating, my brain providing the best scenario it could come up with. Though, I didn't know how it made the leap to fish man. Unless it was Ella's Ursula impression that had me envisioning a whole *Little Merman* scenario.

Calder waved one hand over himself as if that explained everything. It didn't. It explained nothing.

"I am Prince Calder of the Pacificus Kingdom."

"The Pacificus Kingdom?" What did that mean?

"It is the kingdom of merfolk that lies at the bottom of what you call the Pacific Ocean."

"Merfolk?"

"Yes. I am a merman, though I would think the tail would have given that away on its own."

My eyes blurred and my head swam. I slid down the door until I sat on the floor, my knees pulled up to my chest. I must have fallen and hit my head. This was some serious hallucination shit.

“This can’t be real.”

“Denver?” His voice floated over to me as if on a dandelion fluff carried by a breeze, soft, wavering.

I lifted my head to look at him. He was now turned on his side, his tail bent where his knees should be and lifted behind him. “Magnificent.” The word slipped from my lips. I might have wondered if it was out loud except for the knowing smile that Calder gave me.

"You're a merman?"

"And a prince, in case you missed that part." Calder winked.

"Right. Sure. Of course, you are." I muttered. If I ever were to envision what a merprince would look like, Calder was exactly that. And yet he worked as a server in a coffee shop. It didn't make sense. But then his fluke waved in the air. There was no making that up.

I stood up once more, my sight focused on him. The way his ripped body appeared even stronger with the tail attached. I walked slowly towards him, curiosity drawing me in. I'd never seen anyone as exquisite as him. Standing at the edge of the bed, Calder rolled to his back once more, giving me a full view of him. My hand raised on its own, reaching for him.

"You can touch me. I won't bite. Unless you want me to."

I'm a predator. His words echoed back to me. Seeing him like this, it was easy to imagine. And biting...should *not* intrigue me the way it did, but his teasing tone had my attention. With permission given, I was dying to know what he felt like.

I poked his side where his hip was not long ago. The scale was hard but cool to the touch and smooth. I let my finger slide down, running across the overlapping scales. Amazed by the sensation, I flattened my hand, squeezing what should have been his thigh. Calder hummed deliciously in the back of his throat. A sound that had my dick perking up. He caught notice, his eyes landing on my still very naked cock hardening. What was wrong with me? This should not be a turn-on. The guy wasn't human. And yet...

My hand continued to glide over his strange form, but when I slid it back up, the small plates lifted slightly and Calder hissed, his body jerked. "With the scales not against." He said through gritted teeth.

"Oh. Sorry." I continued my exploration, my finger gliding along the rim where human flesh met inhuman tail. Calder sucked in a breath again, but this time it was one of pleasure, not pain.

"Really sensitive. If you keep doing that, I'm going to be ready to explode. But the next time I do, I want to be inside you."

My hand stilled. I met Calder's gaze which was focused on me and even with those milky eyes, a blaze pierced me. He was stunning. Absolutely gorgeous.

And the intensity with which he wanted me had me feeling like I was the most desirable man on earth. And yet, he wasn't human. But he had been when we fooled around before. His words repeated in my head, leaving my ass practically begging for him. I let my eyes drift over him once more. And it was confusing as fuck how interested my body was in this beautiful creature.

"Just come here," Calder said as he grabbed my arm and pulled until I fell on top of him. My chest on his chest, my leg on his *not* leg. The feeling of his cool, smooth scales against my already excited dick was exhilarating. Calder tilted my chin up and he angled his head until his lips met mine. It was tentative at first, testing me, giving me an out. I didn't take it. I pushed myself up until my mouth crashed into his. Fevered with need and desire, his arms wrapped around my back, holding me tightly against him. A groan rumbled in the back of his throat as I rolled my hips against him.

My hand roamed down his side, over the contours of each muscle, and brushed against the seamless flesh where scales protruded from his soft skin. He inhaled against my mouth and it was heady and wonderful.

"God, you are so beautiful. I can't believe I'm

saying this, with you being what you are, but I want you so badly, Calder."

"You can have me, Denver."

"Yeah. Okay. You, uh, can change back, right?"

I felt Calder's smile against my cheek where his lips lingered. "I can. Are you ready for me to?"

I was more than ready. I had only had him in my hand and I needed more of him. But this all came out for a reason and I had to be sure before things went any further. "One question first. Why were you naked at someone's house?"

He chuckled, his chest rumbling beneath me. "I needed to swim."

He said it as if it made all the sense in the world. I pulled my head back to look at him. "To swim?"

"Mmhmm. This—" he gestured to his tail—"is hard to keep contained for too long."

"That's all? You just went swimming?"

"Yes. I thought I was in the clear. I found an empty house with a pool, but someone must have seen me and put out an alert. I didn't hurt anyone, I only needed to be free."

I thought of the times I had gone without playing my guitar, whether of my own doing or through situations that arose, and the itch I had to sneak away and pluck the strings. And that was something I simply did. It wasn't a part of me. That wasn't entirely true. Music *was* a part of me. I felt at home when I could play and sing, not doing so made me feel like a shell of who I was. I couldn't imagine what it was like for Calder to have to hide part of himself.

"Does anyone else know?"

"All of the seas know who I am."

I shook my head. "No. I mean, any, uh, humans?" The word felt strange to say in a context where I had to specify.

"Only you."

"Why me?"

"Because you call to me. I feel something when I'm with you and I'm drawn to you."

My heart might have melted a little. Maybe. "Shit, Calder. How do you say such perfect and bizarre things?"

He answered me with a kiss on my nose, on my cheeks, on my chin. He lightly brushed his lips over my face until they met my own once more. I sunk into him. His hands that wrapped around my back slid down and cupped over my ass, pulling me tighter against him. I purred at the feeling of our bodies pressed together. And yet, he wasn't close enough.

"I'm ready." My voice was thick with need.

"Slide over for me. It's a lot harder to pull back in than it is to set free, especially when I'm this wound up and I don't think I can concentrate with your body touching mine." Calder gave me a gentle nudge on my side. I rolled off of him, wondering how much space he needed, finding it harder than it should be to provide it. I thought of the pulse of energy when he shifted before. Was there a blast radius? Was I safe where I was or should I cross the room? But the thought of leaving the bed that held him almost pained me.

Calder grabbed my hand between us and squeezed. "Stay."

I couldn't do anything else. I turned on my side and watched as he closed his eyes, breathing deeply and slowly. I found myself matching his rhythm. Inhale. Hold it. Exhale. Inhale. Release. He took off his headphones and tossed them to the floor as if our tandem respirating helped him tune out everything beyond us. A moment later a ripple seemed to burst from him, a visible wave of energy that forced my eyes closed when it rushed over me. When they opened again, he lay there looking like the tall, muscled, two-legged man I thought him to be.

“Incredible,” I whispered.

That one word broke the mystical moment and before I knew it, Calder had me flat on my back, settling himself between my thighs. His very human cock was standing tall, ready to go. I gulped. It was unreal. One minute he had been laying there with a freaking tail and the next he was leaning over me ready to conquer me. And hell, I was ready to let him.

I spread my knees wider, letting him get even closer to where I needed him to be. Calder ran a hand down my body, following the trail of hair. I shivered under his touch, arching my back as his fingers brushed along my shaft.

“Whatever you do, keep making those beautiful sounds. I can’t put into words what it does to me or how I feel it in my chest.” Calder said as he stroked me a couple times. I whimpered when he stopped touching me.

“Please, Calder,” I begged. I yearned for him.

He leaned over me, his face hovering above mine. “What do you want? Anything and I’ll give it to you.”

“I want you inside of me.” The words came out breathy and alien as if someone else’s voice spoke through me.

Calder kissed me, claiming my mouth with his.

My hands roamed over his muscled back, loving the way his smooth skin felt. He released my mouth and bent over my chest, kissing his way down the center of me. His hand reached between my legs, cupping me, before drifting further south. A brush between my cheeks, circling, had me anticipating what would come next.

"I, uh, have supplies in my pants." I managed to get out before things escalated.

Calder kissed the inside of my thigh and pushed off of me. "Is that right? So you orchestrated this whole thing to get into bed with me?"

"I only wish I were that smooth or confident but I figured it couldn't hurt to be prepared."

Calder dug around in the pockets of my discarded skinny jeans. When he came back and sat on his knees between my legs, he held up the two packets I grabbed at the last second before I convinced myself to go to the Beanwater to see him.

"It's an admirable trait." Calder grinned wickedly. God, he was gorgeous. And a fish man. I mentally yelled at myself to shut up. *Focus on the gorgeous part.* "I understand the expected safety protocols, but for the record, I cannot give you any diseases."

“That may be. But I just saw you with a tail, so it’s already crazy enough that we are doing this, but I don’t want to have to worry about getting pumped full of fish babies. I’m no seahorse.”

Calder threw his head back and laughed. “You are a lovely surprise, Denver. That’s not quite how that works and I’m no seahorse either. But we’ll do it your way until you change your mind.”

He fiddled with the packets, turning them over in his hand, feeling the edges and their shape. I sat up and took them from him. “Can you really not see what they say?”

“My eyes are adapted to the water. If you were to have your eyes open in a pool, would you be able to see clearly?” I shook my head no. “I can easily see through the depths, everything appearing to me as it would to you on land. The glasses help, though they aren’t perfect. I had to make do with what I could without the invasion of seeing a doctor who would be able to tell that something was very different about my sight.”

“How does that work? You seemed to know each move of the men who attacked me before they did it.”

“With sound and vibrations. Those things play a big role underwater. I have extra cilia in my ears that help detect movement and resonance. But it carries and flows differently in the water. A whale's song can be heard ten thousand miles away. It can be detected even by your human ears, but it is much clearer and crisp to mine, grasping every nuance and detail. Which is why noise can become overwhelming to me above. There's no water filtering it, it just echoes and bounces off of brick and metal, all of it all at once, unless I can pick something to focus on. Like you. You center me so that all else fades away."

I leaned forward and kissed him, my hands going to his hips and pulling him into me. "You are truly remarkable, you know that?"

"I did tell you I'm a prince, right?"

I snickered. "And your humility only adds to your charm."

Calder brushed his mouth over my jaw and followed it to the base of my ear. He nipped at my ear lobe which sent sparks through me. His lips trailed down my neck and nipped at the curve of it. Yeah, we'd had enough talking.

I ripped open the travel lube packet and handed it to him. "Let's start with this. Be careful, it's open at the top."

Calder took it from me and planted his free hand on my chest, pushing me back into the bed. I watched as he slicked his fingers and placed the packet carefully on the bed beside me. He kissed my knee before pushing it up and out. Cool, wet fingers teased me. I pushed out, begging, needing him to do more. When he obliged and pressed a finger in, I gasped. It had been way too long, but even if it hadn't, everything with Calder tonight felt like I'd been waiting for years for him to be touching me like this.

"More, please." Maybe another time I might have been embarrassed by the plea in my voice, but with the way his coated eyes gleamed, I couldn't bring myself to care.

He pumped in and out, before adding another finger, stretching and readying me. My breathing hitched and my heart was beating rapidly. I grabbed the condom packet and ripped it open, handing it to Calder. I watched as he rolled it over his glistening head. He used the remaining lube in the packet and positioned his tip, pausing to look up at me.

"You know what I am now. Are you sure you want to do this? We don't have to."

"Yes, we really do. I need you so badly. Please, Calder." I was hungry for him, starving. And with this beautiful man, merman, whatever he was, looking at me with the same urgency that I felt, I couldn't possibly stop.

"I love the way you say my name like that." He purred.

Slight pressure and he slid in, waiting and letting my body adjust. Inch by excruciating inch until he was seated entirely inside of me. I felt so full, so wonderfully stretched. Calder pulled out and slammed back in, eliciting a loud moan from me.

"Your body makes such beautiful music," he said as he drove into me again. Over and over, brushing over that special spot that had me seeing stars or fishes perhaps. I grabbed Calder's ass with both hands, pulling him, wanting him as deep as I could get him.

After waiting for this for what felt like hours of arousal, eons really, I was nearly there. Calder grunted and moved, I panted and pushed, meeting him with everything he gave me. My whole world was on fire. Pressure was building and I was aching for release.

"You're so close, I can feel the way you are vibrating with it," Calder growled out. He reached between us and stroked me. With him inside me and his fingers wrapped around me, it was perfectly too much. I came hard, gasping for breath and shuddering in the afterquakes rolling through me.

Calder made this humming lyrical sound as he

thrust into me and stilled as he came. When he was done, he leaned down and captured my mouth with his. I couldn't speak, I had no words, but I tried to convey what I felt in the kiss I gave him. Powerful, mesmerized, in awe, content. Sex with Calder was incredible, it almost made me forget that he was anything other than a perfect specimen of a human.

Gone were his long and strong legs and in their place...a tail. There was no other way to describe it. Calder had a *tail*.

CHAPTER 14

DENVER

I wanted to stay there in Calder's arms and never leave them again, but it was already the middle of the night and I was going to need some sleep before work. If I remained in his bed it would have been too tempting to see how many times we could bring each other pleasure in one night. But I'd already left Ella to cover the store two days in a row.

She would understand, she would probably be thrilled with the reason, but I was the manager and owner. It wasn't right for me to continue shirking my responsibilities. Calder watched me as I hunted for all of my clothes on the floor of his room. Damn, it was hard to walk away from him, especially with how I could feel his gaze trailing over me.

After I was dressed, Calder got out of bed and threw the cover in place. "You don't have to get up on my account."

He crossed the room in all his naked glory and stopped before me. "I can't sleep in that bed unless you're in it with me."

"Right. You sleep in the bathtub, which is totally normal." How easy it had been to forget what he was when he had me begging and pleading. "How is that comfortable for you? There's no way you fit in there."

"Not completely, no. But the water is comforting and it muffles the noise enough to let me relax."

Calder stepped closer to me and put his hands on my cheeks, tilting my head back. He closed his mouth over mine, searing me with the memory of his lips, the taste of him.

"Can I see you again?" I asked, a mixture of hope and dread tangled together. One night with Calder and I didn't want it to end, maybe not ever. Not with how perfectly satisfied I felt, the excitement of what he was, and what a unique situation it was. Unless it wasn't. For all I knew, all the princes of the sea were walking around on land seducing humans.

"I'd really like that." The half-smile he gave me

nearly had me swooning. I couldn't get over this gorgeous person looking at me like *I* was the incredible one between the two of us.

"Alright, great." I started to move to the door but stopped and faced him. "Uh, thank you for trusting me, Calder. I promise to keep your secret, no matter what."

"I said that I did, I meant it. I can feel the truth and honor in your words. But I appreciate you saying it. Thank you. Rest well, Denver."

"Rest well, Calder."

The past two days caught up to me and when I got home, I collapsed in my bed. A bed that felt rather lonely without the hard, lean body to lay beside. Shadow jumped up and laid down on my back, so helpful. It didn't matter, though. I was out soon after my head hit the pillow.

My alarm blared far before I was ready. Though it wasn't as long as I would have liked, I slept hard. The kind of sleep that followed multiple orgasms with a partner who knew what he was doing. A sleepy smile stretched across my face at the memory.

Ella was waiting for me at the shop with coffees in hand, bless her. She followed me in as I unlocked the door. I was about to grab a cup from her when she pulled it back.

"Nuh-uh. You can have this when you tell me what happened with your mystery man last night. You tell me he's on the news and then you go off the grid. I didn't see or hear anything from you, no messages, no posts on social media. I half-worried you got yourself kidnapped or killed. But, you're alive and you're here. So what happened? Did you talk to him?"

I couldn't stop the way my lips tugged up at the corners. "Yeah, we talked."

"Oh my God! You got laid." She set the coffee down on the counter and held her hand up for a high five.

"And then some," I smirked and even though it seemed weird considering the amazing night I had, I slapped my hand against hers.

"So how do you go from this guy I met might be a creeper to getting dicked down?"

"Oh, uh, yeah. That wasn't him." I trusted Ella, but there was no easy way to explain what happened or why Calder did what he did. No human explanation that was. A small lie, but easier for both of us.

"Really? But you seemed so sure."

"It was just my imagination. Or over-exhaustion.

Maybe I wasn't fully awake yet and my brain supplied the rest. Like red-car syndrome. You know how once you buy a red car you see them everywhere."

"Oh." Her face fell with disappointment at the lack of juicy gossip.

"Oh my gosh, you'll never guess who he *actually* was, though!"

Ella's green eyes widened, "Who?"

"Beachy Bigfoot." I could give her that much at least.

"Shut the front door! Are you serious?"

I leaned against the counter and ran my hands over my face. "God, he's so beautiful, El. It's hard to believe it was real. That *he's* real."

That was true. Here I was a regular man, standing in a hardware shop, dreaming of the merman I'd shared a bed with. I was in some sort of fairy tale.

"Did you at least get his number this time?"

"Fuck." I didn't remember seeing a phone or feeling one in his pocket when we were grinding against each other. Maybe he didn't even have one. But then, who would he call? All of his people, *not* people, lived underwater. I seriously doubted they had reception down there.

Ella slapped my shoulder and let out a loud laugh.

"Leave it to you to meet the man of your literal dreams only to muck it up. I love you, Den, but sometimes I wonder about you."

"You and me both."

CALDER

I already ached with Denver's absence. A hole, a chasm, quiet and blaring all at once. The sound of him that repelled everything was gone and tidal waves of noise crashed in their wake. There was no better sound dampener than the thrum of his heart beating or the airy breaths of pleasure.

Get over it, Calder, I canted to myself. One night shouldn't knock me off course. No matter how fucking fantastic it had been. I'd only revealed myself to a few humans back home, though they knew of our kind already, they viewed us as gods who walked among men.

I hadn't been sure how Denver would take it. From everything I had seen since being in the city, humans tended to fear anything new and unknown. Even though he was shocked at first, he'd come around quickly. I thought our night would have ended there, strange and weird, and Denver running away to process. Instead, he stayed and gave me his body. He gave me every sound, every movement, every hum, and catch of his breath. To know that I was the one eliciting those things from him was incredible.

I called my tail back in and toweled off. It was my day off from work but I didn't have internet at home, so I got dressed and packed my computer to take to the Beanwater. I switched off between there and the library, if I needed a change of environment. With Denver on my mind, I decided to stick with the coffee shop on the off chance he came looking for me. Perhaps it was wishful thinking but I didn't know how else to get ahold of him.

With headphones on, I made my way to the Beanwater. Erica and Jen were there for the morning rush and waved to me when I came in. I sat at my usual table in the back, as far away from everyone as possible. As soon as I had the internet connected, alert after alert popped up. I subscribed to environmental news sites that often had all sorts of updates about wildfires, power plants, radiation. Humans sure knew how to fuck up their world. But when I clicked on the alert, my heart stopped.

Oil Rig Explosion Off The Coast of California

I scrolled through the information, the time

stamps showing it happened early that morning. *Of course,* the rig had connections to Cal Chem, that name seemed to show up on all the sites. Every time I saw the stories tied to that company my skin crawled and I felt the urge to act.

They managed to get the fire out, but there was still a lot of damage done and oil was actively leaking. Oil leaking into the ocean. I thought of how harsh the water had seemed close to shore from the fumes and chemicals of the boats, but that would be nothing like the effects of black tar oozing directly into the sea. It would take me hours to get there. And what would I do when I did? I didn't know but I couldn't sit here and do nothing. Not when there were beings in danger.

If I could get to the nearest beach, I could swim there faster than it would take me to drive. But I needed to get to the shore first. A bus would take too long, too many stops along the way, and that skin-crawling anxious need to act would make me far too restless to sit on a bus. I needed a vehicle and someone who could drive it. Learning to drive hadn't been a priority to me, not with how little time I had on land. I didn't have any proof of identity anyway and it would bring more questions I didn't need.

Denver! I closed my laptop and went to meet Erica who was behind the counter. "Good morning, Calder. Can I get you anything?" She leaned forward, angling her breasts at me as I felt her eyes rake over my body. We didn't work together since we were on opposite shifts, she was nice enough but she didn't seem to get the hint that no amount of cleavage would catch my attention.

"Good morning, Erica. Is Lee in yet?"

"Not yet, handsome. But I'm sure I can help you with *whatever* you need."

If she leaned any further, she might topple over. "I need to find the contact list that he has for the performers."

"Oh? Is there a certain someone you're trying to reach? Did she forget to give you her number?" She said with a hint of disappointment in her teasing tone.

"Not exactly. I found something that belongs to him and I'd like to return it." Another small lie but it was the easiest way. I had to admit I liked the way she shifted and her vibrations changed with my answer.

"Oh. Him?" Maybe now she would finally get it. "Fine, let me see if I can find it. You know this is breaking privacy rules and all, we're not supposed to give out any of that information."

I reached across the counter and grabbed her hand. "I know. I understand and you can tell Lee when he comes in, so you don't have to feel like I'm trying to get you to do something untoward. He knows that I was with him."

I could practically hear her jaw drop. But she sighed, "I swear all the good ones are taken or gay."

"I'm sorry, Erica."

I felt a whoosh of her hand as she waved it through the air. She went to the office and came back with a notebook. "Okay, handsome. Who's the man that's got you all worked up?"

"Denver Greene."

"Well, damn! You move fast. He was just here two nights ago."

"I just need his number and a phone."

"Why not use *your* phone? Did he block you or something?"

"I don't have one."

"Wait! You're saying you don't have a phone? Like for reals?" Disbelief colored her voice. I knew it was strange when everyone seemed to be connected to their devices day and night.

"Yes, and that's why I'm here asking you for help."

"Oh, sweetie! To have a booty call, one must be able to *call*. It's in the name. Well...texting will do too. Do yourself a favor and get a phone. Anyway, here's your boy's number." She rattled it off.

"Thank you. I appreciate this." I dipped my head and pointed to the Beanwater's phone.

"Sure, go ahead." She indicated and I grabbed it off its stand and went to the back with it. I breathed in deep and dialed the number.

It rang and went to voicemail. I started and stopped a few times trying to figure out what to say in the message. But I'd taken too long and the call ended. *Shit!* I called and again it rang until it went to voicemail.

I still wasn't prepared when it beeped. "Denver? Fuck. What am I doing?" I mumbled and ended the call. Trying to plan what to say this time, I said it over and over in my head. This shouldn't be that hard, but the rings, beeps, and robotic voice were throwing me off.

The phone rang once, twice, three times, and it picked up. I started talking right away this time, "Hi Denver, it's me, Calder. I need to get somewhere and I hope you don't mind me calling you, but I could really use your help. Okay. Thanks, goodbye."

I was about to hang up when I heard Denver reply, "Wait, Calder! What is going on? Are you okay?"

"Oh? You're there?" I didn't expect to hear him after the last few tries, I assumed it went to his voicemail.

He chuckled slightly. The sound both soothed and excited me. "I'm here. What's going on?"

"Did you hear about the oil rig?"

"Yes, it's terrible. I can't believe it could happen again since they put all the extra safety procedures into place after that last one."

"I need to go there."

"To the rig?" Denver asked carefully.

"Yes. I have to see if I can help somehow."

"That's commendable, but a lot of people are already working on it. They have the fire out, so now it's just a matter of containment."

"Denver!" I snapped, sharper than I meant to, but the situation's urgency stole my patience. "I might be able to help in ways that they can't."

"Shit. Right. I almost forgot. Which is weird, that's not exactly something a person should forget. Okay. What do you need me to do?"

"I need you to drive me to the ocean as quickly as

possible."

"To the ocean?" He repeated.

"A beach, a harbor, whatever I can get to the soonest that connects to the sea. I can swim there."

"Alright. I'll be there as soon as I can."

I took the phone back to Erica, thanking her. I opened my computer and continued to read the large font to get as much information as possible. Twenty minutes later I heard Denver's truck pull up and I ran out and got in the passenger seat without waiting.

"Okay, let's go."

"Hi to you too." Denver snickered as he put his foot on the gas.

"I'm sorry. Thank you for coming. You're the only one I could think of. And public transportation would have taken even longer and wouldn't get me exactly where I need to be. I hope this didn't create any problems for you."

"Ella will get over it. She's more curious than anything. She is dying to meet the man that keeps pulling me away from work."

"Hmm. Does she know about me?"

Denver reached across and squeezed my bouncing thigh. His hand on me was comforting and alluring, reminding me of the ways we'd touched each other the night before. "That's not my secret to tell, Call."

"Call?"

"I don't know, just trying it out as a nickname. It's either that or Fish Boy."

"Please *not* that. But Call, I don't mind it." I hadn't had a wordspeak nickname before. Plenty of cants or names below from my siblings and friends, but it was nice to hear something picked for me. "Thank you, I appreciate you keeping my secret for me. I would like to meet your friend, maybe after all of this."

Denver grew quiet, though his hand stayed on my thigh. I liked the warmth of him, the connection it gave us, the way my nerves relaxed beneath his touch. I placed my hand on top of his.

"What do you plan to do when you get there?"

I stroked my thumb over his. "I am not entirely sure. I only know that I have to try to help."

"It could be dangerous." Worry colored the tones of Denver's lovely voice.

"It probably will be. But there are sea creatures and beings that are in harm's way. I may not currently be under my father's command, but I still have a duty to the sea."

"I understand. It doesn't make it easy to think of you putting yourself in jeopardy, but I get that you feel you have to. I think my father would have liked you. He was a Marine. He would proudly go to the frontlines if it meant protecting others."

I turned to face him even as his concentration remained on the road. I could feel a slight tremor in him and a change in his tone. The same feeling that he conveyed with the song he sang at the Beanwater. Sorrow and pain seeped through.

"I'm sorry." I wished I could sing him a song, anything to help ease the ache I felt from him. But the ones I knew sounded better echoed through water. "Will you tell me about him?"

Denver smiled sadly and he slid his gaze over to me. "Maybe another time."

"Alright. Whenever you are ready, I am here for you."

We sat in silence for a while. Well, it wasn't silent, not really. I was accompanied by the music Denver made, the notes within his body and without. His heartbeat, tapping on the steering wheel, brushing his thumb over my jeans, his steady breathing, his contemplative hums as he looked at the navigation device. I took off my headphones, focusing on everything that was Denver. It made the usually loud drive in a vehicle much more pleasant.

He pulled into a parking lot. I didn't hear waves or the rolling of pebbles under their movement, but I smelled the brine of the sea and it called to me. The sense of home when I have felt so far from it for so long drew into me with each inhale.

"Where are we?"

"You said somewhere you could swim from, right? This is a bay that has an inlet connected to the ocean. It doesn't have big boats and isn't too crowded. It's recreational, mostly kayaks and canoes. I thought it might be easier for you to get to the water sooner without a long stretch of sand to have to walk over first or draw attention to yourself. And there are plenty of bushes that help provide a little more privacy from leering eyes. Will it work?"

Denver looked anxious yet hopeful. Leaning across the car, I kissed him. "It's perfect, thank you."

I got out and surveyed the area. It was broad daylight. But as Denver said, there was greenery that went nearly up to the water's edge. I started running towards the water, anxious to dive in and shift with a longing to be fully enveloped by water not tainted by chemicals like the pool and submerged far more than the bathtub allowed. I was pulling off clothes as I went. Shirt, shoes, socks, pants. All these human things were in the way of my true form. My thumbs were hooked under the elastic of my underwear when Denver yelled for me.

"Call! Wait!"

I paused and looked back at him. He was following the path I had taken, collecting all my deposited items. When he reached me, he held out his hand and pointed at my glasses. Right. I wouldn't need those soon, but I would when I got back. I placed my glasses in his palm.

Denver grabbed my neck and pulled me down to meet his mouth once more. A hard, searing kiss. "Make sure you come back, okay?"

A twinge of pain hit my chest as I remembered Marin asking me to promise the same thing, to return. I placed a hand on his cheek, "That's my plan. Will you wait for me?"

"As long as I have to."

With that promise from him, I stripped the final layer of clothing away and smiled when I heard Denver's soft intake at the sight of me naked before him. I kept that sound in my head as I dove into the water. The salt of the sea was a breath of fresh air as it slipped through my gills. All the wrongness that I felt over these past several months was gone in an instant.

My tail came forth and with that first flick of my fluke propelling myself deeper to stay out of sight my entire body hummed with relief and excitement. I pushed and swam as hard as I could. The entry to the bay had a netting across it. The squares were big enough to let fish through easily but small enough to prevent sharks or bigger sea creatures from going into the bay, keeping it safe for them and for human recreational use. I couldn't quite fit so I ripped a strand which gave me enough room to squeeze through. It would still be fine. If sharks felt or sensed a barrier, they turned away.

With the location in mind, I drove myself forward, staying as close to the ocean floor as possible to avoid boats. Even still, they didn't have to see me with their eyes. They had technology that could spot living beings underwater. I whistled and canted a special tune at a high frequency. It was a call for help. One that was answered almost immediately as schools of mackerel surrounded me, forming a bait ball, a large moving mass normally used during predator attacks. I *was* a predator but I was a prince too. The fish recognized me for who I was and were providing cover for me. I swam in the middle and they stayed with me along the way. If anyone was looking, all they would see was the large ball of mackerel swimming at a rapid speed. I was a shadow in the cloak of darkness.

CHAPTER 15

DENVER

I waited. I sat on the pebbled beach, toes mere inches from the water, and I waited. I had no idea how long it would take Calder to swim the hundred miles or so to the oil rig and back. Luckily, I had water bottles and snacks in a storage compartment under the backseat. My dad always insisted I have emergency supplies in case my truck broke down or I got stranded somewhere. As much as he was the type who prepared for anything, I doubt he would have envisioned the emergency being merman-related.

"Thanks, Dad." I lifted my beef stick in the air, raising it to him, before taking a bite. I pulled out my phone to see if I could get updates on the clean-up.

The wi-fi was terrible and it couldn't keep up with the live feed. Instead, I clicked on the short update clips. It took forever to load and even then it kept freezing.

"Multiple agencies are on scene." "Fire is out." "Oil leaking." "Biggest concern." *Gah!* I needed to know what was happening. I scrolled through Google looking for different media coverage. So far nothing about a merman sighting, no red-haired captive caught in a fishing net, no naked man hooked by a fisherman that thought he caught the big one. No men in black suits with alien equipment. What would happen if he got captured? What would they do to him? What if he gets injured? All kinds of scenarios ran through my head, each one worse than the last.

After a while, I checked again, hoping for newer information. I scrolled until a headline jumped out at me. Unusual Fish Activity Near Explosion Site. I clicked on the thumbnail and it went to an aerial view that showed a dark cloud in the water. I cursed my phone when it froze and refreshed, hoping it would buffer and play better.

"When most sea life are trying to flee the waters surrounding the collapsed rig, there seems to be a massive school of fish heading straight for it."

I watched the video intently until it froze again.

Calder. I didn't know how or what he was doing, whether the fish were a distraction or something else, but it had to be him. I was torn between wanting to get somewhere with better reception to see what was happening and staying where I was in case he came back.

I stayed. I hated the thought of him returning and finding me gone. Hours passed and the sun began to dip. I grabbed the blanket I kept in my truck. I always thought it was ridiculous with California weather that I would ever need a blanket, yet here I was. Luckily, it was pretty quiet most of the day. There was only one family nearby who brought their kayaks. I spent the past few hours on my own, staring at the water. I loved water—even if it scared me—and watching it was relaxing, but not when I was worried and anxious and wondering if he would ever make it back.

Ripples that didn't match the patterns I'd memorized caught my attention. My heart raced when I saw a head break the surface. "Calder!"

I launched to my feet, dropping my phone and blanket, and ran into the water. He popped up again before sinking back under the water. A chill ran through me. Something wasn't right. I splashed through the water not caring that I wore my shoes and jeans and ran to meet him. There was a drop-off and I was suddenly waist deep. Calder wasn't surfacing and I couldn't see him getting any closer.

"Calder!" I yelled one more time. A few bubbles came to the surface about ten feet out from where I was. *Fuck!* I dove into the water and swam as hard as I could until I reached him. The need to help him drove my fear of dark water away. He was sinking and not fighting it. Had he merely worn himself out or was it something worse? I swam down until I could hook my arms under his and pushed off the bay floor, kicking with all my might.

Come on, Calder, help me out! I thought to myself. I wasn't strong and he was dead weight. I cringed at the word choice, praying it wasn't true. The surface was within reach but I couldn't quite make it. My lungs burned. If I held on to him, we would both be in trouble. Frustrated, I let out a yell under the water, using the last of my air.

Calder stirred and suddenly he was pushing us both up, weakly, but we rose all the same. I gasped for air as soon as I broke the surface. He was right behind me but lost his momentum. I caught him and kicked until we were shallow enough that I could stand. I huffed, trying to catch my breath, my arms circling his chest. Calder drew in a deep breath as well. I dragged him backwards until I couldn't carry his weight anymore. I collapsed on the shore, Calder half out of the water. The fluke of his tail only partially concealed.

"Calder, Call, babe? Are you with me? Are you okay?"

He started coughing and spasming. He rolled to his side and puked a thick black substance. *Oh shit!* What was I supposed to do? Taking him to the hospital was probably out of the question. A veterinarian crossed my mind, but even then it would draw unneeded attention. The first thing I needed to do was get him out of here. I couldn't have someone find him like this.

I bent over him, brushed his hair out of his face, and whispered in his ear. "Hold on, Call, I'll be right back. I promise."

I hated to leave him but he was far too heavy for me to be able to carry. I wished I had the muscles to heft him over my shoulder, but I couldn't. The family nearby! They were sitting around a bonfire pit, holding sticks over the fire. I startled them when I ran up to them.

"Hi. I'm so sorry to ask this, but my...boyfriend hurt his leg and I need to get him up to my truck.

Could I possibly borrow one of your kayaks to help move him across the sand?"

The dad stood up, concern on his face. "Uh, yeah, sure. I can help too."

"Oh, no! Thank you. He's, well, he's already really embarrassed, he had a little too much to drink and he's feeling pretty sorry for himself. I think he would kill me if someone else saw him in that state."

"Right. Okay. Well, if you change your mind, I'm here."

"Thank you, truly. I promise I'll get it back to you as soon as possible."

"Sure. Glad we could help. Take the yellow one, it's already loaded on the cart." The father pointed out the one farthest up the shore.

Hallelujah, it was on wheels, even better. I grabbed the handle at the front and wheeled it across the beach to where I left Calder, grateful for the hedges that provided some privacy. He hadn't moved and the sight of him curled up at the water's edge was heart-wrenching. "Please be okay."

I got the kayak as close to him as I could. Now for the hard part. "I'm going to get you out of here but if you have any strength left, I could use a little help."

I crouched down and grabbed under his arms and

pulled with all my might. Despite the chill in the air, sweat poured off me as I hefted his back over the edge of the kayak. I winced at how uncomfortable the position seemed, but it was all I could manage. I grabbed the blanket I had abandoned and draped it over his tail and tried to figure out the best way to handle him. Where did he bend, how did he move? I looped my arms around the middle of his tail where I imagined his knees would be. He was slippery, even more so with the oil I realized now coated his skin and scales.

It turned my stomach to imagine him swimming through that and the black he had thrown up. I reached into the deepest part of me, using every last bit of strength I had and lifted, bending and pushing him awkwardly into the kayak. I got him wedged in enough that he would be movable. "Sorry, Call. It won't be long."

Making sure the blanket covered his tail as best it could, I pulled the kayak up the bank to the truck. I wanted him in the front by me so I could keep an eye on him, but he wouldn't fit like this. One more awkward push and shove onto the floorboard of the truck's backseat, bending his tail until it fit and I closed the door, trapping him in. I wiped the oily residue out of the kayak and ran the cart back to the family, thanking them profusely. With reassurance that everything was fine, they waved me off. I *hoped* everything would be fine.

I drove as quickly as I could without drawing attention. Calder hadn't shifted back and I didn't need to get pulled over for something stupid and have him be seen. I tried to think about what I could do for him. I had zero experience in the care of mythological marine creatures after a man-made catastrophe. I needed to get the oil off him, I knew that much. It had to be clogging his pores or whatever he had. He'd thrown some up, which was gross but probably a good sign. At least he got it out of his body.

As I made a mental list of the things I thought we would need, I changed course and drove to the shop. With inventory fresh in my head, I knew exactly what I would grab and where to find it. I parked in the back, grateful to be away from the streetlights and any prying eyes that might peek in at my passenger in the back seat.

Leaning over the seat, I looked at Calder whose chest was moving, but barely, his smooth skin had a pallid tone that I didn't like. "I'm coming right back, I'm just going to grab a few things and then get you somewhere safe. Keep hanging on."

Luckily it was after hours and the store was empty. I unlocked the door and put in the alarm code, before running around the shop. I grabbed a wheelbarrow and threw the rest of the items into it. Within five minutes, I had the alarm set, door locked, and I was back in the truck. I had never been as grateful for the shop as I was at that moment.

Originally, I planned to take Calder back to his house but it was too far. My place was closer but it was an apartment which meant less privacy. Thankfully, I was on the ground floor, I doubted I could have gotten him upstairs.

After parking, I maneuvered the wheelbarrow to the side of the truck. I opened the door and rushed forward to catch him as he fell back. The momentum gave me barely enough oomph to pull him into the wheelbarrow—at least his butt and back were in—his tail hung over the side. I grabbed a tarp which was much bigger than the throw blanket I'd used before. I wrapped his tail, carefully picking it up, so it wouldn't be dragged on the ground or be seen.

I whispered apologies as I loaded the rest of the items beside Calder and closed the trunk. He groaned when I hit the edge of the sidewalk. "Sorry, Call, almost there." At least that meant he was conscious. I got him inside and rolled the wheelbarrow to the bathroom. Shadow meowed and wove around my legs. "You're not helping, buddy," I said between my teeth as I tried to keep the cart from tipping over. It wouldn't fit through the bathroom door, so I stopped.

I leaned down over Calder. "Are you awake? We've got a few steps left, do you think you can hold onto me?"

He coughed and blinked, his eyes even paler beneath the milky film that was naturally there. His arms lifted and wrapped around my neck, weak, nothing like when he had me pinned to the bed last night, but it was more movement than I had seen in him since he first surfaced. That was something.

"Okay, bear with me for a second. I got you, Calder."

I gripped him around the waist and hauled with all my strength, his arms tightening around me. I managed to get him out of the wheelbarrow and upright, well as upright as someone who couldn't stand could be. The translucent fluke fell to the ground behind him and I walked him backwards, over the small slider frame for the walk-in shower. My back hit the wall and I slid down, Calder crumbling with me. I leaned him back until he was resting against the wall

"Are you alright?" I asked, brushing his hair behind his ear.

Calder moaned but nodded his head slowly.

"Okay. I'm going to get some supplies."

I carefully stepped over him to fetch the orange gallon of soap. It was made to cut through oil, but didn't have any chemicals and was biodegradable, so I hoped it would be safe to use on him. I filled up a plastic wash basin with warm water and grabbed a sponge. Returning to the shower, I knelt beside him.

"I'm going to get that oil off of you. The soap has granules in it that cling to oil to help remove it, but if it's too rough, let me know. I'll see what else I can find."

Calder blinked his eyes open and looked at me. With the slightest indication that he understood, I got the sponge wet and pumped the pumice soap onto it. Wanting to be gentle but also needing to be thorough, I began with his shoulder and worked my way down his arm. When he didn't react or stop me, I continued. Scrub, rinse, soap, lather, scrub. I dumped and changed the blackened water several times.

When I finished cleaning his entire body from

shoulder to tail, I put some soap on my hands, rubbed them together, and carefully massaged it into his face. I grabbed a towel and wiped his face so it wouldn't drip into his eyes or mouth.

"I'm going to wash your hair now. Are you doing okay? Do you need anything?"

"I'm...okay." The painstaking way he got the words out tore at me, but still, they were the first he said and I was relieved to hear his voice again.

"Liar," I said and a hint of a smile formed on Calder's face. I'll take it. "I'm going to sit behind you, it'll be easier that way.

Calder managed to slide himself away from the wall and I positioned myself behind him so that my legs were on either side of him. He leaned back against me. I rubbed soap all through the long oil-slicked red hair, sliding my fingers against his scalp, scrubbing all the muck out of his silky strands. Calder sighed.

"That...feels...nice."

I leaned forward and placed a kiss on his cheek, before getting back to work. When I moved his hair away from his neck, I caught sight of a skin flap I hadn't noticed before. Three actually. Thin parallel lines curved with his neck. I bent my head to the other side and noticed he had the same there as well. The edges were darkened, residue beneath them. I ran a finger lightly over them. Calder shuddered.

"Are those what I think they are?"

"Gills. Yes. Clogged."

"Can I...is it okay for me to touch them?"

"Mmm." Calder rolled his head to the side, giving me better access.

I rinsed the sponge out thoroughly, not wanting any of the pumice to get into his gills, and wiped them as gently as I could, lifting the flaps and cleaning beneath them. I was both curious and, honestly, a little weirded out by them. But once I had them wiped clean, Calder grabbed my hand and pulled it to rest on the center of his chest.

"Thank you." He whispered as he leaned his head back against me. His voice already sounded better.

"Is there anything else I can do?"

"Water."

"Uh, to drink or to be in? I'm afraid I don't have a bath, just the shower."

"The shower will do."

Not wanting to separate from him, I stretched up and turned the handles to both the hot and cold and moved the wash basin outside of the stall. I sat in the shower with him as water flowed over us. Me still fully dressed, him still with tail. Calder tilted his head from side to side, letting the water run into his gills. He coughed a few times, hacking up more black, but then he relaxed and sunk against me.

A while later, Calder patted my hand as if to say, he was ready. That pulse of energy came from him, forcing my eyes closed, and then the very naked man with two beautiful long legs was tucked between my own.

"Are you going to be alright, Call?"

"Yes. I think so. Really tired."

I was starting to shiver in my drenched clothes, sitting in the shower. I carefully moved out from behind him. Calder looked completely worn. If I was going to get him out of that stall, I needed to do it while he was awake. I offered my hands and he took them. He used me to pull himself up, but wobbled when he stood. I wrapped a towel around his shoulders and had him lean against the bathroom wall, while I toweled off his hair.

With that done, I pulled him gently to my bed. He climbed in and I couldn't help but admire how beautiful his damp red hair looked on my pillow. I chastised myself for the timing of that observation after all that had happened. I got out of my wet clothes at last and dried off. As tempting as it was to crawl in naked next to Calder, I grabbed a pair of gym shorts, wanting to be ready in case his condition changed. I sat in bed beside him, leaning against the wall. Calder rolled over and laid his head on my thigh, placing his arm over my leg. I ran my fingers through his beautiful hair and I felt him melt into me.

I sat in the shower with him as water flowed over us. Me still fully dressed, him still with tail.

Denver's heartbeat, his breathing, and the hum of the muted television accompanied my sleep. It was enough to keep me under and drown out the world beyond us. Enough to let my exhausted body rest.

I woke with my cheek on his thigh and my hand tucked underneath him. His warmth and the smell of him were comforting. He felt like home in a way that the sea didn't. I blinked hard, trying to cast off the sleep that held me captive.

It wasn't merely sleep, some outside force was keeping me in place, a weight on my hip. I felt several little pinpricks through the blanket that covered me. I reached out nervously and my hand landed on something furry. Reluctantly, I pulled away from Denver, stretching my stiff neck as I tried to get a better view. A black blob was perched on my hip, golden eyes peering at me. When I moved my hand over the creature, it began to purr. A scratchy tongue licked my hand, making me smile at the strange sensation.

I turned to look up at Denver and saw him sleeping, sitting up against the wall. Everything he did for me flooded my thoughts. There were some blanks in my memory, but I had flashes of moments between him pulling me from the water to him washing me tenderly in his shower.

I'd never felt so weak before. The thick oil that coated my skin and had gotten into my gills was suffocating me, weighing me down. It was miserable. I wasn't sure what would have happened if Denver hadn't taken care of me. I probably would have gotten better, eventually, though he got me out of the water to breathe fresh air, which I desperately needed. And the way he cleaned the oil off me had gone a long way towards helping me heal.

When I sat up, the furry blob stopped purring and got off me. I leaned over and kissed Denver's cheek, brushing his fallen black hair out of his eyes.

"Thank you," I whispered.

Denver stirred and a sleepy smile formed. "You're awake?" He said as he wiped his hand over his mouth. "How are you feeling?"

"A little sore, but much better. Is it just me, or does it smell like oranges everywhere?"

Denver let out a laugh. "It's not just you, or it is I suppose. That was the soap I used on you. God, Calder! I was so scared. I had no clue what I was doing."

"You did an amazing job. You have good instincts. I'm sorry I put you in that situation, though."

"Don't you dare be sorry. What you did was nothing short of heroic. I was watching the news while you slept and they kept talking about this miracle that happened. No one can explain it, but the oil leak was sealed. You stopped it from spreading and causing a lot more damage."

If any creature endured even a percentage of what I felt, it was too much. And yet, I should have done more. I should have gotten there sooner. I'd been distracted after the time I spent with Denver, blissfully unaware of the world around me. But that was a luxury I couldn't afford. I didn't get to be unaware or distracted. Perhaps if I'd gotten the alert as soon as the fire happened, I could have kept it from getting as bad as it did.

If I couldn't make a difference being on land, then what was I even doing here? I might as well be back home, securing our kingdom's future through an *alliance*. Getting wed to Taneesh and never knowing freedom or a heart singing to mine again. The ache of that fate that awaited me settled deep within, even deeper than the ache in my body from yesterday's events.

It was inevitable though. All I'd done was buy myself time. I was no freer on land than I was at sea. But I had to hope that if I could prove to my father, and to King Katal, that I had more to offer than to act as a symbol of union then they would change their minds. To do that, I needed to find a way to make an impact. And that wasn't likely to happen in the arms of a man I didn't want to leave.

I dragged my hands over my face. "I need to go."

Denver touched my arm, concern vibrating from him. "You can stay. Rest. You've been through a lot."

I got out of bed and nearly stumbled, my legs struggling to carry me. Denver came around and wrapped an arm around my waist. "Hold on, Call.

Take it easy for a minute."

Leaning on him, I breathed him in, his scent filling me, the sound of him echoing through me. If I stayed, I would never leave, not with how good it felt to be in his presence. I steeled myself as I faced him and cupped his cheeks with my hands. "I will never forget what you did for me. Truly. You are a remarkable person and I am glad to have known you."

Denver stiffened. "What? What do you mean? That sounds like a goodbye. Like for good."

"It is. It has to be."

"What the hell? We are just getting started. How can this be over already? After everything that's happened?" Pain and confusion flowed through Denver's vibrations and I hated making him feel that way.

"It's *because* of everything that has happened. There is too much at stake, too much I need to do, and not a lot of time to do it." I tilted his head back and pressed my mouth to his, savoring his taste, searing it to my memory. My closed eyes burned.

I pulled away, leaving him standing frozen in shock. When I reached the door, he called out. "Wait, Calder. You can't go..."

"I can't stay." I cut him off without looking back

at him and turned the knob.

"No. Shit. Just...you can't go...like that. You're naked."

I looked down at myself and shrugged. Humans and their nudity. Denver pushed the door shut, stepping in front of me. "All your stuff is in my truck. I was too focused on getting you inside last night that I didn't bring it in. Give me a minute and I'll grab everything for you. You can't go strolling out in the buff or you will be stopped for sure."

"Alright."

I stood awkwardly and waited for him to return. My certainty that I was doing the right thing waned with each article Denver carefully handed me.

"Can I at least give you a ride?"

"No, that would make this even harder. Goodbye, Denver." With my headphones on and glasses in place, I got one last look before I thanked him once more and left him behind.

"Fuck!" I punched the wall on the outside of his building, the impact far greater than it would have been underwater. The sting on my knuckles was nothing compared to the ache I felt with the lack of him though. My heart felt hollow without his singing to mine. It would have been better if I had never known what that felt like.

I caught a bus and took it to the library close to home, not wanting to face anyone at work yet. I'd be there for my shift later anyway. With my laptop that Denver returned to me, I hunkered down and studied every article and media that I could find on the oil rig event. Not one mentioned a merman, only the strange bait ball activity that no one could explain. The mackerel had done their job perfectly and masked my presence from any radar and cameras. While they were prey for many creatures, and I'd had my share of them as meals, it still hurt knowing that not all the fish that accompanied me made it back out.

The oil clogged the water, choking them, even as they stayed in tight formation to protect me while I worked. It took longer than I thought it would to find the leak and seal the hole and by then, I had absorbed too much of the tar too. When we made it back to safety and the school dispersed, I felt the heaviness and stress they carried.

What if there was an oil leak in or around the kingdom, how many merfolk might be affected? What of the elderly and the small ones that would not be able to protect themselves as easily? This was a certain threat to our kingdom and others. Something *had* to be done about it.

Every thought was a riptide pulling me and dragging me around. The poison in the water. Denver's kiss on my cheek. The companies that seemed to bypass safety protocols. The way he scrubbed every inch of my body. The politicians who sided with industries that were known to cause harm. His fingers massaging soap into my scalp. I felt as if I was being ripped in two. Anger and determination at war with the longing to be with someone whose compassion and tenderness made me forget the problems of the world.

I stayed at the library until I had to go to work, and once there, I had a hard time focusing on the menial tasks of making and serving drinks. Strange to go from taking action and facing a threat to waiting on people and talking about the weather.

Lee pulled me aside after a while, "Is everything okay with you? You seem a little distant tonight."

"I apologize. I'm fine, I have a lot on my mind is all."

"Okay. This probably isn't my place to say anything, but Erica mentioned the musician. Did something happen?"

My heart clenched at the thought of him. "No.

Nothing happened, nothing is going to happen."

Lee rippled with sympathy. "Well, I know I'm your boss but I'd also like to think I could be a friend. And I get the feeling you don't have a lot of those. So, I'm here, if you want to talk about it."

"I appreciate that. The timing wasn't right, that's all. And yes, I consider you a friend. Thank you, Lee." He was probably the only friend I had that didn't know I wore a crown. He acted out of kindness and not because of what a connection to me might be able to do for him. Though, Denver had been the same. He wanted me before he knew who I was. No one here expected anything from me, except their lattes and biscotti. I did miss them though.

My siblings, my parents, and my friends, however real or not they were. Having Denver even for a brief time reminded me of what it felt like to be connected to someone and of how isolated I'd become.

It seemed like a lifetime ago since I raced my siblings through kelp forests, played with dolphins, or lazed around talking of romantic pursuits. How Marin and I would dream of what we could do if we didn't have the responsibility of the crown upon us.

As I grew older, folly and games gave way to meetings and decrees. I was to follow my father's tail strokes, training to take his place should the need arise. Though Marin managed to steal me away from time to time.

I wondered how he was getting along without me. It shamed me to think that he hadn't crossed my mind nearly as much as he should. Coral too, though she was several years younger than us. I loved her dearly, but my relationship with her was different than what I had with Marin. I sighed as I tried to push them from my mind. I would see them again in half a year.

I wasn't normally so unfocused at work, had even mixed up a few drinks for customers and had to redo them. While serving coffee was the furthest possible thing from my purpose on land, I strived to do it well. It was ingrained into me early on that no matter the task, you should commit and follow through. Another reason I didn't need the distraction that Denver provided.

For the next month, I did as I had before Denver popped into my life unexpectedly. I worked, I studied, I went home alone. The last one was the hardest part. Denver's scent lingered in the bed I never slept in and couldn't bring myself to wash. It became a reminder, a trophy, like the toys I kept on the small shelf in my living room. The days got easier though as I filled them until I had no room left to think about him. It was working well for me. That is…until he stepped out on that stage again.

CHAPTER 17

DENVER

I was in a funk. A big, wallowing funk. Had been since the whole Calder thing. Back to my day job, to normality. To hammers and shovels and tape measurers and customers and regular non-mythical people.

I found myself staring extra long at each new person I saw, looking for a hint of gills at the back of their necks, even though they hadn't been visible in Calder's human form. I looked for filmy eyes and headphones, both of which I saw on occasion and it got my hopes up for a moment. Though the old man with cataracts or the teenager blasting music weren't likely to be anything other than what they seemed.

Still, I looked. As if there were merfolk walking around buying supplies for home improvement projects.

Ella snapped her fingers in front of me. I might have spaced out, staring at a red-haired man that passed by the shop. His hair was strawberry blond and short, nothing like the deep red strands that I'd wrapped around my hand. "Okay, loverboy. You gotta snap out of it. It's been weeks since you saw the guy."

I scrubbed my hand over my face "I know. I'm trying. I can't seem to shake him though."

Ella whistled, "That must have been some dick if it's got you all twisted up like this over it."

It was. I still fantasized over the way it felt to have Calder inside me, but not only that, simply being with him. The way he held me, touched me, kissed me, made me feel as if I belonged with him. But that was only a small part of it. The sex had been great, but it was everything else that came with it. The way my world expanded when I was with him. The way I felt special for owning the attention of such an incredible being. The way it felt like I was now living in black and white when I once had a taste of technicolor.

"I guess for a minute there, I thought we had something. It gave me hope."

"That's not a bad thing. To have hope. You've been stuck in the doorway of life, afraid to take a step out into it. You met a guy, you stepped out. Maybe it didn't work out, but it's still a step further than where you were. Don't get yourself stuck there. Take another step and another, and maybe someday you'll be running again. Running towards something without hesitation."

I bumped my shoulder against Ella's. "You're like a guru, a power-tool-wielding guru."

"Damn straight. Leave it to the lesbians. We can fix houses *and* hearts." She tugged on her open plaid shirt and held her head high. "Besides, there's other fish in the sea."

I snorted at her choice of words. Not like him, there weren't. But she was right. Even if things weren't meant to be for me and Calder, it gave me a taste of life again. And I wanted more.

"Oh, and by the way. You might want to check your voicemails." Ella called out as she walked to the back of the store.

"What did you do?" I shouted, before realizing a customer had walked in and looked at me funny. I apologized and stepped away before pulling out my phone to see I had a missed call from The Beanwater

Brew. My heart started racing. The last call I had gotten from there was Calder, asking for a ride and a handful of rather amusing voicemails that I couldn't bring myself to delete. Was it him? After all this time? Was he finally calling me again?

The customer approached me, asking where he could find a laser level, and I reluctantly put my phone away. I spent ten minutes discussing the pros and cons of different brands and products with him before he finally picked one out, all while trying not to show how impatient I felt. I was dying to check my messages. What if he needed my help again? My dad always insisted on giving every customer your full attention. That was what brought people back. Especially to an independently owned shop like ours when they had big box stores they could go to and maybe save a couple dollars. Customer service and knowledgeable employees who didn't rush customers off were what made them willing to pay a little more and come out of their way. After I rang him up, I snuck away to my office before anyone else came in. As soon as I was out of sight, I pulled up the voicemail.

"Hi, Mr. Greene. This is Lee Robertson at the Beanwater Brew." I had a whole roller coaster of emotions within the two seconds of hearing his voice.

Relieved that Calder wasn't in trouble or needing help, disappointed that it wasn't him wanting to see me, all while I should have been glad to hear from the manager. "I have some dates coming up and was hoping I could get you in to play for any or all of them. Give me a call when you have a chance and we'll see if we can put something on the calendar. Thanks, talk to you soon."

I put a pause on looking for gigs since everything went down with Calder. Lee called me a while back but I never returned the call, it was too fresh at the time. He could have easily moved on after I blew him off. But here he was, giving me another chance. And I needed it. If I was going to keep taking steps, as Ella said, that needed to include my music too.

I called the Beanwater, hoping and praying that Calder didn't answer. I might have to see him when I went, but I would cross that bridge when I got there. Luckily, Lee picked up and I breathed a sigh of relief. It sounded like he wanted me to come in weekly, a regular on Saturday nights for the next two months. And he was going to pay me. It might not be much, but it was a huge step. With the hardware store closed on Sundays, I could work early on Saturdays, play music, and still have time to relax the next day. Even if it meant seeing him, it wasn't something I could turn down if I had any hopes of getting my name out there with my music.

With the details arranged, I walked out of my office feeling a lot lighter than I did earlier. When I told Ella about my conversation, she slapped me on the arm hard enough to hurt. "Well, look at you, taking another step. Good for you Dennie."

I spent all week practicing in every spare second I had. I felt really good about the first gig I did at the Beanwater and wanted to make sure I could continue to deliver, especially if they were giving me their prime spot each week. Butterflies swarmed inside me as I got closer to the coffee shop. It wasn't the music I was worried about, though. It was the red-haired beauty that might be working there.

When I walked with my guitar to Beanwater's back door, a chill ran down my spine at the memory of my last time in that alley. My head was on a swivel as I clutched my case to my chest, secretly wishing Calder was by my side in case anything happened. *Damn!* Not what I wanted to be thinking before I saw him again. Luckily, no muggers crept out of the shadows or guns held to my face. I made it inside without incident.

Once on stage, I scanned the room, barely seeing the decent-sized crowd that was there. My eyes landed on his tall, athletic frame and even though his back was to me, I could practically feel him stiffen as if he could sense me. But then, he probably could. Even in our short time together he was very attuned to me. Calder seemed to free himself from the temporary paralysis and continued working, not ever looking back at me.

That was fine. I wasn't here for him. We had an incredible, life-changing weekend that would make me question reality forever, but it was fine. Totally fine. Clearing my throat, I greeted the audience and kicked off my first song.

It wasn't the best set I'd done, I caught myself drifting a few times when Calder came into my line of sight, but it had been well received. Hopefully, no one noticed but me, though I had a feeling Calder would know any hitch or note that didn't hit quite right. Lee thanked me, paid me, and I left without ever saying a word to the prince among peasants.

It sucked, but I survived. Of course, my traitorous dick had other ideas in mind, especially when I thought of Calder whispering in my ear, *If I'm distant, it's because I'm barely in control right now*. I wished that was the case tonight. His aloofness merely an act to keep from attacking me instead of outright ignoring me. I could do this though. There was much more at stake than a fantasy come true in a man, but a fantasy I've been working towards my whole life.

I practiced even harder through the next week ensuring that nothing could distract me or pull me out of my music. I wouldn't let Calder get in the way of my dream. The Beanwater made posters with my picture on them. It was a surreal moment when they tagged me on social media, seeing my name and face on official promos. When I got there the following Saturday, the place was filled, standing room only. The audience was into it and I fed off their energy, letting it fuel me as I sang my hardest and played my best.

The only time I almost slipped was when I caught Calder with his headphones around his neck frozen in place. I knew what that meant for him, to be so lost in the music that it drowned out everything else around him, despite the coffee shop being crowded and loud. And fuck if that didn't make my heart do somersaults.

When I was done with my set there was a thunderous applause and it gave me a natural high. I was flying, soaring on the audience's love. I waved as I got off stage and made my way to the restroom. I stood there at the sink, splashing water over my face, feeling quite proud of myself.

The door opened and suddenly he was there in the reflection, standing behind me. I gasped, turning around until I was face to face with him, or nearly with our height difference. Somehow he was even more gorgeous than the last time I'd seen him. He stared down at me from behind those thick lenses, the black frames only highlighting the intensity in his dark blue eyes. Calder's gaze dropped to my mouth. I couldn't help the reaction I had to him or the way my tongue ran across my bottom lip as his filmy eyes were locked onto me.

Not even a heartbeat passed and he was on me, pushing me into the counter, his mouth on mine, devouring me. My mind screamed that I shouldn't allow this, that I should stop him, but the rest of me...God, I wanted him so badly. My arms snuck around his back and I clung to him. I could feel his hardness pressing into my hip and I was right there with him. I'd never been kissed so ferociously as if we would die if even air came between us.

When he let up at last and we both caught our breath, the head above my shoulders finally regained some control. I pushed him back. "What the hell,

Calder?"

"I'm sorry. I couldn't help it. I am so drawn to you. I've never felt such a strong pull to anyone like this."

It screwed my brain up to hear him say things like that. It was heady and powerful and confusing as hell. "You're the one that walked away, in case you forgot. I thought things were good between us and you dropped me like none of it mattered."

Calder took a step closer, but I held my hand against his chest, trying to keep some distance, even though everything in me ached to feel him against me. "It mattered."

"Well, you have a shit way of showing it."

Calder's shoulders dropped with a heavy burden that seemed to press down on him. My heart ached for him, and yet, I couldn't let myself get crushed too. "You're right. I have such limited time, and what happened just brought that to the forefront. I didn't mean for you to get hurt too."

My ears perked up on the last word he said and asked softly, "Who else got hurt?"

"Walking away from you was devastating. Seeing you, hearing you, feeling your presence last week, it nearly killed me."

"Then why the games? If you want me, why can't we give this a try?"

Calder shook his head and put a little more distance between us. "It's not that easy. I only have a few months..."

"And then what? What happens in a few months?"

"I have to return to the sea. My time on land has a deadline."

That sucked the air out of the bathroom. He had to leave? "What do you mean?"

"I made an arrangement with my father to spend one year on land in order to find a way to help our kingdom from above. But when the year is up, I must return."

"But don't you want to return? I've seen how difficult things are for you on land and the need you have to be in water."

Calder sighed and ran a hand over his face. "It's not that simple. I have responsibilities as a prince. Things that I can't walk away from. I'm not free to do whatever it is I wish to do. Not like you."

My head snapped back, "That's not fair. You have no idea what I've been dealing with. You're not the only one that has to do something he doesn't want to do."

Calder reached out for me, but when I pulled away, he looked defeated. "You're right and you're wrong. I don't know your story, but I know your heart. I know you're the kind of person who will go out of their way to help someone. I know you have a passion that bleeds through every word you sing. But all the things that make you who you are...I'd like to get to know that too."

I threw my hands in the air. "Well, which is it? You can't be with me? You want to get to know me? I can't handle this hot and cold bullshit. So you either need to decide we can make a go of it or you need to leave me alone."

"I should leave you alone, it would be much easier that way. There's no future for us. But I don't know if I can."

The pain in his words was palpable and I couldn't resist getting closer to him. I'd never had someone want me so badly that it pained them to think they couldn't. If he let me go, I could move on, but I might always wonder what it would have been like to be with someone like him.

I rested my hand on his arm and he lifted his eyes to meet mine. "What if we didn't think about the future?"

"I don't understand."

"If we both want to be together, why can't we do that? Be together. For as long as we can. We live in the moment and be with each other in the time that we have."

Calder shook his head. "I don't know. That might make things harder when it has to end."

"My father got sick. When we got his diagnosis we knew a time would come when he wouldn't be able to do anything on his own. He could have given up right then, but instead, he lived every moment while he still could, before cancer took his ability to walk or get out of bed. And it gave me a few more good memories with him that I wouldn't trade for anything."

Calder smiled wistfully. "I'm very sorry that you lost him, but I'm glad to know that you had that time with him."

"Thank you, I appreciate that. But to my point, you have a few months. You can do a lot in that amount of time or you can count it as over already and not even try."

Calder lifted his arms and rested them on my shoulders. "If you're willing, I think I'd like to try."

I wrapped my arms around his back and tilted my head up. "If we do this, we do it for real. No more pushing me away."

"Alright." Calder brushed his lips across mine. "Will you come over tonight?" I was about to protest, but he added, "Just to talk. As I said, I want to get to know you more."

"Okay. Talking sounds nice."

CHAPTER 18

DENVER

Waiting was both harder and easier than it had been the last time I sat in the Beanwater until Calder's shift ended. This time there wasn't the intense sexual charge between us, it lingered still, but it was tapered with promise and wonder. When he looked at me as he passed by my table, I didn't feel as if he would attack me and have me begging for release, but I felt a new thrill at knowing that what he wanted was more than simply satisfying a sexual appetite. He wanted *me*, all of me, and that made me feel strangely giddy.

When he was done, the manager waved us out with a knowing smile as Calder's hand found mine, interlocking our fingers. Holding his hand felt wonderful and normal and big all at once. I caught our reflection in the window of the Beanwater. He was so much taller and stronger than me, but we looked good together. It was mostly him, though, he looked like a god, even with his hair in a tight bun and his glasses on. A sea god walking around on earth, and I was an average nobody who was lucky enough to have his attention.

We made it to his house with minimal groping, mostly light touching of legs and hands. If we'd done any more, it would have been harder to stop the momentum and we would have ended up naked and not talking. We'd done that already, and we would do it again, I hoped, but now was the time for us to look beyond how perfectly our bodies fit together.

The last time I'd been in his house, I'd only taken a brief glance around, too distracted and needy for Calder. If we were going to get to know each other, I wanted to know what he surrounded himself with. I set my guitar case down by the door, not willing to leave it in my truck in case something happened. I hung my pork pie hat on it and wandered around the small place. The brick walls were nearly empty, not even a TV, except for one small shelf that held three very distressed-looking toys.

I crossed the room with Calder following behind and stopped in front of the shelf that sat above a fish tank. The tank contained what looked like seaweed in it, which was odd, but it was the contents of the shelf that held my attention. On it sat an old GI Joe action figure, a purple My Little Pony toy, and a Paw Patrol pup. It was a strange collection and nothing that I would expect of a prince from another realm.

"What are these?"

"They are my most prized possessions," Calder said and I might have laughed if it weren't for his serious tone.

"But they're just children's toys."

"I assumed so."

"So what makes them special? I can't imagine they were gifts." A mental image of a mer king giving a toy wrapped in a box to his son brought a smile to my face.

"No. They are treasures. Things I found among trash floating in the ocean."

I looked over my shoulder and saw the affection in his eyes for these random toys. "What made you keep them?"

"I've been told my entire life about the evils of humanity. And there is plenty of evidence to support that, but these toys...I always felt like they showed more than we gave people credit for. That they could design such bright and fun things and create simply to bring joy had to mean there was something more to them."

"There's a lot of good in this world if you look for it. Acts of kindness, people trying to help, art, music."

Calder wrapped his arms around my waist and I leaned back against his chest. "Yes. I've seen things I never expected to since coming on land. And heard things too. One musician in particular." He kissed the side of my neck. I longed for him to keep going, but I didn't want us to get ahead of ourselves. We were meant to be getting to know each other.

"Do you have a favorite?" I asked.

"I do. Want to take a guess?"

I stared at the three very different objects, but there was something about the way the pegasus was placed in the center and a little in front of the others. I reached out and grabbed it, surprised to find it heavier than I expected. I shook the purple-winged pony around and heard something inside.

"Sand. To weigh them down so they don't float away." Calder took the toy from me and traced a finger over the wings. A simple motion but one I imagined he'd done numerous times. "Are they real? Horses with wings?"

"You know...if you had asked me a couple weeks ago I would have been able to say with absolute certainty that they aren't. That it's all stories and fairy tales. But then I met a being who shouldn't exist either. So there's no way to know for sure, except to say that there aren't any known sightings of one."

"So it's possible?"

I marveled at the childlike wonder in his tone. Even knowing him for such a brief time, already my world was different. Who knew what other mysteries and legends surrounded us? Things unseen and unknown. "Yes, it is."

Calder replaced the pony on his shelf with utmost care. His reverence for the simple items was endearing and so unexpected. Each new thing I learned about him fascinated me more. I grabbed Calder's hand and sat him on the couch.

"It just so happens my most treasured things are with me as well. Since you shared yours, I figured it only right to share mine."

I could feel his eyes follow me as I went back to his front door where I left my guitar and hat. I grabbed both and returned to the couch, sitting next to Calder, our knees barely touching.

I set my hat on the wooden coffee table and opened my guitar case. Calder had been wearing his headphones around his neck since we first got inside. He set them on the table next to my hat. There was something about seeing them together so casually that did funny things to me. I imagined coming home from work on any given day and seeing our things laid out together. *There's no future for us.* I tried to shake off the thought and stay in the moment. That's what he and I would have to do. Enjoy the moment.

I pulled my guitar out and instinctively strummed the strings. Calder smiled and leaned back against the couch. "That's the guitar you were trying to protect when you were attacked. What makes it so special?"

"My dad was a lover of music, so much so that he named me after his favorite musician, John Denver. But the man had no knack whatsoever for it. Tools he knew, he could build anything. Music, on the other hand, he couldn't find a beat if there was a laser beat finder. He always said his favorite instrument to play was the radio.

"But when I showed an interest in it, he did whatever he could to support me. He figured if he couldn't teach me or help me grow my talent, he would give me the best tools he could because having the right tools for the job was the most important part. My dad watched video after video, read book after book, and then insisted we do it together. He and I made this guitar together. There is no other like it in the world. This one was bent and formed by my dad's own hands. It was a labor of love. It would have killed me to lose it to those guys in the alley. So you stepping in that night not only saved my life but the thing most precious to me."

"I'm glad I could be there when you needed it. It's lovely. It sounds like you had a really special relationship with him. What about your mother?"

I shrugged. "I never knew her. I'm not sure what happened, my dad never talked about it. Whatever it was hurt him too much, so I left it alone. It was always just the two of us. Father and son, but even more than that, he was my best friend. And now it's just me." That ache that accompanied the thought crept in.

"He's still with you, in your memories, in your heart, in that guitar."

Most of the time I could believe it. But some days were harder than others when I wanted to call him up and tell him something stupid that happened or hang out in the office at the shop with him and talk about weird things customers asked. I couldn't say anything with the emotion that clogged my throat. Instead, I strummed the guitar once more.

"Will you play something for me?" Calder asked. I met his gaze and with the way he looked at me, I couldn't possibly deny his request.

Down, down, down, up, down, up. As my fingers found each chord, the old familiar song that my dad loved came through. A smile stretched my cheeks as I remembered him wailing and hitting all the wrong notes whenever it came on the radio, and later when I played and sang it for him. Even now, with Calder beside me, I was singing it for Dad.

As I sang the John Denver classic about going home on country roads, a tear escaped. Calder sat on his knees, leaned in, and wiped it away with his thumb.

"You are so beautiful, Denver." He held my face in his hands and kissed me sweetly.

I gave him a half-smile, reveling in the awe in his words, and teased, "You can barely see me."

His hand slid down, resting over my heart. "I see you here. I feel every word and note that comes from you and it is the most beautiful thing I've ever known."

I choked on emotion once more and cleared my throat, setting my guitar back in its case. Trying to steer myself away from the intense feelings, I turned the conversation back to him. "What about your father? What's he like?"

Calder shifted, sitting back, and looked pensive for a moment. "He is as much a father as his position allows. But your children can't be a priority when you have a kingdom resting on your shoulders. Still, there were a lot of good times. As I grew older, more was expected of me, and he became more king than father to me, a mentor in leadership more than a parent. I understand it, not even a king is free, not really. But it was nothing like what you had."

I moved across the couch, resting my head on his chest. Calder put his arm over my shoulders and I tucked in next to him. "Tell me a good memory."

"Before Coral came along, she's sixteen, it was just my brother, Marin, and me. Marin is a year younger than me. He and I have always been close. My father used to get us boys into all sorts of trouble. One time he showed us how to make a squid squirt its ink. So we rounded up a bunch of them and took to squirting them at each other until the three of us were black from head to fluke. My mother was so mad. And we had to apologize to the squid." Calder's chest shook as he laughed with the memory.

I smiled wide, it sounded like such a normal thing, a father and sons playing and making a mess, except this was a king and princes and an underwater world that seemed so unreal. "You had to apologize to squid?" I snorted.

"Well...yeah. They were distressed and it wasn't fair. I never felt so stupid as I did saying sorry to cephalopods, but my mother was making a point. Each life is precious, we take what we need for food and resources, but there is no reason to treat something like that. Everything in the sea is about balance and that needs to be carefully maintained for the benefit of all creatures that live in it. And as the royal family, it is our job to lead by example."

"I've apologized to furniture for bumping into it." I offered.

Calder laughed and I loved the way it felt hearing it rumble through him. "Thanks, that actually makes me feel a lot better about the whole thing."

I grinned, happy and content. Being with Calder like this was nice. In the short time since we met, we'd done heated and intense, heroics and heartache, and now we were simply us, together.

"What about your mother? What's she like?"

"She's the only one who can put the king in his place," Calder stated matter-of-factly.

"So she's a badass?"

"To put it lightly, yes. She's fought at my father's side, despite his wishes for her to remain behind. She is his equal."

Is that the kind of partner Calder would need? A warrior who could hold their own? "I'm not a fighter," I mumbled.

Calder rubbed his hand up and down my back, "Not every fighter uses weapons. But what you did for me when the oil made me sick, you fought. I know it was no easy task, and yet you fought with everything in you to take care of me. I would be honored to have someone like that as my partner."

I squeezed my arm around his waist, a silent thanks for his reassurance. "Is that something that happens a lot? Fighting? Battles?"

"Mmm. Resources are dwindling and it's created a lot of tension between the kingdoms. There has been a lot more fighting within the last few decades than there has been in a very long time. But...there are plans in place to try to change things."

Calder's body tensed up with the last part. I

wondered what it was that upset him. Ending wars should be a good thing, right? I considered asking him about it, but I didn't want to push it. If he wanted to tell me, he would.

Changing the subject, I said, "Fighting aside, it's so strange to think that there's this whole world beneath the surface, different people, uh...*not* people, societies, warriors, kings and queens...princes. What I wouldn't give to see it for myself."

"I would show you the entirety of the oceans if I could."

That sounded amazing. I would love to see Calder's world, the one that he was made for, to see him in all his glory. "Do you have a favorite place?"

"I have a couple. Sometimes I'll go to the deepest parts of our kingdom, so deep that there isn't any light. It would be complete darkness if it weren't for the creatures that inhabit it. Even my eyes that can see through dark waters would be blinded down there without them. It can be disorienting so it's warned against, but I did it anyway. It's eerie but incredible, like standing in the middle of the inky black sky, stars twinkling around you. Only it's not stars twinkling, it's different types of fish that create their own lights either to lure in their prey or to confuse their predators. Darkness all around you, a flash here, a spark there, a glimmer of light beyond. There's nothing like it."

"Wow. I've read about anglerfish and they look terrifying, but the way you describe it, I'd almost like to see it. And the other place? What kind of terrors do you seek there?"

"No terrors. It's nothing much really, but it's mine. There's a cavern that I've claimed as my own. Though I suppose in a way it's for the same reason I go to the deep, to get away. To have time to myself without having to be a prince. The toys on my shelf, they were stored in my cavern, along with a lot of other human things that I have found."

"You have a treasure trove?" I asked, smiling against his chest.

"It's no treasure to anyone but me."

I imagined a cave full of children's toys and the tender way in which Calder handled them. That this big, strong warrior of a man, *mer...man*, could care for such simple things only endeared him to me even more.

"What's your other thing?" Calder asked.

"What other thing?"

"Your most treasured things, plural."

Right, I'd gotten so caught up in hearing about this magical, mystical life under the surface that I forgot how it started.

I pointed at the coffee table, "My hat." The hat and the note stuck in the ribbon band. But I was feeling light and happy and I didn't want to think about it right then. I wanted to stay in the little bubble that we were in.

"I'll tell you another time. Right now, I just want to enjoy this." I squeezed him once more.

Calder slid a leg onto the couch and I shifted to give him room. His other leg came up and he leaned his head on the armrest. He pulled me back down until I was laying right on top of him. My face above his heart and my legs on his legs. Calder's arms tightened around me and I sunk into him.

CHAPTER 19

CALDER

Being with Denver was equally wonderful and terrifying. I loved every second with him and feared it ending. I'd nearly told him of the arrangement when he asked about fighting among merfolk. But what then? What would he think if he knew I was no more than an object bartered off to someone else? Would I lose his respect? Would I lose him? I wanted to do what he said. To live in the moment. I only wished that this moment could be frozen and we could stay in it always. Him, in my arms, his body on mine.

We slept on the hard couch, him laying on me. It was wonderful getting to talk openly about my life, my family. I haven't had much more than small talk in nearly six months. And Denver, the more I learned about him, the harder I fell. When he sang for me, I could have died blissfully happy right then and there. It touched me so deeply. His beautiful soul poured out of him with each note he sang or played.

The sun had broken through the curtains. I hadn't rested solidly. My neck was at a weird angle against the side of the couch and my tail itched beneath my skin wanting to be freed. Denver's presence, his scent, his weight, his sound, relaxed me whenever I woke, lulling me back under each time.

He yawned and tilted his head up to see me. A sleepy smile stretched across his face when he met my eyes. "Good morning."

Waking up to that smile made any discomfort worth it. I reached up and ran my hand through his short black hair. "Good morning, Denver."

He pushed up, dragging his body against me until he could reach my face, and kissed me. The slight movement was enough to bring the semi I'd had all night to full hardness. Denver grinned and pushed his body once more. I felt him press against my belly. Heat stirred in me as he slowly slid down my body. He pushed my shirt up and kissed my stomach, a kiss, a lick, as he continued lower. It made me very glad I hadn't slept with my tail out, because I had a much different need now. I *needed* Denver to keep going.

He unzipped the khaki pants I'd slept in and pulled my cock out of the briefs beneath. When he looked back up at me, I could smell and feel his excitement and it was a rush.

"Mmhmm, good morning indeed." His words whispered over the sensitive tip. The thrilling sensation was followed by a swipe of his tongue across my head. I groaned and arched my back. Denver ran his tongue along the length and back up twirling it around me, driving me to madness before his mouth enveloped me, wet warmth coating me. He took me in as far as he could, moving up and down, wrapping his tongue around me. Each movement, each sensation, each hum in his throat that vibrated around me, pushed me closer and closer to the edge.

I rubbed my fingers over the soft, short-trimmed hair at the back of his head as he worked me. "Mmm. You feel so good!"

Denver added his hand to the action, pumping in tandem with the movement of his mouth. The building tension was almost too much and when he hollowed his cheeks, he drew everything from me. I deflated against the couch, empty and satisfied.

Denver crept back up and leaned over me. The smell of me on him was intoxicating, I grabbed the back of his head and smashed our mouths together. Kissing him, tasting the tongue that had tasted me. "Mmm. I like waking up with you."

I reached between us, wanting to help relieve him too. What I found instead was a wet spot on his jeans. I could feel a wave of heat as embarrassment wafted from him. "Sorry, I have been thinking about you all night. I was halfway there before I even started. It didn't take much."

I grabbed his cheeks and tilted his face up to me. "Don't you ever be sorry for being turned on. That is fucking hot. Although, I was hoping to return the favor."

"Yeah, I'm not opposed to that. There'll be time later." He brushed his lips on mine and then his stomach growled.

I chuckled. "Maybe breakfast first."

Denver pushed up and sat between my legs. "Probably a good idea. Only...I'm not really decent anymore if we go out."

"So we stay in. I can cook something."

"You cook? How does that work? There are no ovens or stoves in the ocean, right? What *do* you eat exactly?"

I laughed at the disbelief in his tone. "No, we don't have underwater fires going, no barbecues either. We eat what the sea provides us. But I've had to make some adjustments on land. Fish, shellfish, mollusks, sharks. Too much time has passed between their harvest and being eaten, not like eating it fresh. So, I've learned to tolerate it cooked. I don't eat beef or meat from land animals, my system can't handle it. So, I stick with seafood, fruits, and vegetables. Though, I have found that I rather enjoy dark chocolate. As long as it doesn't have dairy in it, it doesn't bother me."

Denver laughed, "Chocolate is magical, and I usually like mine a little sweeter, but I don't mind it dark either. As for me, I like pretty much everything. I am definitely a meat eater, though. Is that going to bother you if I eat it in front of you?"

"Not at all. You should be able to eat what you enjoy, I just know what my body can handle and what it can't. But that being said, I'm afraid I don't have anything like that on hand." I was going to have to figure out what kinds of things he liked and stock up. That was assuming he would be coming over again. We agreed to do this for real, which meant we might get to have a lot more nights and mornings like this one. As much as I tried to fight it, I wanted nothing more than that.

"Whatever you would make for yourself will be fine. I'm afraid my diet has consisted of a lot of frozen meals lately anyway."

"Alright." I kissed him on the nose and stood up, stretching. I felt a lot looser since Denver worked his magic on me. Loose, light, content. "I have a washer in the bathroom if you want to throw your stuff in.

"Thanks, that's probably a good idea."

I grabbed my glasses that I'd set on the coffee table last night and went to the small kitchenette. Staring in my fridge, I tried to decide what would be the most appealing to him. I pulled out a salmon filet, kale, and zucchini. I shrugged as I prepped and hoped it would be alright.

Denver called from across the room, "What's this blobby thing in the tank?"

I turned to see him leaning in front of the glass tank that sat below the shelf with the toys on it. "Coral made me that bag to carry what I needed when I left home. She stitched it together out of seaweed. If it dries out, it will get brittle and crumble, so I keep it in salt water."

That bag and the plastic figurines were the only things I'd brought with me, and the note contained within the bag. I kept it wet too, hating that I may need it again when I return. I tried hard to ignore it, but it mocked me. A ghost in my room, my future haunting me.

I plated the seared salmon and vegetables. Denver came over wearing a towel and I tried not to think about how easily I could whip it off him. He wrapped his arms around my waist, kissing my shoulder through my shirt. "She sounds sweet. I always wondered what it would be like to have siblings. Though Ella's probably the closest I've got to a sister, but we didn't grow up together."

I grabbed the plates and headed to the small table, sunlight shining in through the window. "Siblings are complicated. You love them, you hate them, they drive you crazy, and they are your confidants. But yes, Coral is sweet. She has a very giving and generous spirit. Marin can be a handful sometimes. He tries too hard at everything. Making a joke, he takes it too far. Training to fight, he doesn't know when to stop. Parents ask us to do something, he tries to outdo me. But I love the guy. And I know that I naturally get the attention as the oldest, but more is expected of me as well. Marin wants to be seen, he wants to be the one that is talked about or given honor. I also know he would do anything for me. He took it hard when I left."

"I'm sorry. It must be difficult to be away from them." It was. The hardest part about being on land. Denver cleared his throat, picking up his fork. "This smells delicious. Thank you."

We ate and lounged around while Denver's clothes were washed. We talked, we kissed, we touched, we laughed. It was easy and light. After I changed my clothes and he got dressed, Denver gently placed my headphones over my ears. It was a simple thing, but I found it very sweet that he thought about it, doing it automatically before we left the house.

We went for a walk around town, me in my headphones, he in his hat, our hands clasped together. Something I'd watched countless couples do. A simple, everyday, normal thing, that I didn't realize how badly I wanted. It felt so right, spending time with him and touching each other casually.

I'd never had a relationship. Not like this. I'd slept with several males and the occasional islander, but having a relationship when you were a royal wasn't easy to do. It was hard to know who wanted to get close to you to get closer to the throne or if something was genuine. With Denver, I had no doubts whatsoever.

It was a perfect day. A day where I didn't have to be a prince, I didn't have to think about the future and what it held for me. Gone were the worries of pollution, corruption, and evil corporations. I got to simply be with a man I cared for deeply. I wished it didn't have to end.

"I have to go, Call. I wish I didn't, but I do. I didn't expect to be gone so long and never made arrangements for someone to check on Shadow."

"Shadow?"

"Yes, my cat."

Oh, right. I vaguely remembered waking from exhaustion with a small beast on me. "Oh? Do you think he's alright?"

"Oh, he'll be fine, he's just over-dramatic about his food. I don't doubt there are crumbs in his bowl he could eat if he wanted to, but he won't. And when he's mad about his food, he tends to take it out on me and pukes in my shoes."

I grimaced. "That does not sound pleasant."

"No, it's really not. Especially when I'm trying to leave for work and stick my foot in my shoe to discover the present he left me."

"So you have to leave then." I tried not to let the disappointment sound in my voice, but now that I had Denver back, I never wanted to let him go.

He folded his hands behind my neck and stared up at me. "Yeah. So...what do we do now? When can we do this again?"

"I don't know how this works. But I would spend every night together if we could."

Denver pressed a kiss to my cheek. "Damn, you say the sweetest things. A lot is happening at the shop this week or I would be very tempted to take you up on that. How about I call you in a few days and we'll see what we can do?"

I shook my head. "I don't have a phone."

"Right. Of course."

"I don't have anyone to call. The only one that would need to get a hold of me is the Beanwater, but I'm there most days anyway. It seems like a waste of money. Something I never really had to think about before."

"Hmm...well, that won't do."

"You'll be back on Saturday to perform, right? We can make a plan for after. Perhaps I can come to your house this time so you don't have to risk Shadow spew."

"Okay, that will work. It's going to feel like an infinitely long week without you. I have to admit, though, I've been dreaming about having you in my bed again. Only more conscious and feeling better than you were last time."

In his bed sounded like exactly where I wanted to be. Well, I would prefer something a little wetter, but it held appeal all the same. I leaned down and kissed him hard, wanting to make it last on my lips long enough to get me through a week without him.

CHAPTER 20

DENVER

"You promise to behave?" I narrowed my eyes while I pressed the lock button to keep her from getting in.

Ella held her hands up innocently. "What? I'll be a perfect angel."

"As long as it's not an avenging angel. Be nice to him, please."

"Okay, listen, Dennie. The guy has been giving you the runaround. Every time I've asked you about him, I get all these weird, conflicting answers from you. Sure, he saved your ass, but he also broke your heart. And you're just running back to him?"

"Weren't you the one that told me I needed to run towards life?"

Ella sighed. "Yes, to something good. Not a mind-fucker. You don't need that."

"El, he's special. He's got a lot of stuff he's been dealing with, but I like him, a lot, and we're giving this a real shot. Can you please try, for me?"

She crossed her finger over her heart. "I'll try. That's all I can promise."

"Thank you." I clicked the unlock button and she climbed into my truck.

We chatted off and on as I drove us to the Beanwater. She smacked my arm a few times when I wasn't paying attention. But it was hard to stay in the present when my thoughts were consumed by the man I'd been dying to see all week. I couldn't wait to feel his strong arms around me, to play in his beautiful hair, to touch him and be touched by him.

With each mile that brought me closer to him, the butterflies got more aggressive. I was so anxious to be with Calder and take him back to my place. I shifted in my seat, trying to will away the excitement growing in my pants while Ella snickered beside me at my obvious discomfort.

Instead of going through the back which led straight to the small stage as I normally did, I took Ella through the front. Calder must have sensed me the moment I walked in. He turned around and a wide grin broke out. God, it felt amazing to have someone look at me like that. He excused himself from the table he'd been helping and walked across to greet us. When he stopped in front of me, he stared at my lips but managed to keep from attacking me on the spot. He had to be professional, I got it, but I didn't have to like it.

"Well, fuck, you're pretty!" Ella exclaimed.

It was enough to shake Calder from his focused attention on my mouth. He let out a surprised laugh. "Uh, thank you."

"Calder, this is Ella. Ella, Calder."

Ella reached her hand out. Calder surprised her when he grabbed it and placed a kiss on the back of it, instead of shaking her hand. I pursed my lips as my best friend tried to figure out what to do with the unexpected formal greeting. For all she knew, he was some guy that worked in a coffee shop. She knew nothing of the prince that he was.

"It's very lovely to meet you, Ella. I know you are important to Denver, so it means a lot to know someone that is special to him."

"Yeah, same. To you."

Out of the corner of my eye, I saw a hand shoot

up, trying to call for attention. Calder dipped his head slightly, "Excuse me. I hope we can talk more later."

"Yup, we'll talk. I can promise you that." Ella said. At that, Calder turned and went to the table. They hadn't called out verbally but somehow he knew exactly who and where it had come from. Had he heard the rustling of the man's arm when it lifted? The subtle clearing of a throat? I would never cease to be in awe of the amazing things he could do.

I faced Ella with an expectant expression. "Well?"

"The jury's still out. He's...odd. I can see why your descriptions were confusing. I'm not quite sure what to think of him. But holy hell, the chemistry is explosive. If he were a chick I would chain my U-haul to that crazy train and ride it until it crashed and burned. Go out in a blaze of glory."

I snorted. "I'm hoping for something a lot less dramatic, but thanks."

"Oh no, hun. A man that complicated, it's going to be epic one way or another, no middle ground."

"Weeell, this has been great. I'm really glad you're here." My tone dripped with sarcasm. "I gotta go get ready for my set."

"Go kick ass, Den."

"Thanks, El." I winked at her.

When I began playing, Ella cheered embarrassingly loud. I even caught Calder's smirk at her level of enthusiasm. It would have fit better at a Crow's Nest concert, not a coffee shop. It meant a lot that she was here, though. She'd been begging to see me perform for a long time. Before my dad got sick, I was too self-conscious to have someone I knew in the audience. But she had been a big part in getting me back here, encouraging me to keep trying and keep playing.

Song after song, obnoxious applause after obnoxious applause, and I was happy. Ridiculously happy. Eager too. Each note I played got me one step closer to being with Calder. An ache grew within me. Being so near to him, knowing he was mine, yet not being able to do anything about it was torture. But I took that agony and poured it into my music. When I finished my set, the rest of the audience showed their appreciation, even if it wasn't quite matched with Ella's. Still, I felt great. It was a good set and I was buzzing with anticipation.

I found myself shoved against the counter, Calder's leg pressed between mine as soon as I got off the stage. One glance across the room and I could practically feel the need rippling out of him. I gave a quick nod in the direction of the restrooms and here we were.

"Mmm. Are you going to attack me like this every time I sing?" I asked through kiss-swollen lips.

"I might." He kissed me once more for emphasis. "As soon as you started, this happened." Calder placed my hand on his hardened bulge. I gave him a squeeze and pulled my hand back before we got out of control. We were nearly there already.

"Later," I whispered in his ear.

Calder let out a dramatic sigh. "You're right."

With great effort, we walked out of the bathroom, trying to look casual and not like we were seconds away from tearing each other's clothes off and going at it. He returned to work and I to Ella.

One glance at me and Ella snickered. "You're looking a little sex-crazed there."

"Am not. It's just the adrenaline rush of performing." I brushed my hands over my clothes, trying to look perfectly kempt, all while my cheeks burned red.

"Uh-huh." She smirked. "You did awesome up there. I'm so proud of you."

I smiled. "Thank you, I appreciate that. Maybe next time just bring it down a notch though?"

"I cannot make any promises. So what's the plan from here?"

"Calder should be getting off pretty soon."

"Yeah, I'm sure he will," Ella interrupted, her eyes gleaming with amusement.

The thought got my dick's attention. I sure hoped so. And me right along with him. "He's coming back with us. Well, to my place."

Her brow shot up. "Oh? You're having a sleepover and I wasn't invited?"

"Maybe next time." I winked.

When Calder was finally done, he grabbed his laptop bag and walked out with us. Ella looked him over and said with a grin, "You packed light for a weekend."

Calder flashed his eyes to me. "Did I need to bring clothes?"

Ella cackled and my cheeks flushed, "No, I suppose not."

Calder leaned down and whispered in my ear. "Did I say something wrong?"

I turned to face him and wrapped my arms around his neck, pulling him down to me. "Not a thing. I can't think of anything better than being naked with you." I followed that with a kiss so he knew

I meant it.

Ella cleared her throat. "Can you two keep it in your pants long enough to get out of here?"

"I cannot make any promises." I echoed her words back to her and she flipped me off with a sly grin.

Ella opted to sit in the back so Calder could sit in the passenger seat. His hand reached over and grabbed mine. I love the way he gravitated towards me, needing to touch me. Ella sat in the center and leaned forward to be able to talk to us more easily.

She began interrogating Calder on his history and he gave a story about growing up on a small island, that this was his first time in a big city. All answers that I knew to be half-truths. Ella seemed suspicious at his unusual tale but she relaxed as the ride went on.

When I pulled in front of her place, she got out but came around to Calder's window. She leaned in and stared him straight in the eye. "You seem like a nice guy and you are clearly into Dennie. But so help me, if you hurt him, I will bury you and plant a garden over your grave."

"Noted. It's good to know Dennie"—he slid his gaze over to me with a hint of humor at the nickname—"has a friend like you looking out for him.

It was a pleasure meeting you."

Ella shook his outstretched hand. "Okay, don't go getting yourselves into any trouble. See you Monday, Den."

"Goodnight, Ella. And thanks." I met her eyes and she gave me a little nod of approval.

"I like her. She's a warrior."

"Yes, she is. She's been there for me through a lot but especially since everything with my dad. I got really lucky when she walked into our store and asked for a job about five years ago. He took a liking to Ella right away. And when we started working together and realized we were both queer, we clicked. We've been tight ever since."

"Will you take me to see your shop? It's something that is a part of you and I'd like to know every part I can."

I glanced over at him. "I'd like that. But maybe not right now. I have other plans for tonight."

Calder hummed, "Mmm, me too. I've been thinking about you all week."

His hand went to my thigh, sliding higher and higher. One simple touch from him and I was already straining against my zipper. I was so ready for him. Luckily, I didn't live too far from Ella. I sighed in relief when my apartment came into view.

This time, I walked hand-in-hand with Calder to my door instead of pushing him in a wheelbarrow and trying not to tip him over. I weirdly felt nervous having him over. The last time didn't count. I was too busy trying to keep him alive and then everything imploded after.

Calder squeezed my hand, "I'm sorry. I won't run out of here again."

It was strangely comforting that he was able to read me so well. I took a deep breath and squeezed back. "Okay."

I opened the door and Shadow was there immediately. Instead of greeting me as he usually did, he went straight to Calder, sniffed his leg, and rubbed against him. Over and over, from the side of his mouth to his ear.

Calder chuckled. "This is Shadow?"

"Yeah. I've never seen him like that with anyone. Normally he hides when people come over. When I brought you here before, I was causing too much of a commotion. He was curious but he didn't get too close."

"He slept on me. I couldn't see him clearly before, because I didn't have my glasses on. But when I woke up he was on my hip."

"The traitor. He rarely sleeps on me."

Calder set his laptop, glasses, and headphones down on my dining table and pulled me in close. His muscled arms wrapped around me. My hands went to his chest, feeling his defined pecs beneath his work shirt. Calder tilted my head up and crashed his mouth against mine. I loved the way he kissed me as if he could draw me into himself and become a part of him.

He was as hard as I was, his erection pressing against my belly. I rolled my hips against him, eliciting a moan from Calder. A sound I wanted to get lost in.

"I'm a little sweaty from working all day and performing tonight. I'm going to take a shower. Want to join me?" I'd had him in my shower before but it was the furthest thing from sexual.

Calder pulled a face, "You naked and wet definitely holds some appeal, though I must admit the shower isn't my favorite."

"I don't have a bathtub, sorry. But I think you might like it...if you give it a chance." I winked at him before grabbing his hand and leading him to my bathroom, kicking my shoes off along the way. When we got there, I turned the hot water on and stripped. Calder's eyes were fiery behind the film in them as his eyes roamed over my naked body. I knew he couldn't see me clearly but it must have been enough, especially when he zeroed in on my eager cock. He licked his lips and soon his clothes joined mine on the floor.

After checking the temperature, I stepped into the shower and dipped my head under the water, letting it flow over me. I wasn't usually this bold and confident when I was naked. But the way Calder reacted made me forget my insecurities.

"Beautiful." He said as he stepped in, watching me but not coming any nearer. Water drops bounced off of me and hit his legs and feet. He took a deep breath as if steeling himself.

I moved out of the water, closer to him, my wet body pressing against his. Calder's hands went to my ass, squeezing me and pulling me tighter.

"What is it about the shower you don't like?" I asked as I traced every part of his chest, circling his nipples, one after the other. His firm body fascinated me, I wanted to memorize every inch of him.

"It's a tease, to feel the water but it not be enough to soak or swim in. It makes me want to shift."

I turned in his arms and pressed my ass back against him. Calder's hands roamed over me, the water barely splashing us. I was hoping to get soapy, our bodies slippery, sliding against each other. I didn't want to force him if it made him uncomfortable though. I was happy to have him touching me however and whenever it happened.

I leaned my head back and he kissed the side of my neck. "What does it feel like?"

Calder nipped my earlobe and scratched his cheek against my bearded one. "What does *what* feel like? This?" He thrust his hardness against my ass, nearly making me forget what I had asked.

"What does the need to shift feel like?"

"Hmm. As you are human there is no real way to convey what it is like, except..." Calder turned me around and pushed me against the tiled wall, surprising me. Though my dick twitched with excitement.

He began kissing his way down my chest, licking my nipples, twirling his tongue over my navel, until he was on his knees before me. The sight of him knelt, staring up at me with a devilish look in his eye was beyond arousing. He teased my tip until he took me into his mouth. My hands went to his long red hair, wrapping it around my fist as I braced myself against the shower wall. An embarrassingly loud moan fell from my lips as he began to bob his head, taking my length.

"Call, that feels incredible, don't stop."

He continued to work me with his mouth and tongue. Sucking, pulling, and when I almost couldn't take anymore, he popped off. He squeezed my base, tight enough to cut off my release, but not so much that it hurt. I was panting and desperate when he stood back up, wishing he would finish the job. Maybe he wasn't ready to, that was okay, but I needed to. I reached down to stroke myself to completion, but Calder grabbed both of my hands and held them over my head.

"No. Not yet."

"Please, Calder, I'm almost there," I begged. My whole body was tense, ready to break apart, stuck in a climax that was held inside.

Calder kissed me lightly. "That. That is what it feels like."

My brain went completely empty, the only thought in my head was the need for release. "What do you mean?"

"The need to shift. Even now, with the water splashing me, it brings me to the brink. I've had a lot of practice controlling it. I let my tail out most nights in the tub, but it isn't the same. I need to stretch, to swim, and that urge makes me feel as if I will rip apart."

"Fuck. That's intense. I'm sorry. We can get out of the shower if that will help."

Calder pushed his hips against mine, my hands still pinned above me. I groaned and arched into him but he pulled away, leaving me aching for him.

"What will help is if I can swim."

"Okay. Can we finish this first and we'll figure something out?"

Calder grinned wickedly. "No. I don't think so."

"What?"

He leaned next to my ear, the warm whispers of his breath making my dick cry out to be touched. "You can come when I can shift. Then we can both have release together."

"Fuck!" I let my head fall back against the wall. "How soon until we can get somewhere you can swim?"

Calder tilted his head. "That depends on you. I could find us a pool but you probably don't want to risk getting caught. There's the bay you took me to."

"Maybe, if I drove fast," I grumbled as I tried to reach for him, but Calder held me in place. I'd never been so turned on and so frustrated all at once.

Calder kissed me, smiling against my lips. "So

what do you think? Should we stay here in the shower"—he rubbed himself against me, stirring the ache once more—"or do you want to go for a swim?"

Stay, naked and wet with him torturing me until I had no will left of my own, or get dressed and leave? I never wanted clothes on more than I did right then. "You are an evil man."

Calder released his hold on me and walked out of the shower, "But alas, I am no man."

I stared at his firm ass, appreciating the view before I peeled myself off the wall at last.

Urgency drove me as I found a pair of swim shorts and tugged them on. Calder put on his pants and nothing else. The clothes wouldn't be staying on long anyway. I grabbed a shirt, simply because I felt weird about driving shirtless. There was always the fear of getting pulled over half-dressed. With flip-flops on, I walked out, not waiting for Calder. I heard him chuckling behind me as he locked and shut the door.

When I got to the truck, he stopped me and kissed me hard, ensuring that the raging hard-on that tented my shorts didn't have a chance to soften. God, he was hot, and I was bothered. So very bothered.

With the kind of motivation I had and Calder stroking me through my shorts while I drove, I made it to the bay in almost half the time as I had before. It was late, the gates were closed. I stopped in front of them, feeling like I was going to scream if I couldn't get him into the water soon, needing him to finish what he started. He said that's what it felt like for him. The need, the pull, if it was anything like how I felt now, I understood his mad naked leap through the neighborhood to get to a pool.

Calder got out of the truck and removed his headphones. He turned his head as if he was concentrating on something. I heard a high-pitch whine and then nothing. Calder looked in every direction, listening for something. Then he went to the gate and broke the lock with ease, pushing it open and letting me drive through. Once I was in, he closed the gate behind me.

When he got back in I stared at him in awe. "What about cameras? Do you think they'll look for us?"

"No. I took care of those first. We're clear."

"You are amazing."

"I'm a prince." Calder winked.

"Yeah, an evil prince."

He chuckled and patted my leg before sliding his hand up higher, making sure I was still ready, still anxious. With no one else there, I pulled my car as close to the water as I could. Calder was already out, stripping from his pants, his glasses and headphones left behind. He walked gloriously naked in the moonlight. Such a beautiful sight. I tore my shirt off and left it in the car, but kept my sandals on as I walked down the pebbled beach.

Calder stopped at the edge of the water and turned back to face me. He beamed, radiant and stunning. He indicated for me to follow and he walked in the water until he was deep enough to dive in. He went into the water a human with two legs. A moment later, his fluke broke the surface and came down fast, sending a wave of water at me.

I kicked off my sandals and ran into the water, desperate to see him, touch him. It was late at night, but the full moon cast enough light over the surface that I could see it rippling with movement. The water itself though was dark and all those old childhood nightmares of sharks came creeping back in. My confidence decreased rapidly the further I had gotten from shore and the longer it had been since I'd seen Calder.

A whoosh of movement under my feet nearly had me jumping out of my skin. But then Calder popped up right in front of me. His long red hair draped on either side of his face. I could feel a flutter of water around me and I couldn't help darting around looking for fins.

Calder placed his hand on my cheek. "Your heart is racing, are you okay?"

"It's the dark water. I've probably seen Jaws too many times. It makes me nervous when I can't see through it."

He slid his arms down my back, wrapping them around me. My instinct was to kick my feet to hold me up, but I realized he was keeping me above the surface. I attempted to relax as I placed my arms around his neck, trying hard not to cling to him in a panic.

"Don't worry, I can see through the water just fine. And remember what I told you that first night together?"

"That you're working undercover on classified coffee missions?" I asked in a ploy to distract myself.

Calder chuckled. "Perhaps. But the other bit."

"You're a predator?"

"I am. And I promise you that there is nothing in this water that I can't protect you from. Besides, you've seen me command fish. Do you honestly think I would want anything around us to get in our way?"

"So you're saying you've cleared the area so we won't be bothered?"

"It's only you and me, the moon and the water. That is all."

I looked around and realized it was true. There was no one in sight, no *thing* in sight, but him. "Okay. Just you and me."

Calder leaned in and kissed me, everything else disappeared. The fear, the uncertainty, the dark water, and even the moon above. Calder became my entire world at that moment, held in his arms, his body flush against mine, his lips melded to my own.

"Hold your breath, Denver."

"What?"

"I've been dying to see you properly and my vision works best underwater. Will you let me see you?"

How could I refuse? I'd gotten to see all of him, yet so far he'd only seen blurry versions of me. But what if he didn't find me as beautiful as he thought me to be? What if he realized I'm an average guy with nothing spectacular about me?

Calder cupped my face, stopping my train of thought. "I promise you nothing can change how much I admire you, except now I will get to visualize you better when I can't see you clearly."

"Alright." I drew in a deep breath and next I knew his tail wrapped around my legs and he pulled me under. Panic started to seep in as I was drawn into the darkness. He held me beneath the surface, his face right before mine as he stroked my trimmed beard and he sang. I couldn't understand it but it was beautiful. It wasn't words but a series of tones, long and short, humming and surrounding me. It was comforting. The way it vibrated through me, I felt it reach every part of me. It was as if I was cocooned in sound that whispered to my soul. It calmed me and made me feel like I was home.

I didn't know how long we remained under the water, him staring at me, touching my face, singing, but I wished I could stay in that moment with him forever. But my chest constricted as I started to run out of air. I jerked in a panic, needing to reach the surface. Again, Calder's hands held my face and he brought his mouth to mine. I wanted to push him away, to scream that I wasn't like him, I needed air. Except...suddenly, I didn't.

My lungs relaxed as they expanded. Calder was breathing into me, breathing *for* me. I threw my arms around him, holding him to me, and took in the moment. With him, I could stay underwater. I wouldn't drown, I wouldn't run out of air, I wouldn't be attacked by anything that could be lurking. Nothing could hurt me if he was with me. I was safe. In his arms, in the water, it was the safest place I could be.

He released me at last and brought me to the surface. I launched myself at him, tackling him backwards, but he managed to keep us upright. "Thank you for helping me push past my fear. That was incredible. *You* are incredible."

"And you are even more beautiful than I imagined. I love the way your black hair flows around your forehead in the water. And your green eyes catch the moonlight and hold it in them as if you held the very moon behind them. Thank you for trusting me."

"I do. I trust you. I know you won't let anything happen to me out here. What were you singing? It made me feel warm and safe and...loved."

"It's called a cantonation. It's how we communicate underwater. Song and sound travel much easier and clearer than trying to speak words. Each note, each hum, or whistle conveys meaning. What you felt was what I was canting to you."

"So your song was telling me I'm safe?" Calder

nodded his head. "And warm?" Another nod. "And..."

"Loved?" He prompted. It was my turn for a head nod, not sure I could speak in words or in cants to respond. "Hmm. Let's see if you can understand this next one."

Calder ducked back under the water without bothering to clarify what he said. Did that mean he loved me? It was too soon for that, wasn't it? But my heart didn't agree. It seemed to be on board with the idea. I felt a vibration roll through me and I ducked under the water to get the full effect.

I no longer felt simply warm. Heat bloomed beneath my skin. With each hum and cant that came from him, I felt an ache building in me. The same ache that Calder started in the shower and continued during the frustrating drive here. I was getting hard without being touched, his song alone calling to me. Calder broke through the surface looking rather pleased with himself.

"And how did that make you feel?"

"Horny," I replied bluntly, my mind confused by my body's reaction.

Calder grinned. "Mmhmm. Do you want to know what I was canting?"

"Hell yes."

Instead of answering, he dipped below the water. I felt his hair swish against my belly and his fingers pulled my shorts down, exposing me. I gasped when his mouth closed around me. His hands held my ass, keeping me above water, while he licked my head and took me in. Water swirled around my balls, between my legs, the sensation strange yet alluring as Calder drew me in deeper. A flick of his tail drove him onto me, causing me to moan loudly.

Calder kept us suspended as he continued to work me. He controlled every movement. I was in complete surrender, merely existing and holding on to him. He never surfaced, he never let up, his mouth suctioned around me. Reason and logic tried to tell me that he needed to come up for air. But he didn't. He'd shown me that. I told reason to fuck right off and stayed in that moment with him.

My entire body tensed, the build-up that started at my apartment had me near bursting. When I came harder than ever before, Calder stayed in place, taking all of what I gave him. If he hadn't been holding me up, my limp body would have sunk into the bay. I would have laid on the seafloor and died with a smile on my face. I felt completely numb in the most amazing way possible. I barely felt him putting my shorts in place once more.

When his face was before me, I collapsed against him. My head on his shoulder, my arms around his neck, as I tried to catch my breath. I didn't even attempt to hold myself up, trusting that he had me.

"Fuck, Call." I had no other words. My capacity for wording had been sucked right out of my body.

CHAPTER 21

CALDER

He rumbled against my chest, laughter rolling through him. It was infectious, his joy brought a smile to my own face. I tilted his head back and kissed him hard, squeezing him to me. His legs circled my tail, feet brushing against it as if he couldn't stop himself from feeling me. It was intoxicating. Not only did he not recoil from me but he sought me out.

"Did that really just happen?" Amused awe bled through his words.

"It did," I said as I nipped at the side of his neck, unable to resist another taste of him. It killed me having to wait after starting things in the shower. While I meant to be teasing him, edging him, motivating him to get me to the water, it backfired. It was as much torture for me, doubly so, the need to shift and the need to give Denver pleasure nearly overwhelmed me.

Denver leaned back and looked at me, "So what did you cant to me that caused that reaction? I mean I'm not complaining, but shit, that was intense."

I stroked the side of his face. "I told you that I had a promise to keep and explained in detail what I planned to do to keep it. Fuck, Denver, you tasted amazing."

"Damn! That was the hottest moment of my life. It made the pain in getting here worth it." So worth it. "And you? Are you feeling relieved now that you're swimming?"

"Very much. I needed this. The last time I got to swim was to the oil rig and well, that hadn't been exactly enjoyable. Thank you for bringing me here. It's even better having you with me."

Hearing him and feeling him in the water made each note that rang between us even stronger. And seeing him truly for the first time...I wished that I could keep him underwater for all time, simply to feast upon the beauty of him. His short, black hair, his thin cheeks covered in the perfect trimmed beard, his green eyes. *He* was perfect.

"And thank *you* for keeping your promise." Denver half-smiled. It made me want to dive right back under and feast on the rest of him too. But now that my tail was out I had to use it.

"Mmm. That was entirely my pleasure. And when we get back I plan to show you how much I appreciate that you did this for me. But first, I *do* need to stretch and swim for a bit. Remember, nothing is out here but you and me. Right?"

"Swim as much as you like. I'll be here when you're ready."

I kissed him soundly and dove back under the water. I stayed within the bay, it was plenty big enough and I wanted to remain near him. His steady pulse stayed with me as I alternated between swimming hard and fast, really working my tail, and coasting happily along the floor of the bay. I could hear Denver kicking in the water, no longer afraid of whatever might be lurking unseen.

I'd felt his panic when he first got in and felt it ease when I held him and breathed air into him. He gave himself over to me completely, trusting me. That was a heady thing. To have someone place that kind of faith in you. I could have easily dragged him to the depths and he would have been powerless to stop me. Denver trusted me and that was something I never wanted to break.

A sound reached my ears that had me grinning stupidly and propelling myself towards him. He must have dunked his head underwater and was making noises. It sounded like he was blowing bubbles at first but then it changed. Was he attempting to cant? To sing? It was gibberish and yet it compelled me.

When I popped up in front of him, he let out a startled gasp at first and then laughed at himself, looking sheepish. "Sorry, I didn't see you coming. Still weird to have something in the water with me, even if I know it's you. Did you hear me?"

I chuckled, "I did. You called to me."

"Did I? I mean, did I actually say something?" His eyes rounded with wonder.

I let out a loud laugh. "No, love. It was utter nonsense but it was the most fucking adorable thing I've heard."

"Oh." The look of disappointment on Denver's face added to my amusement. "Can you teach me?"

"I'm not sure it's that easy. It's more felt than taught. But I can promise you no matter what kind of noise you make, if you are in the water and you need me, I will come to you."

"Anytime?"

I nodded.

'Anywhere?"

"The sound of you is imprinted on my heart. Wherever you might be, the water will carry it to me and I can find you."

"Incredible. How did I get so lucky?" Denver whispered. He backed up as his feet touched the ground below. I followed, caught in the invisible net he cast out, helpless to do anything but move with him. When it was shallow enough, Denver sat back on the rocky beach, and I pushed myself between his legs. His body the cushion between the rocks and my tail. I laid on top of his chest, my tail hanging in the water, hoping I wasn't too heavy for him. Denver's arms wrapped around my waist, his fingers dancing over the sensitive part where skin met scales. I crashed into him. Our tongues entwined as we lay there half in, half out of the bay.

"I've stretched enough. And now there's something else I need." I kissed under Denver's jaw and brushed my lips against his Adam's apple. The rumble in his throat was heavenly.

"Oh? And what's that exactly?" Denver said with

a tease.

"I need to be inside you, to feel you around me, to hear our bodies together." My words came out thick and rough.

Denver blew out a breath and I could feel his response pushing against my tail. "Shit, yeah. I think it's time we go. Let me grab some towels and your clothes. You going to be ready?"

"More than ready," I growled and called my tail back in. It was much easier this time, having been sated with the swim; my tail and cock aligned with the same goal. *Denver.* I walked back to the car, saluting the moon as I went.

Denver held a towel in hand and stared, his eyes roaming over me, lingering on my erection. "If you keep staring at me like that, we aren't going to make it back to your house."

"Mmm...tempting. But I think I've handled all the risks I can manage for tonight. It would be my luck security rolls around while you have me bent over the hood of the truck."

I took the towel from him and rubbed my dripping hair, very nearly ready to do as he said. "You paint quite the picture."

With new motivation, our drive home was nearly

as urgent as the one to the bay. We got back to his place and crashed into each other once we were inside. Shadow licked my legs and wove between them as we tried to walk to Denver's bedroom. It didn't take long before our clothes were shed once more.

I kissed Denver hard and turned him around. He rubbed his ass against my groin, eliciting a moan from me. "On the bed, love."

Denver did as I said, laying on his back, arms folded beneath his head as he watched me. I looped my arm under him and flipped him over. An excited squeal slipped from him and it went straight to my dick. I lifted his hips until his ass was in the air, his face on the bed. I spread his cheeks and tasted him. Exploring him carefully. I kept going until he was groaning and begging for more.

"Lube?" I asked.

Denver pointed to the bedside table. I left the beautiful sight of him long enough to retrieve it and return. "Do you want me to use protection?"

Denver turned his head back to look at me. "You said you can't share anything with me?"

"That's right."

"And no fish babies?"

I chuckled. "No fish babies."

“I want to feel you, Call. Only you. Please. I need you so badly.” For every song he sang with his heart, the ones filled with memories and longing and love, the pleading tone in his voice might be my favorite one so far.

I lubed up, situating myself between his knees. I lined my tip with him and pressed forward through the initial stretch as Denver purred. When I was fully seated inside of him, his warmth and tightness hugging me, I began to move. Each thrust, Denver met fully and pushed back, as if he couldn’t get enough of me. I grabbed his hips and rocked forward, the wonderful music of our bodies ringing through his apartment.

Denver hummed and moaned and it undid me completely as those sounds struck every fiber of me. He reached under him and stroked himself. I wasn’t going to hold him back as I did in the shower. We both needed this. I lunged into him once more and held him in place as I came inside him. Denver followed right after and he pulsed around me, working the rest of my climax from me. We were both panting and sweating. Denver’s legs gave out and I crashed against his back. He reached behind him, his hand on my back, holding me in place.

“You felt so fucking good, Denver.”

"Mmm." His wordless response had me smiling. I kissed the center of his back and got up at last. Already missing the feel of him against me. I returned with a damp washcloth, cleaned his limp body, and threw it on the floor. I climbed into bed next to him and Denver turned around to face me. Even blurry, I could see satisfaction written on his face. He tucked himself against my chest. Everything I felt for him was big, bigger than I ever imagined.

"When I first saw you on that beach, my Beachy Bigfoot, I dreamt of you doing exactly that," Denver said.

"Oh? And was it what you thought it would be?"

"So much more, beyond words." His lips brushed my chest.

"Remember the way the cant made you feel?" I whispered against his black hair.

"Ready to blow my load?" Denver said sleepily.

I snickered. "No, the other one."

He was hesitant as he fought through the exhaustion seeping into him. When he said the word, it was barely a whisper. "Loved?"

"Yes. That. I do, you know." I kissed his forehead. Denver sighed happily and snuggled even closer to me.

Denver pulled his head back, surprise widening

his sleepy eyes as though he finally heard what I said. "What do you mean exactly?"

"That I love you."

"But I'm a nobody, and you're...well, you're a prince, as you like to remind me. Among other things."

"You are not a nobody, you are a very special person. From that first moment you performed, your heart sang to mine and I knew. I tried to deny it, but it was always there. You played my heartsong. And it's only grown stronger the longer I've been with you."

"A heartsong?"

"Yes. It is a connection between hearts, an imprint. A chord that rings for us alone. I will always know the sound of you and will hear your call."

Denver sat up and looked at me, astounded. "But, it's all...so soon. Isn't it? I mean that's not normal."

I sat up beside him. "Is anything about us normal?"

He shook his head slightly. "No, I suppose it's not. I mean, it definitely isn't normal having a boyfriend who can blow you underwater and not come up for air."

I smirked, even as I got stuck on the word, *boyfriend*. It was such a human term but I understood the meaning. And it was something I'd never had. I rather liked the sound of it. Instead of drawing attention to that word, I focused on the rest of what he said. "Is that a complaint?"

"Oh hell, no. That was fucking fantastic."

"So maybe *not normal* isn't a bad thing." I reached over and ran my hand down his arm, enjoying the way he reacted to my touch. "Denver, I'm not trying to pressure you into saying something you don't feel or pushing you too far. I simply wanted you to know that what I feel isn't something that is going to change. But it's fine if you don't feel the same or if it's too soon, I'm not expecting anything."

Denver's hand landed on mine, stopping its movement. "I...didn't say that."

My eyes shot to his. "What do you mean?"

"It's fast and insane and you're not even human, and yet, I have never felt this way about anyone before. You consume my thoughts when we are apart and I bask in your presence when we are together. And I think maybe...what I feel isn't normal either."

I grabbed his face and pressed my mouth to his. He didn't need to say the words and perhaps it felt too soon for him, but I could sense it in him nonetheless. We sank back down into the bed, Denver tucked against me, his head on my chest. No more thoughts spoken out loud but sang with every breath and beat of our hearts.

The last time I'd been in his bed, he sat up and took care of me all night while I recovered. This time I held him after we lost ourselves in each other, confessing our not-normal feelings, and it was more perfect than I could imagine. His body started to relax and before long, tiny snores rose from him. There was no place on earth or at sea that I would rather be than there with him like that. His rhythmic breathing was a lullaby, the sweetest song in all of history. One that pulled me under and whispered dreams of love and hope that I had no right to. My brain tried to remind me that anything with Denver was temporary while my heart laid claim and refused to budge.

When I woke in the morning my chest was weighed down. Denver was tucked in next to me, his head on my shoulder, his back pressed against my side. Once again, amber eyes stared out from a black void. Only this time, Shadow was on my chest, inches away from my face, instead of on my hip as he had been the last time I slept in Denver's bed. I reached up and patted his head, the cat purred instantly. It was practically automatic, one touch on his soft fur and his motor started. Shadow licked my hand and rubbed his head on it. I chuckled. I hadn't spent much time interacting with land mammals. And certainly never one so close to my face. Another pat and he stretched out his claws and dug them into my skin. I hissed while he purred even louder.

Denver shifted at the sound, turned towards me, and asked sleepily, "What happened?"

I pointed at the cat whose claws were going in and out, poking into my chest. Denver reached over and scratched the cat's ear.

"I thought purring meant happy, so why is he trying to dig inside of me?"

Denver laughed. "He *is* happy. They knead like that to show pleasure."

"Can he *not* be quite so happy?" I grimaced as tiny little daggers pinched my flesh.

"He normally does that with soft blankets or pillows. But he seems to have taken a liking to you. Though, I know that doesn't feel great on bare skin. I'm sorry. Maybe I can help." Denver shooed the cat away, who seemed to glare at him as he hopped off me. He leaned over me and kissed the spot on my chest that had several red marks on it. "Better?"

Having his lips on me would make anything

better. "Not bad. But I think you may have missed a spot."

Denver roamed over my chest, being sure to cover every inch of me with his tongue, his lips, his teeth. Him sinking into my skin was a thousand times better than Shadow's murder claws. We stayed in bed, tasting and devouring each other until Shadow's relentless cries got us up at last. He was a needy little thing. But then, I was feeling pretty needy myself. Denver was the kind of person that made cats *and* mermen desperate for his attention.

I followed him into the kitchen, even as the black cat wove around us. Denver pulled out a can and popped the lid. The smell made me crinkle my nose. "*What* is that?"

"It's *Oceanfish Dinner*. It's cat food. Usually, Shadow gets dry kibble but sometimes I give him a little treat and he seems a little jealous this morning."

I leaned closer and smelled again, "I don't know what kind of fish that is, but it didn't come from the ocean."

Denver snickered. "It's a mixture of things, gravy, cheese, fish bits. Who knows. But he loves it."

"Do cats typically like fish?" I watched him put a dollop in a bowl on top of dry food pieces.

"Oh yeah. They go crazy for it. Cats are carnivores, so any type of meat, really. But there's something about seafood that they love more."

His eyes snapped up to mine and widened before he let out hoots of laughter. "Oh my God!"

"What? What happened?" I looked around, despite everything being blurry without my glasses, as if the answer was behind me.

"That's why he likes you so much!" Another bout of laughter.

"What? Why?"

"Fish boy?" Denver said in a teasing tone.

"I thought we agreed that you wouldn't be using that nickname," I replied flatly.

"Okay, right. But there is truth to it. I bet he can smell the ocean on you, just like seafood."

I looked down at the black furry beast as he greedily ate the fish mash Denver had given him with disturbing snarly, smacky sounds. "He's not going to try to eat *me*, is he?"

Denver bit his lip trying to keep from laughing again. "I think you're probably safe. Though, he has been known to bite a toe on occasion but more out of annoyance than out of the need to consume."

"Maybe I'll bring him a real fish sometime as an

offering."

Denver stepped in close and held my hips. "If you did that I think he'd be your friend forever."

"I'll settle for not being on the menu."

Denver smiled wide. "You are a predator, prince of the seas. There is nothing in the water that you can't handle. Yet, you are worried about being eaten by my cat." He leaned forward and pecked a kiss on my lips.

"At least in the ocean, I know what I can trust or not. But he is an unknown to me. Besides, he was watching me while I was sleeping and that's just..." I shuddered at the thought.

Laughing, Denver placed his hands on my cheeks. "You are not normal, but I love you for it."

My heart leapt at the words, the furry fish-annihilator forgotten. He'd hinted at his feelings last night when I told him what he meant to me, but to hear him say the words out loud was different. Denver seemed to consider what he said that had given me pause. Was it merely a phrase that rolled off his tongue, did he not mean it? No, not possible, not with the powerful vibrations I felt ringing through him. Should I call attention to it or pretend it didn't happen? A thousand thoughts swirled in my head as we stood there, staring at each other, neither of us speaking.

He cleared his throat and stepped closer to me. So close that we were bare chest to bare chest and I had to tilt my head down to look at him. His hand slid from the side of my face to the back of my neck.

"I do. It surprised me to say it, but I do love you. Some logical part of my brain is probably screaming at me, but nothing about you, or us, is logical. I don't think I've ever said it and meant it before with anyone, outside of my dad and Ella. But I mean it with you."

I wrapped my arms around his waist and held him tight. "You have no idea how happy it makes me to hear that. I love you too." I bent my neck and kissed him, letting our mouths whisper and speak of all of love's promises, wishes, dreams, and hopes.

"So what happens now? What do *boyfriends* do?" I asked, one side of my lips tugged up at the funny term.

Denver shrugged. "Uh...brunch?"

CHAPTER 22

DENVER

Driving Calder home at the end of the weekend was the hardest trip to make. I didn't want our time together to end. After our adventure to the bay, we spent the rest of the day doing almost normal couple things. We ate, we kissed, we cuddled, we made love. I had more orgasms in the past few days than I had in months. Everything with Calder was intense. The way he looked at me and saw into my soul. The way he hung on every word I said. The way he heard every word I *didn't* say. The way he treated me as if I were the greatest treasure that could be found on land.

When I got to his apartment, I grabbed what I bought for him and walked him to his door. I stopped in the door frame, knowing if I crossed the threshold it would be even harder to leave. Calder leaned against the jamb, headphones around his neck, glasses on, staring at me through his filmy eyes, seeing way more than his vision allowed. Even merely standing, doing nothing at all, he was gorgeous.

"I got you something."

Calder's brow creased. "You didn't have to get me anything. Being with you is gift enough."

I very nearly melted into a puddle of goo right there on his doorstep, but I managed to keep it together. "Well, it's not *just* for you, it's for both of us. It's more selfish than anything."

I held out the box. Calder eyed me as he reached for it. After sliding the lid off, he pulled out the device within. I watched as he turned it over in his hand until he hit the power button and the screen turned on.

"A phone?"

"Yes."

"Thank you, that's very kind, but I've been fine without a phone. I'm not sure I need one."

I stepped in closer to him, putting my hands on his hips, tracing the invisible blue line that would appear when he shifted. "I programmed my number in it already and I have yours. You told me that if we were in water, you would hear me anytime I called. Well, on land, I want to be able to hear *you* if you call. Besides, as your *boyfriend*, I would like to be able to talk to you or send you messages. If I had to wait all week to hear or see you again, it would feel like an eternity."

A slow smile stretched his lips. "That does sound nice, I would very much like to hear your voice as often as I can. Thank you, this is very thoughtful."

After I showed Calder the basics, he kissed me hard, ensuring I wouldn't forget the feel of him while we were apart. I was five minutes down the road when my phone rang. His name popped up on my truck's bluetooth and I grinned like an idiot.

I hit the button on my steering wheel. "Hi, Call."

"Hi, love."

"Are you missing me already?"

"Incredibly so, you have no idea."

With the heat in his voice, my shorts tightened and I was about ready to turn around and let him pound into me one more time. I replied with a thick voice. "I have some idea."

"I'm not sure this phone thing is going to make anything easier when hearing your voice in my ear makes me wish I had your body under me."

"Fuck me," I mumbled and adjusted myself.

"I wish that I could."

"Damn. I gotta hang up or I'm not going to be able to drive. But Calder?"

"Yes, love?"

"There's more that we can do on the phone than just talk."

I could practically hear the growl in his throat. "Alright. Call me when you get home and you can tell me more about that."

I white-knuckled it the whole way back. After giving Shadow some attention, I climbed into bed and called him. Somehow Calder over the phone was nearly as intense as he was in person. When it came to describing what he would do to me, long gone was any awkward hesitation he had with normal human interactions. He was every bit the commanding prince only I knew him to be. It felt as if it had been his hand that brought me release instead of my own.

The next morning Ella was there extra early, impatiently waiting for me, hands on her hips. "Well?"

"Well what?" I asked nonchalantly, knowing she was eager to get the low down.

She punched my arm in answer. "Ow." I rubbed it. I was surprised I didn't have a permanent lump from all the times she hit me in the same spot.

"You took your boy home. How did it go?"

"It was...nice," I said with a big smile.

"Nice? A man like that is *not* nice?"

"But he is though. He makes me feel really special."

"That's great, I'm happy for you. But come on!"

"What do you want to know exactly? That he blew my mind?" Among other things. "Or that Shadow loves him?"

Ella snorted. "Shadow loves him? Your cat?"

"Yes, it's a sordid love affair that frankly, I'm quite jealous of."

"You are so weird"

I shrugged. "You asked."

"I was hoping for something a little more juicy than that."

"Like the fact that I have the most beautiful man on the planet for a boyfriend and I keep pinching myself, wondering if I'll wake up and discover it was some elaborate dream prison where I was kept in a state of bliss so that I wouldn't complain while demons feasted on my soul?"

Ella shook her head and pushed past me when I unlocked the door. "I don't know what he sees in you."

I put in the alarm code. "Me neither, to be honest. But damn, I feel like I hit the jackpot with him."

"So...boyfriend huh?" Ella asked as she powered on the register.

I couldn't stop the wide grin from breaking free. "Yes. I really like him. I've never been with anyone who makes me feel the way he does."

She came around the counter and put her hand on my shoulder. "All kidding aside, I *am* happy for you and I know your dad would be too."

My eyes misted. "Thank you."

***

We fell into a routine over the next two months. The spring brought new life, new hope, and possibilities. Talking, sexting, the Beanwater, weekends spent at his place or mine. It almost felt...normal, like we were any new lovesick couple caught in a bubble that seemed unburstable. We could almost be that except for the times we drove to the bay and stayed underwater longer than was humanly possible. It had become our place. Quiet and secluded at night and the security system wasn't a problem for Calder. It was truly unique having a whole world of our own.

Being with Calder was easy. It was complicated

and strange and surreal, but it was the easiest thing in the world. Each time I saw him after being apart for any length of time, he attacked me as if we had gone years without the other. I was madly, deeply, and wonderfully in love. And yet the longer we were together, the more we felt the ticking clock hanging over us. Most of the time, we could pretend it wasn't there, but occasionally I would catch a wistful expression on his face. I knew it appeared on mine as well.

It had been three months since I started making a weekly appearance at the Beanwater. The cover charge for my performances had increased due to the size of the crowd. Which also meant bigger checks for me. Nothing to retire on, but it was affirming to get paid for doing what I loved. It was hard to fathom that things had gotten to this point when four months ago I had to force myself to return to the stage.

Lee pulled me aside after I finished performing. "Mr. Greene, I'd like to introduce you to someone."

A man in a navy suit and tie stood beside him. He was dressed way more business-like than the clientele that frequented Saturday nights at the Beanwater. He held out his hand to me. "Hi, Mr. Greene. My name is Alex Steiner. I work with the Legacy and Lore Label."

Legacy and Lore?! They were one of the biggest folk record labels in the US. *Don't freak out, don't freak out.* My heart raced as I shook his hand, but I tried to keep my voice level. "Alex, please call me Denver. It's great to meet you. What can I do for you?"

"Well, I think it's more like what I can do for you. Let's have a seat." The man smiled and my mind went a thousand different directions as I followed him to a table. Calder caught my attention, worry creasing his brow. He was sure to have noticed the change in my pulse or vibes or however he seemed to know my emotions before I did. I raised my shoulders. Lee walked up to him, indicated our direction, and patted him on the shoulder. I could see him relax visibly. What did Lee tell him? Did he know what this was about?

"I've seen you play twice now," Alex said. "It's a great set. You put a lot of heart into your songs. Do you write them yourself?"

"Yes, sir. Every single word has been bled out of me."

"It's noticeable. And the one about the father and son, I can admit that made me cry both times I heard it."

"Thank you. That one is particularly special to

me."

He bobbed his head and pressed his pointer fingers together. "With your talent, what are you doing playing in a joint like this?"

"I like the Beanwater. Mr. Robertson has been good to me. I took a break from music for...personal reasons, but he's given me a place to let me find myself again."

"And have you...found yourself?"

I slid a glance to Calder. His support and encouragement, the confidence he gave me, the way he reacted to my music. The way the god of the sea made me feel like I was a god on the guitar. "Yes. I believe I have."

"Good. Your music is solid and I think you have a future ahead of you. One where you're playing much bigger gigs than cafés."

'Thank you. That's kind of you to say."

"I'm not just saying it. I'm telling you I have an offer for you for something bigger. *Much bigger.*"

Holy shit! An offer? What did that mean? "Then I would say that I am definitely interested in hearing more."

Alex smiled and leaned back, he waved his hand for help and Calder came striding over. My lips tugged up. His presence soothed the palpitations that threatened to launch my heart out of my chest in anticipation. After he took the drink order, he turned to leave, but I grabbed his hand. When he faced me his expression lit up my whole world. Whatever this was about I wanted him with me for it.

"Do you mind if he joins us?" I asked the music scout opposite me.

His brows arched in surprise. "Sure? I don't usually get folks who want to consult their barista."

"This is Calder, my boyfriend."

Alex gave me a half-smile. "I see."

I shrugged. "Like I said, the Beanwater has been good to me."

At that, he laughed and indicated for Calder to join us. Calder insisted on grabbing Alex's drink first, needing the job to be fulfilled. When he took his place beside me, his hand landed on my leg beneath the table, keeping it from bouncing wildly out of control.

"Alright, well, let me get to the point. Legacy and Lore hosts an annual bluegrass and folk festival by the sea in San Diego. We have all the top names from our label, but we also feature indie and lesser-known artists. Thousands of people attend for the headliners, but they come early and vibe all day. A spot in the festival gets your name and your songs in front of the audience that buys this brand of music."

"My dad took me once. It was an incredible experience. So many talented musicians and bands all in one place."

"And it's an experience you still remember, right?"

"Completely unforgettable."

"How would you like to be a part of that experience?"

My mind was reeling, but before I got my hopes up too high, I needed to make sure I understood what he was saying. "How do you mean exactly?"

"I mean that I have a spot for you if you want it. I think you're just the kind of talent we're looking for. And if you do well at the festival, you'll have a great shot at making a career out of this."

I slumped back against the chair, trying to process everything. It was a lot to take in. One minute I was happily playing a nice evening set at a coffee shop, and the next, everything I ever dreamed of was being offered to me. I had no words.

"So, what do you say? You ready to expand beyond the Beanwater?"

My brain was screaming yes. My mouth and body

hadn't caught up yet. Calder gripped my leg and leaned forward. "Yes. He'll do it."

"Smart barista." Alex winked. "So, Denver, is that a yes?"

I nodded my head, snapping out of my frozen state of disbelief, and shook his hand emphatically. "Yes, oh my gosh, yes. Thank you, Mr. Steiner. I can't tell you what this means to me."

"It's your music and your talent, kid. I'm merely a conduit between you and your future fans. Come by this address to sign paperwork and we can get your name on the line-up. You can even bring your barista if you'd like." Alex smirked as he handed me a business card.

I took it numbly and thanked him. Once he left, I turned and leapt at Calder who caught me with ease. "I can't believe that happened."

Calder squeezed around my waist, my toes off the ground. "You deserve it. I am so proud of you, love."

He set me back down but I still felt like I was floating on air. "You'll come with me, right? I don't want to fanboy and miss anything important."

The gaze in his eyes told me he would have kissed me if we weren't standing in the middle of the place where he worked. He straightened, brushing off his apron. "Of course. I would be honored to. You are going to be extraordinary."

CHAPTER 23

CALDER

That evening, Denver came over to my place, still in awed shock over what happened. He chattered excitably, reminiscing on the festival he'd gone to with his dad, and talking about all the musicians he saw that he still listens to. I loved hearing him talk about music. The passion he had for it was a unique syncopation that sang through his whole being. It was clear how much it meant to him. Though I could listen to him talk about anything simply to bask in the timbre of his tenor voice.

Denver sat between my legs, his back against my chest as he looked up the festival on his phone. Gasping with each name he recognized. "I can't believe I'm going to be sharing a stage with them. It's so unreal. I've always dreamed of playing there, but I didn't think it would actually happen."

"Of course, it's happening. You are quite gifted." I hugged my arms around his waist.

Denver rolled his head to the side, showing me pictures over his shoulder. It was a beautiful venue; the ocean in the background, open fields where people could sit with folding chairs or blankets. I imagined merfolk drawing near in the water to hear the voice of the man I loved. Wouldn't that be something? If only I could take him home and profess that he was my mate and my family would welcome him as their own. My heart ached at the thought of what could never be and I tried to shake it off to stay in the moment.

It was getting harder and harder. Sometimes I looked at him and envisioned a whole future for us, only to have it yanked away by the reality I had to face. When Denver said his dad chose to make more memories before he was no longer physically able to do things, I thought it would be enough. I *wanted* it to be enough. But every moment, every day spent with Denver had me wanting more and more of them. I was greedy for him. Yet, it would end all the same. No matter how I clung to him, it wouldn't last. But the memories I was making with him would stay with me forever. When I had to relent to the destiny given to me, I could hold on to the time spent with Denver, the same as I held him in my arms even now.

"It's a three-day festival. The headliners only perform once, different big names on different nights, but some of the newer sets might get a couple time slots, the crappy ones no one wants. Hell, I don't care if I play at 3 AM when the audience is all two sheets to the wind, it will be a thrill just to be there."

"That Alex guy seems to want to put you in front of people. I think you'll be given a great slot."

"Here's hoping, but I'll be happy to get whatever I get. What are the dates? I'm going to need to make arrangements to have the store covered." He flicked his finger, scrolling back to the top and he froze. Despair replaced the excited vibrations that had been flowing off him only a moment before. "I can't do it."

"What? Why?"

"It's in three months."

"That's plenty of time. You know your music backwards and forwards. You even sing in your sleep, which is adorable by the way. You got this."

He set his phone down next to my headphones and his pork pie hat on the coffee table and turned to face me. "*Three months,* Call. Mid-August."

My heart sank like a stone. I'd first come on land mid-August. My year would be up and I would have to leave. The date that we had an unspoken agreement to never speak about. The end of us. We could remain blissfully happy as long as that date stayed far from our thoughts. The selfish part of me wanted every second of Denver to myself that I could get. But it was his dream. I couldn't let him sacrifice when I already had to. One of us should get to forge his path.

"Listen to me, Denver. You *have* to do this. Your music is important. It's a part of who you are and it's a gift you need to share with the world. I would never forgive myself if you gave that up for me. It would make this whole thing pointless."

"But there's bound to be meetings, rehearsals, run-throughs. All the time I'd have to devote to this would take me away from you."

I grabbed his face in my hands. "I will be by your side through it all. But this is a huge opportunity, you can't walk away from it. And besides, it will give you something to focus on after I'm gone. I expect you to become a name everyone knows."

He slumped against my chest and sniffled. "How am I going to do it without you?"

"The same as you've always done, by pouring your heart and soul into your songs. You did that before me, you can do it after me too." I tried to infuse strength I didn't feel into my words. Each one hurt to say.

"I don't want there to be an *after you*."

I rubbed circles on his back, even as my own chest constricted. "Don't let what will come steal from what is now or what can be. You and I both went into this choosing to live each moment while we had them. And if I get to leave knowing that I got to see you rise to your dream, that is something that will stay with me forever."

"I need you by my side for this."

"You don't. You can do this. But I will be with you as long as I can. Don't you think you owe it to your father and his memory to see this through?"

Another sniffle, Denver sunk even lower, until he curled up between my legs, his head resting on my thigh. "I can't do it."

"You can, love."

He stared up at me, I could smell the saltiness of his tears. "Let's say I go, and someone is interested in giving me a chance. What then? I have the store. The store that my father left to me. That was *his* legacy. He built that place. He wanted it to be the two of us together. I can't just throw it all away."

Denver sounded completely defeated. He once told me I didn't know what kinds of responsibilities he had, I hadn't considered the burden he carried with the shop or the obligation he held to continue it. I saw it as something that he did, not something that he *had* to do. "You're not throwing anything away. You are moving towards something important to you, like the shop was to him. But that shop isn't his legacy, *you* are. His spirit lives on in you and from the kind of man he sounds like he was, he wouldn't want you drowning in something you didn't love. He would want you to soar."

His body shuddered and he drew in a deep breath, but his words came out soft and broken. "I just wish he were here. He should be here for this. It doesn't seem fair."

I continued my circles on his back. I hurt for him. I wanted to make everything good and right and easy for him, but I couldn't make his father not be gone. "It's not fair. I'm sorry, love."

I held him and felt tears dampen my pants. I looked around feeling helpless, wishing there was something more I could do for him when my eyes landed on his hat. I tilted my head. "Tell me about your hat."

Denver sniffled and sat up, looking at me with confusion. "What?"

"You once said that your guitar and your hat were your most treasured items. I know about the guitar, but you never told me about the hat."

Denver wiped his cheeks with his hands and leaned forward, grabbing the hat, and holding it in his hands. A small square of paper was tucked beneath the red band. It was always there. Every time I saw him wearing his hat, the paper remained.

"My dad bought it for me from a vintage store. He said every musician needed their signature piece. My eyes landed on the hat and it called to me. I just knew it felt right. I wore it and a scarf for my first performance, feeling all pumped. I looked the part of a singer, but my nerves were all over the place. I nearly couldn't go out on that stage. My dad said I needed a lucky charm. Something to focus on and give me strength. He ripped a piece of paper out of my song journal, wrote a quick note on it, and gave it to me."

"What did it say?"

Denver took the square out from under the band and handed it over to me. I held it as if it were a precious artifact. It was. Something precious to the man I loved. I unfolded it with great care.

"To my bravest, beautiful boy. I believe in you and am so proud of you, no matter what. Love, Dad."

Denver smiled wistfully. "*My bravest, beautiful boy.* He always called me that. I *hated* it as a kid. It embarrassed me whenever he said it. And he had no shame in saying that in front of all my friends. Completely mortifying. But that day on stage, it seeped into me. I felt brave, I felt beautiful, and I knew that even if I choked, it wouldn't change the way he saw me. It helped give me the courage I needed to perform in front of strangers. And every time since then, I've worn my hat with his note tucked in and heard him calling me his bravest, beautiful boy."

"You carry him with you every time you sing."

Denver bobbed his head, his finger playing over the note as he tucked it back into his hat. "Yeah. I feel him, his words, when I wear this."

"And you'll be wearing that hat when you're playing at the festival," I stated it as a fact.

Denver sighed. "I don't know. He also wanted me to be a part of the hardware store. He built that from the ground up. It doesn't seem right to turn my back on it."

I reached over and hauled Denver into my lap. "From everything you've told me about him, I think your dad would be more hurt knowing that you stopped chasing *your* dreams because of what you think *he* wanted. But with the guitar he made you and the note in your hat, he gave you everything he could to help foster your music. You would be honoring him by doing what's important to you."

Denver tucked his head against my neck and another tear escaped and dripped down my neck. "Okay. I'll do it."

"He would be so happy for you."

"Thank you, Calder."

I kissed the top of his head. "Anything for you."

The next day, I went with him to the office that housed the record label putting on the festival. I checked every document thoroughly making sure there wasn't anything they were trying to sneak by Denver. While the negotiations I'd been involved with as part of the king's council in the sea courts were usually verbal, I knew my way around tricky wording. Even if I couldn't see it through with him, I wanted to make sure he was set up for success. It hurt thinking about not being able to see his career grow, to leave it all behind, and wonder what he might be up to. But at least I could know that I did everything possible to help him before I left.

July. One month left and I was getting restless. The days were longer and hotter. I wasn't used to feeling so hot and worn, the sea remained the same cool temperature throughout the year. The sun oppressed me as much as the clock did. Had I accomplished anything in the time I'd been on land? Outside of Denver, was there anything of note that I could take back to my kingdom?

It all came down to policies. Policies that needed changing. The people that made those policies didn't want to hear the opinion of anyone uneducated. I'd seen it time and again. The average person that tried to stand up for something was knocked down by men who knew words, big words, and used them like weapons, hurtling them without care. Breaking down the person who brought passion and heart and sound reasoning.

It was why I spent so much of this year studying. If I hoped to be able to stand up to them, I needed to be able to fight back with the words they loved so dearly. I knew it wouldn't be an overnight process. Changing the world, the mindset, the way things worked. But still...I had done nothing. And now I would be returning to the sea in a month with zero to show for it. It wouldn't change anything though. This year had been an indulgence of a petulant prince, and at the end of it, I would still be forced to wed no matter what I might have accomplished.

What kind of husband will Taneesh be? Will he let me pursue things of my own? Would I have to seek permission or would I be an equal partner and have Taneesh's support? I bristled at the thought of losing the independence I'd grown accustomed to on land. I sighed and checked my phone.

I had been reluctant about the tech at first. The hum that accompanied electronic devices was grating at best. Though, I quickly learned the benefits outweighed the annoyance. Not only was I able to talk to Denver or bring him pleasure from a distance, but it also had internet when I didn't have access at home for my computer. I set it to get notifications from the environmental news sites I followed, not wanting to have a big delay as I had with finding out about the oil rig. If I had known sooner, I could have stopped it from getting as bad as it did.

A ping went off and I checked it to see a story about Cal Chem. I sneered as soon as it popped up. I had been following them for months. It was a long-established manufacturer whose name often came up in the news in conjunction with pollution and environmental risks. It was suspected that Cal Chem was illegally dumping their chemical waste in a bay very similar to the one Denver and I swam in. There had been a lot of denials and red tape, but it seemed as if the by-product in the drums had a signature that matched what the company was handling.

There was proof. Actual proof. And yet they had to drag out the process through the legal system. Would they get away with it? Would it get swept under the rug like so many other things they'd been accused of? Money was the biggest word that talked and Cal Chem seemed to have lined plenty of pockets.

The restlessness I felt at the little time I had left was bubbling up into an urge to take action. I was trained to fight. The possibility of war was an undercurrent always flowing beneath the surface. I was a prince, a warrior, not someone who should be sitting on the couch watching as the world turned to shit around me. I grabbed my keys and headed out the door without a real plan but a need to move. Anger and dread fueled each step.

I got on the bus and scrolled through the history of the company, seeing article after article that reflected a history of wrong-doings, and yet they still stood. My phone rang in my hand, Denver calling. With the mood I was in, I was tempted to not answer. But it was him and I craved his voice more than Shadow craved fish.

I tried to steady my voice and answered, "Hi, love."

"Hey Call, I'm currently hiding from Ella after passing off an annoying customer. The look she gave me was scary. I'd much rather talk to you anyway. What are you up to?"

Hearing him made everything seem better and worse all at once. I could get lost in the moment with him, but the clock roared in the back of my mind. So much left undone, so little time. A resolve settled in me at what I needed to do. "I'm out."

I could hear his breath catch and I immediately wished I had said something different. "What's wrong? What are you doing?"

I sighed. I didn't keep anything from him. Well, that wasn't entirely true. I never told him about the engagement. He didn't need to know *that*. But I didn't want to hide from him. "I'm trying to make something right."

"Did something happen? Are you alright?"

The last eleven months pressed onto me. "I'm just tired, Denver. Tired of not being able to help or make a difference."

"Okay, where are you? I'm coming to you."

"I'm on a bus on my way to Cal Chem."

"I'll meet you there. Promise me you won't do anything before I get there."

I didn't respond. I couldn't or I might have lied to him. I stared out the window, watching as blurry buildings passed by. I checked the GPS and saw that I would be there in about twenty minutes. The rest of the ride there was used to learn everything I could about the facility. The closer we got, the more determined I felt. I didn't know what I was going to do exactly, I'd have to figure it out once I got in. But these monsters needed to be stopped and I was going to be the one to do it.

The call for my stop rang out and I pulled the cord. With headphones on and hands in my pockets, I walked off the bus with my head down. I tried to keep a quick pace, but not so much that it drew attention. Rounding a corner, I got off the main road and headed for the security gate. From the videos I saw, they had three entrances. One for the public, a private one for the executives, and the one that was used for shipping and receiving. That was the one I wanted. I turned left, following the hedge-covered iron fence. I was about to listen for and manipulate the cameras when I heard a truck pull up. I knew its distinctive hum and screech, my heart and mind battling for reaction. Was I relieved, happy, excited, or disappointed that he was here?

A door slammed, "Calder! Wait!"

I couldn't resist him. The worry in his voice hooked into my heart and I couldn't dismiss him either. When I heard Denver running towards me, I stopped. I didn't move forward or back or turn around, merely froze in place, until he grabbed my shoulder and pulled me to face him.

"I'm here. Talk to me. What's happening?" Every vibration rang with concern for me.

"Have you seen the news? Do you know what they've done?"

"I've seen it. It's awful, they need to pay for the damage that's been done."

"Yes. They do." I said flatly. I started to turn away but Denver grabbed my arm and tugged me back, holding on to my arm.

"Wait. What are you planning on doing?"

"Let me go, Denver." I kept my voice low. He and I both knew that I could easily pull away from him. Physically, at least, Mentally, not so much.

He stepped right in front of me, his hand still gripped on my arm. "No. Not until you tell me what you're going to do."

"If I tell you, then you'll let me go?"

Denver's shoulders slumped. "I can't guarantee that, but I'm listening."

"I've gotta get in there."

"And what happens when you do?"

"I'm going to figure out a way to shut them down. Maybe I'll destroy their equipment so they can no longer produce their poison." Maybe I'd burn the whole place to the ground.

"There's gotta be security. What about that?"

"I can handle the cameras."

"Sure, but a place like this is likely to have human guards as well."

I figured as much. "I'm prepared to handle that if it comes up."

Denver sucked in a sharp breath. "You can't be serious. Those people are just doing their job."

"Their job protecting criminals?"

"No, Calder. I can't let you do this! There are other ways. But this is too risky. People could get hurt. *You* could get hurt. And what if they capture you? You go to prison, get screened, they find out you're not human. Then what? You endanger all of your kind by revealing yourself. Is that what you want?"

I'd considered the risk. The entire ride here I thought of the possible outcomes. I couldn't get in, I couldn't get out. I got caught, maybe even killed. But a warrior always faced the fact that they might not live through a fight. But I hadn't thought of what would happen if they discovered what I was. I couldn't allow that to happen. My resolve began to deflate.

"No, of course, I don't want that. What else am I supposed to do? I feel so...lost." The last word barely slipped from my lips.

Denver wrapped his arms around me and I crumpled against him, my head resting on his shoulder. "You're not lost, Calder. I'm here with you."

"It's just...I've done nothing. All this time on land, it's almost over, and I have nothing to return home with. No great tales that might influence their decisions. No accomplishments. Nothing to show the asset I can be outside of..." I managed to stop myself before I said anything about the marriage. "I will return to the destiny that awaits me and all of this was for naught. I wasted a year of my life...for what?"

Denver pulled away from me and I could feel his heart change, could feel the hurt that crept into him. "It wasn't for naught. You've learned more about people than you allowed yourself to know before. You've learned more about yourself too. Everything was decided for you back home, right? Your path stretched out ahead of you with no say given to what you can do. But you've lived a year for yourself. Making your own path, finding your own way. That's something."

All it did was help me realize how much I liked having independence and how much I dreaded it being taken from me. Would I be free to come and go as the husband of Taneesh? If it had been the other way around and my parents had been the ones to suggest the marriage, I would have hated it still, but I wouldn't have felt so powerless. But as I was being *given* at the request of King Katal, it felt as if I would be shackled and kept against my will. A prize, not a partner. But I couldn't voice any of those concerns to Denver.

In my silence, he reached up, stroking his thumb over my cheek. "And what about us? Was that a waste?" His voice trembled with pain and it made the ache in my chest sink into my belly.

I grabbed his hand from my face and held it in mine. "No, love. I could never think that. You are the very best thing that's happened to me. You've made me feel like the man I want to be and not who I *have* to be. You've been there for me at my most vulnerable. You were my strength when I was weak. You soothe me and center me and I have cherished every minute we've spent together."

"I have too. You've helped me feel alive again. I was stuck after losing my dad, but you brought all this beauty and wonder into my life. Opened my eyes to see things and experience things I never imagined I would. You've made me feel loved and courageous and no longer alone. I love you, Calder, and I am so grateful that I've gotten to have this time with you. So don't go throwing that all away for some desperate need to be a hero. Not all fighters use weapons, right? Or is that just some bullshit you said to make me feel better?"

I shook my head. "I meant it."

"You are a leader that I would gladly follow anywhere. You are strong, passionate, and you have a beautiful heart. But if you go in there, that is one place I can't follow you. You will lose yourself, and even more...you will lose me."

"I. Can't. Lose. You." The words came out as broken as I felt. I knew I would soon anyway, but I didn't want it to end like this.

"Then don't," Denver said firmly.

I wrapped my arms around him and felt a shudder through my body, as hot tears stung my eyes. "What am I supposed to do?"

Denver rubbed his hands up and down my back. "I have an idea. Will you come with me?"

"Of course." I sniffled.

"Okay, let's go."

I pulled back enough to meet his gaze, before pressing my lips to his. "Thank you for finding me, for helping me remember myself. I love you, Denver."

"You helped me find myself too. I think that's what a relationship is meant to be. When one can't see the way, the other will help light the path."

"Light the way, love."

We drove for a couple of hours, mostly in silence, until I insisted he play his music. Denver told me he felt weird listening to his songs being played, but I needed them to wash over me. I would have gone through with it if he hadn't stopped me. Would I have been able to live with my conscience if I'd hurt any people there? I'd stopped Denver's attackers that first night, and had no problem harming them, but I'd been defending *him*. If I had gone into that factory, I would have been the attacker. Not some do-gooder, some vigilante.

I would have been the villain. That wasn't who I wanted to be. Even as a ruler, I wouldn't have wanted to attack first. Words could be weapons for both bad *and* good, and I would like to think I would use the skills I learned in negotiating and debating before those of weaponry and fighting.

The road Denver took followed the coast, the salty air calling to me, making me long to walk out into the water and dive through the waves. I would be returning to the sea all too soon though and never coming back. I wasn't quite ready yet to let her draw me in.

Denver turned onto a small road where I heard the distinct sound of sea lions barking. Their tones were concerning; pain, fear, worn. What was this place? A wooden sign on the side of the road said "Sea Lion and Marine Mammal Rescue."

"What are we doing here?"

"Ella has a few friends that do a lot of ocean clean-up, like when we were on the beach picking up trash that day you first came ashore. One of them works here. They answer calls for endangered marine mammals. Mostly seals and sea lions that get tangled up in fishing gear, or get injured, or pups that get stranded and are suffering from malnutrition or dehydration. When they can, they rehabilitate them and release them back to the wild. And when they are too weak or sick to live safely at sea, they stay here where they are cared for and used for education programs."

"This is great. I didn't know there was something like this."

"You've been watching the wrong news, Call. Yes, there is bad shit happening, and there are things that can be done about it, though change can take a long time. But there are also really good things happening too and ways to help that feel more tangible and less like you are taking on the whole world."

It did feel like I was taking on the whole world. Two worlds actually. Above and below. I focused on the cries of the animals, fighting against the weight of my thoughts that threatened to bury me.

"Can we go in?"

"Yes. I was already planning on bringing you here and got Ella to put me in touch with her friend. Come on."

He led me by the hand and we were greeted and given a tour. There was a group of people working with the pups in the nursery, others were training and playing in a pool of water. I longed to jump in there and swim with the sea lion that was regaining its strength with a half-eaten flipper. My own tail itching and prickling beneath my skin. When we came to the veterinary clinic, a pup was in severe distress, making my discomfort pale in comparison. It was recently brought in and they were preparing to sedate it so they could do a full assessment. I listened as it cried for its mother, lost, hurt, afraid. It tore at my heart.

I walked right up to the table, between the

doctors, much to the confusion of the medical staff. Someone asked me to step back but Denver told them to give me a minute. I couldn't heal the little one, that wasn't something I was capable of, but I might be able to help. I canted to it. Though the sound was different above water, it understood all the same. With a whistle and hum, it looked at me and paused. I continued canting as I stroked its head, rubbing the spot right above its nose and between its eyes. The sea lion pup relaxed, no longer thrashing. I could feel its heartbeat regulate, even as it still reacted to the pain it was in. He pushed his head up into my hand, seeking the comfort I gave him.

I could feel all eyes on me, wondering what I did. I gave no answers to the questions they surely had, instead saying, "Alright, he's ready. You can administer your medicine and continue your exam. He's injured, but not too badly. It's more that he's scared and misses his mother than anything."

The pup kept his nose pressed into my hand until the sedatives coursed through him and his head drooped back to the table. I stepped away, giving them room to work, happy that I was able to help him. Maybe it wasn't taking down an evil corporation, but at this moment, what I did made a difference. Even if it was to one small scared sea lion pup, it made a difference.

"That was incredible," Denver whispered to me as we walked out of the clinic. My head was swirling in a new and different way. No longer stuck on the urgent need to start a battle, but satisfied with what I'd done, wondering what else might be possible.

"Excuse me!" Jo, Ella's friend called out.

I turned to face her, "Yes?"

I could feel her eyes scanning over me, trying to work out what or who I was. "How did you do that? What did you do exactly? I've never seen someone be able to calm an animal like that."

The truth sat on the tip of my tongue. That I sang the song that belonged to all beings within the sea. I longed to share myself and speak freely, but after the reminder Denver had given me about exposing myself and my kingdom, I knew I couldn't.

"I grew up on a small island. We have a very close relationship with the creatures that shared our home."

"That was truly amazing. I would love to learn how to do that. It makes such a big difference when treating animals if they aren't in distress. Do you have an interest in animal rescue?"

"Yes, you could say that."

"We're always glad to have volunteers and someone with your unique skill set would be a huge asset to us."

"I admit, I will be returning home soon. But I would love to come again before I have to leave."

"You are welcome any time."

She shook my hand and returned to check on the pup. I stood at the entrance to the facility, feeling a sense of peace and purpose. So much different than how I felt outside of Cal Chem, fueled by anger and negativity. Too bad it came so close to when I'd be leaving. To think I could have spent a year rescuing marine mammals instead of slinging coffee. My gaze slid sideways to see Denver staring at me. But if I had, I wouldn't have met him. If only I had more time, with him, with the rescue, on land. There were so many possibilities I hadn't known to look for before, only now I wouldn't have a chance to do anything about it.

"Thank you, Denver. This was truly special."

"*You* are special. You are capable of doing so many amazing things, I am in awe of you."

"The same goes for you. You have the gift of your music. Now, we need to get you back, so you can work on getting everything ready for the festival. But thank you for stopping me from doing something I would regret and showing me a better way."

CHAPTER 25

DENVER

One week. It hung over us both like the pendulum in the pit. Closer and closer with each swing, watching the end draw near. It swung so closely now, it whispered over our skin as it passed by. As much as I tried not to dwell, it brought up a lot of feelings from the end of my dad's life. Knowing it would come to an end soon, hoping to hang on longer. It was heavy and somber. It felt ridiculous that I should compare Calder leaving with the death of my father. But it was there all the same.

I was at his house where I'd spent the afternoon playing my new songs for him. The ones I would debut at the festival. And when I was done, he made love to me so tenderly, I nearly burst with the emotions building up within me. It was as though he were capturing every moment, every touch, every kiss, every inch of my body to keep for when we could no longer be together. We were both quiet when we were done, clinging to each other as if we couldn't bear to be apart for even a second of the limited time we had left.

After some time, Calder shifted in bed, agitated, his body tense. I understood it too. The deadline that we had on our relationship pressed in so heavily that it made it hard to simply be in the moment together.

"My head is too loud right now. I'm going to soak in the tub for a bit. Is that okay?"

"Of course, Call. Whatever you need."

I stayed in his bed, staring up at the ceiling, listening to the water fill in the tub. The splash he made when he sank into it, the thwap of his tail unfurling, the sigh that came with the release of it. Sounds that I had become accustomed to. Like the sizzling of a pan, the brewing of coffee, the rustling of sheets, the squeak of the floorboard, Shadow meowing. All part of the music of our life together. Without the sounds of him occupying the space I was in, it would soon feel a lot more hollow.

I couldn't stay in bed either. I walked to the bathroom door and stood against its frame, admiring him in all of his beauty. His dark blue iridescent tail that shimmered with any light that hit it. His muscular frame that held me so easily. His lustrous red hair that flowed around his submerged face. His eyes were closed, his gills moved on occasion. He was a breathtaking sight. The wonder of him would never cease. I wished that I could capture him like this. Hmm. I went and grabbed my phone, came back, and snapped a picture. I stared at it for a while before locking it behind a password so no one would accidentally stumble on it. That picture wasn't for anyone else, only me.

Calder broke through the surface and flicked his eyes to me. "Enjoying the view?"

"As a matter of fact, yes. Very much." I smiled, trying to push past the heavy thoughts that had been plaguing me.

"Are you alright, love?"

"My head is too loud too."

He reached his hand out over the side of the tub. I crossed the room and placed mine in it. He tugged enough to tip me over the side of the tub, until I was laying on top of him, my legs on either side of his tail, not caring about the water that splashed over the side. I slid over until I was halfway off him, tucked into his side. Calder dipped below the surface again and I couldn't help but stare at him with admiration. How had such a wonderful being chosen me?

I held my breath and laid my head on his chest, my mouth and nose underwater, one ear sticking out. Beneath, the water muffled everything, except our hearts that beat in tandem echoing through the tub. Above, the world beyond the two of us seemed so big and overwhelming. But here, in the tub, there was a peace that settled between us. I understood why he needed to rest in water, the way it made everything feel and sound different. It was like a weighted blanket that pressed down, giving the right amount of security and calm.

Calder canted soft and lyrical, a whisper compared to the times he sang to me in the bay. My heart filled with warmth and affection. Even if I couldn't understand it, I knew he was telling me how much he loved me. I melted against him as long as I could. When I couldn't hold my breath any longer, I pushed myself up, leaning my head against the side of the tub. Calder stroked my arm, another gesture that made me feel how much he needed me and my presence. We stayed in that tub—me above, him below—until my skin turned pruny and I started to shiver. I dipped my head beneath, kissed his soft lips, and told him to stay.

If my body were equipped to remain in water as his was, I would have gladly stayed suspended with him forever. Reluctantly, I got out. Instead of grabbing a towel, I went to the bed and pulled the blanket off, wrapping it around myself. It was warmer, but it also smelled like us, like him. And I needed to be infused with it. In a blanket burrito, I wandered around his small place, memorizing every little touch.

Pausing in front of the tank on top of his dresser and the small shelf above, I grabbed the pegasus toy and held it in my hand. The reverence that Calder had for such a simple thing made it feel as if I held the world's most priceless object. I traced her wings with my finger as he had, before putting her back with the other two toys.

My eyes drifted down to the kelp bag kept in the tank. In all the times I had stared at it there, I longed to touch it. I didn't know why it compelled me. It was nothing more than seaweed, but still, it was a strange thing. I reached into the cool water and poked it, yanking my hand back quickly. I half expected it to turn into a creature and bite my finger. I laughed at myself for being so ridiculous as I stared at the greenish-brown sea leaves sewn together. The stirring in the tank I had caused by my quick movement made a flap fall open.

I angled my head trying to see what it looked like inside. There was something within. I dipped my hand into the tank once more, carefully reaching into the bag. My fingers touched something thin and wavy. It was a paper of sorts with some kind of writing on it. I pulled it out to get a closer look. Strange scrolling letters were imprinted on the organic material. Why hadn't Calder told me about this?

I squinted, trying to make sense of the unusual script. The more I stared, the more it started to come into focus, shifting into something I could understand.

By Proclamation of King Vasa of the Pacificus Kingdom. Safe passage is requested for his son, Prince Calder.

Besides his teasing remarks about being a prince, it was easy to forget that he held such a high position. Seeing it written out was surreal. He genuinely was a royal in a kingdom beneath the sea.

Calder, heir to the Pacificus Kingdom and

betrothed to Prince Taneesh, son of King Katal of the Indico Kingdom. Any harm that comes to him will be met by the full force of both kingdoms.

My heart lodged itself in my throat as I read that word over and over. Betrothed. Betrothed? Betrothed! I gripped the strange paper in my hand tightly, as my vision swam. Perhaps I read it wrong, perhaps my mind was filling in words when it was challenging to read. It couldn't possibly be right.

"What are you doing?" Calder called from across the room. I had been so focused, I didn't even hear him get out of the tub.

I faced him, holding the proclamation in my hand. He blanched. The only time he had looked that pale was when he was recovering from oil sickness.

"What is this?" My words came out sharper than I intended.

Calder crossed the room, stopping a few feet away. "I can explain. It's not what you think."

"It says you're betrothed. Does that mean the same thing it does up here?"

"I, well...yes." Calder's head dropped.

"Then how the fuck is that not what I should be thinking? All this time, every second we've spent together and you are engaged?!"

I didn't trust my knees not to buckle as the weight of it pushed in on me. I stumbled backward until I felt the edge of the bed behind me and sat down.

"Please, Denver. It's not...I." He shook his head, not getting any actual words or explanation out.

"Are you going to tell me that it's not true? That you're not engaged?"

He came over and slumped down to the floor in front of me, sitting naked, his eyes cast down. "I wish that I could, but I can't."

"So this whole thing with me was what? A fling? An affair? Have you been cheating on your...prince with me?"

Calder looked up at me, tears floating in his filmy eyes. "It's not that at all. I wasn't given a choice. It's an arrangement that was made between our fathers, to unite our people. It's a political move, not one born of feelings or affection. I haven't even seen him in years."

"That doesn't change the fact that you're supposed to be getting married."

Calder reached out for me but I leaned away from his touch. The devastation I saw in him nearly had me closing the gap between us, but I couldn't.

"When my parents told me, I lost it. They married for love and I foolishly hoped that I would get to do the same. But they need this partnership with Katal. Our kingdoms have spent too much time fighting each other but we need harmony instead of the division that has been there for too long. They told me there is no other way. The king demands a marriage to show our kingdoms as a united front. I didn't want it. I still don't. The only thing I could think of was to ask to come ashore and seek out ways to help our kingdom."

"And when you return, you're not just returning to your duties as a prince?"

"No. We are to wed. It is set."

"And you never thought to tell me this?" Anger, hurt, betrayal, and confusion swirled around inside me.

"I couldn't. I didn't want it to poison our time together. I never intended to fall in love while above, but I did. You gave me the one thing I always hoped I would have and now I have to leave it behind and return to a fate I don't want. I wish there was a way out of it. Denver, you mean so much to me. I wish I could stay with you forever. You're all I want. But I can't see it. I can't see how I can change the minds of kings that have been made up."

Calder wrapped his arms around my legs and

pressed his cheek against my knee. I should push him away. It would be the logical response to the duplicitous life we'd lived these last few months. But they had been the greatest months of my life and Calder was clearly broken over it. He was a prince, as confirmed by the scroll in my hand, and yet he groveled at my feet, desperate and broken and my heart ached for him as much as it did for me.

"This is a lot. I don't know what I'm supposed to do." I mumbled, even as I ran my fingers through his long hair. He lied to me. Maybe not outright, but he withheld information I should have known. What would I have done if he told me at the beginning that he was engaged? Even if it was an arrangement. He told me we had no future. He told me he had to leave, he had...responsibilities. I never pried or demanded to know more about what that entailed. Would he have told me if I asked him? How many times had I seen him looking pensive and lost? Was he thinking about his future husband? My stomach soured at the thought. The only husband I wanted to see him with was me. *Fuck!*

He sat back and stared up at me, his face wore a lifetime of emotions that far exceeded his twenty-four years. "I don't know what to do either. I've dreaded returning since the day I left. And having you in my life made that even harder. But I am not a free man, Denver. I don't get to choose. But you have given me memories that are precious and beautiful and I will never forget them. You are a part of me, your song is etched into my heart."

I stood up and paced the room, overwhelmed and overcome. We had a week left. I could have been happy finishing out our week blissfully unaware of what exactly he was returning to. I couldn't unlearn what I'd learned though. I didn't doubt Calder's feelings for me. Just as he was always able to read me, his affection for me was a second skin he wore, visible for all to see. But I couldn't go back to pretending I wasn't the other man.

My clothes were in a pile beside the bed from when we undressed the night before and he worshiped my body. Without thinking, I started getting dressed. Calder cleared his throat as if he were trying to dislodge a lump in it. With all my clothes mostly in place, I grabbed my wallet, keys, guitar case, and hat. Numbly, I glanced around the room, trying to see if anything else of mine was there. I wouldn't be coming back here ever again. The thought burned behind my eyes and roiled in my belly.

Calder crossed the room and before I could pull away, he wrapped his arms around me. As much as I wanted to fight it, I needed to be enveloped by him one last time. I sunk into him, my cheek pressed against his neck. Breathing in his scent, feeling his body, feeling his love one last time.

"I love you, Denver. That was never a lie. If I could choose, I would choose you. You are the partner I've always wanted, that I've always dreamed to have." I felt a tear drop against my cheek as his body shuddered against mine.

I wanted that too. I wanted him to pick me. A year ago, I wouldn't have been able to imagine being ready to marry, but with Calder, he became my home. A future with him was something I could easily envision. Except it wasn't written in the cards.

"I love you too, Calder. I wish you all the best with your...husband." The last word came out with a sob. I pulled out of his embrace and left before I lost the will to do so.

CHAPTER 26

CALDER

With Denver gone, my life on land felt empty and meaningless. There was a hole, a big gaping, pork pie hat hole. I threw my toys into the bag along with that cursed note and prepared to return to the sea. I technically had a few days left, but what was the point?

The only thing that stopped me was the poster for the Legacy and Lore Festival. Denver brought it over, before our fallout, excited to show his name in the line-up. The festival. It was his dream. At least one of us should get to have one and I was glad it was him.

A text came the next day from a number I didn't know. Which didn't mean much, I only had a couple programmed in.

Unknown: What the fuck did you do to him?

If I had to guess...

Me: Ella?

Unknown: Damn right it is. Denver is devastated, you fucked with my friend. And the worst thing is he won't talk to me about it.

Me: I'm sorry. Truly. I have to return home in a couple days, and I don't think I will be able to come back. It's something we always knew would be coming.

We would have had to end anyway. It would have been so much harder to leave him if we were both still in our perfect love bubble. Maybe it was better this way. Maybe he could hate me and move on. The thought of him hating me was the worst pain I'd ever felt, but if it meant he didn't stay stuck pining for what we could never be. It was for the best.

Ella: That's bullshit.

I sighed deeply. It *was* bullshit, and it wasn't at the same time. Denver was free where I never would be.

Me: Can you do me a favor?

Ella: I don't owe you shit.

Me: No. You don't. But I know you care about Denver. Promise you won't let him stop playing and singing. He was made for it and the world needs his music.

Ella: That's a promise I CAN make. But it's for him. Not for you.

That was all I could hope for. At least I knew Denver had a friend like her in his life. He deserved the loyalty she gave him. He deserved...everything. I only wished I could have been the one to give it to him.

With my lone bag, I left all my earthly belongings behind. Including the phone. I left the first house I had of my own. The first kitchen where I learned to cook for myself. The first human bed I'd ever slept in, swathed in the smells of Denver and me. That was the hardest thing to leave. His scent infused into my daily life. A scent that would be washed away when I returned to the sea.

With a heavy heart and leaden steps, my two legs harder to move than ever before, I left my life. I'd said my goodbyes at the Beanwater already. Lee wished me well and told me I had a place with them if I ever was able to return. Friends, a job, a home, a life I never would have thought to have a year ago. I didn't expect to become attached to it.

I took the bus one last time, watching the interactions of the people on board. Observing all the little things that humans did without even thinking about them. The way they touched their hair, crossed their legs, smiled at strangers. Our histories taught us to fear and hate them. That they were our enemy, at war with the ocean. But now I knew that it wasn't the whole of humanity, but a few.

I wouldn't miss the noise that accompanied civilization, or the way my vision was affected, but I would miss it. I wasn't returning the same prince I left. This year on land changed me. Denver changed me.

It was dark when I got to the beach which was perfect for my needs. I looked around and when I was sure no one watched, I stripped out of my clothes, leaving only the speedo I once found in the ocean and wore when I came ashore. With my bag on my back and naked except for the small swimsuit, I walked out into the sea. The touch of briny water brought about a mixture of emotions like never before. The pull to shift, the rightness of being where I belonged, except it felt wrong for the first time in my life.

I swam out past the waves, the water washing over me as my body burned with the need to let my tail out. When I was deep enough and far enough away from the shore, I removed the swimsuit. I tucked it into my bag in case I needed it, and I called my tail free at last. I pumped my fluke, driving me through the water, the ocean carrying away the tears that fell from my eyes.

Home beckoned me, but going back made it final. If I had one day of freedom left, I would use it. I changed directions and headed south. I pushed hard, harder than I needed to, letting the burn in my muscles cover up the throes in my chest. I followed the coast, avoiding boats along the way. When I sensed I had gone the right distance, I turned inland, heading to shore. It was a much bigger port and busier area. I had to pull my tail back much sooner than I would have liked, for fear of being seen. With the swimsuit in place once more, I began the treacherous swim to land with music wafting over the water. It was the compass that guided me.

It grew louder the closer I got. Too loud without my headphones, but I didn't care. Beyond the sandy beach was the festival. Stages, screens, speakers, and thousands of people filled the place. I was exhausted, having pushed my legs too much, but I still pressed forward, slogging my way through the sand. I got as close as I could without a ticket to enter. It was enough. I could see the stage through foggy eyes.

A strum of guitar almost made me drop to my knees. I knew that guitar. I knew the sound as if it had been made for me as much as him. He sang and I basked in the sound of him. His voice flowed over the crowd, amplified by speakers, louder, bolder, stronger than ever. It hit me with such an impact, it could have knocked the whole earth off its axis.

Denver was beautiful. Doing what he was meant to be doing made him more beautiful than ever. And when the song finished I had to cover my ears with the ferocity of the cheers from the crowd. I smiled wistfully. They loved him. They loved the man whose heart sang to mine. They loved him and he would be okay. He would get through this and live a beautiful life, following his dreams and hopefully finding a new love someday. As much as it pained me to think of him with someone else, I wanted him to be happy more than anything.

My skin tingled and my heart raced. I felt him. As if for that one moment Denver saw me, connected with me across the spans of people. I heard it in the slight skip of a note he knew in his sleep. I canted one last time, quiet and shallow in the air. I doubted it would reach him, but it didn't matter. *My heart will always be yours.*

CHAPTER 27

CALDER

I was spotted by a guard who lowered his head at the sight of me, while his partner zipped towards the palace to deliver the news of my return. I swam past him with little acknowledgement. I didn't intend to be cold but I wasn't myself. The closer I got, the more my thoughts ran wild. As I neared the center of the kingdom, merfolk filled the area waving and cheering. It was all I could do to plaster on a forced smile as I swam by.

My eyes stayed locked on the path ahead of me. The lights of the palace a stark contrast to the surrounding areas. How strange that the place I was raised should feel foreign to me. The murmuring cants of merfolk hit my ears so much differently than the chattering clientele at the Beanwater. I kept my head high as I pressed forward to the awaiting king and queen. I had to push past the slight hitch in my movement. My parents. My brother and sister waited at their sides.

It was good to see them. All of them. My family had been what I missed most while I was gone. Coral looked more mature, her body developing into that of an adult female's. Marin wore two braids of copper hair that framed his face. His shoulders seemed broader, his chin more square. A whole year. I'd missed so much with them. What would they see when they looked at me? Did I appear different?

My mother looked as beautiful as ever, her bronze skin glimmered, her yellow hair that flowed around her face, the crown of pearls that was woven into it. She beamed as she looked at me. And for that brief moment, I allowed myself to feel joy at being reunited. My father's red hair which was much like mine had grayed considerably since I left. Far more silver streaks than red now. I lowered myself before him.

Prince Calder, your kingdom welcomes your return. My father canted loud and strong, his voice filling the entire region, and cheers erupted.

A swish of my fluke had me rising to nearly his height. To go higher than him in front of an audience would be a sign of disrespect. I'd spent a year not having to dwell on such fine details like where and how I held myself.

We shall host a party in celebration along with our friends and allies from the Indico Kingdom.

I stiffened at that. What did that mean exactly? Was this happening already? I had barely returned and I was to be served up to my...betrothed?

My mother must have seen something in my expression, her lips pressed into a flat line. A look I was all too familiar with. It meant there would be further discussion in private. But here, before the beings in our care, we needed to act with discretion and not betray our position. I dipped my head in understanding.

After the official statements and welcomes, I followed my family into the palace, where the doors were closed behind us. It offered some privacy, muffling the sound, though we still needed to speak carefully.

As soon as we no longer had witnesses, I was tackled by my siblings who laughed and squeezed me. I felt a smile stretch across my face for the first time since Denver left.

You've gotten so big, Coral. You've turned into a beautiful young female. She beamed and did a twirl for me, her salmon blonde hair flowing around her.

Marin whacked me with his fluke, hard enough to sting. I held my hands up. *What the hell kind of greeting is that?*

That's for being gone and passing the diplomatic duties onto me. I swear if I have to sit through one more meeting about krill counts I'm going to lose it.

I smirked at that. I knew he didn't mind it. He'd been pestering our parents for a while, trying to convince them he was ready to take on more responsibility.

Calder. The cant from my mother was stern. I'd have to finish catching up with my brother and sister later. I swam up to them, lowering my head. I didn't know what to expect; an interrogation, a lecture, a warning. Finding myself sandwiched between the king and queen in a tight embrace was the last thing I imagined.

It's good to have you back, son. We missed you greatly. My father's soft song in my ear made my heart lighten.

They released me from their hold, putting space

between us. My mother scanned over my body, swimming around me. *Are you well? Did you encounter any trouble? You look a little peaked. Are you sick?*

Heartsick perhaps, though there was no cure for that. *I'm just really tired, it's been a long trip.*

Right. Of course. My father said with his hands behind his back. *I expect you to fill us in on what you discovered being among the humans. But that will come in time. Get some rest. We have a party tomorrow.*

About this party? I asked.

My mother gave a barely noticeable shake of her head. *It cannot be changed and you* will *be there. Your engagement will be announced with you and Taneesh side by side.*

Why so fast? Can't I have some time to myself before I am named as his fiance?

You've had a year! My father bit out. *I believe that was more than generous.*

My heart dropped like a stone heavy enough to drag me down into the depths.

We will discuss this further after *the party.* My father's tone conveyed finality. Conversation over. So they wouldn't tell me more until *after* I was officially engaged. Fuck!

Dismissed, I wove through the palace, attempting

to be cordial with the beings I passed as I made my way to my room. The room was bigger than the house I rented and yet it felt confining, closing in on me.

I took my bag off and set it on a shelf rock, the sand-filled toys weighing it down, and collapsed against the spongy seabed that hugged around my body, helping me feel weightless and cozy, unlike the hard, unmoving beds above.

My eyes burned and my head pounded. All that time away didn't change a damn thing, merely delayed the inevitable. The only thing I gained was knowing love and being loved. At least I had that once in my life. Not everyone was lucky enough to have that soul-deep connection I felt with Denver. I wished I could call him or text him, but there were no phones down here. No way to communicate. Though it was probably better that way. If I was able to hear his voice it would be a lot harder to face my impending marriage.

The water whooshed with the opening and closing of my door. I didn't bother to look, I knew who it was. I could feel him. Marin laid down beside me, head resting on his folded arms as mine was. *Are you alright?*

I blew a breath out of my mouth, a habit from

being on land. Bubbles floated above me. *If I'm being honest...not really.*

What's it like up there?

Mostly it's loud.

Marin snickered before turning more serious. *Did something happen to you? Did they...hurt you?*

No. It's nothing like that. It was surprising. I met some good people. It's just a big adjustment coming back, especially with everything happening.

Marin turned on his side to face me. *It might not be so bad. The king and prince have been here for a few days. I've bumped into Taneesh a couple of times. He seems a little withdrawn perhaps, but he was nice. Besides, he's easy on the eyes.*

I cocked a brow. I'd heard many of his exploits with females over the years but never heard him talk in such a way about males. *Is that so?*

Marin shrugged, not adding anything to the statement, his response to the topic similar to the one he gave a year ago. He turned it back to me. *What are the men like up there? Are they good lovers? Did you meet anyone?*

Yes. I met someone.

"What are you moping around for? You had a killer set at a huge music festival. You're already getting calls. This is your moment, Dennie. Your dreams are coming true."

I knew Ella was trying to be supportive but I couldn't pull myself out of it. "He was there."

"What?"

"Calder was at the festival. I'm sure I saw him outside the perimeter."

"Sweetie, there were thousands of people there. You probably saw some random person with red hair. Our minds can easily trick us into seeing people we love."

I shook my head. "It was him. I could sense it. I could feel his stare on me."

"Everyone was staring at you, Den. Because you were on stage, playing your heart out. But let's say it was him. Does that change anything?"

I slumped in the office chair. "No. I suppose not. We still can't be together."

"Why not?"

"It's...complicated."

"Well, uncomplicate things. If this guy is really your soulmate, you can make the long-distance thing work. It sucks, but it's doable."

"He's unreachable."

"That's bullshit. In this day and age, there is nowhere on the planet that is unreachable. So maybe you can't call him, you could go old school and send letters. It'll be a great story to tell your future grandkids."

God, I wanted that with him. A future, a family, whatever that might look like. And yet, he would have that with someone else. Everything hurt. It would almost be easier if he wanted his marriage. It would hurt like a mother fucker, but I could get over it. But knowing he came and saw me play, knowing he dreaded what he faced, knowing the depths of what he felt for me. It was excruciating. We were torn apart by the vastly different worlds we lived in. And I was alone in it. Nobody could know. I glanced at Ella. My friend, the only family I had left. I trusted her with my life.

"I'm not sure they have delivery service to the bottom of the Pacific Ocean."

Ella tilted her head. "Melodramatic much?"

"It's where he lives."

"At the bottom...of the ocean? What does that even mean?"

"Listen, Ella. I'm going to tell you something and it's going to sound outrageous, but I swear it's true. And I need your promise that it will never go anywhere. You can't tell anyone. Ever."

"Okay, one; that's hurtful that you would even suggest I might share a secret. And two; this sounds juicy, I am so here for it."

"I trust you, El. That's why I'm going to tell you. It's not my secret to tell, but I just need someone to talk about it with. The only person I could have is gone now."

Her expression softened as she put a hand on my arm. "Whatever it is, you can talk to me."

I bit my lip and bobbed my head slowly. "Calder

is...not exactly human."

"Okay. *Not* what I was expecting you to say. What does that mean...exactly?"

I looked around, despite knowing it was only the two of us in the office. We'd already closed the shop for the day and I had been trying and failing at finishing the end-of-day paperwork, my ability to focus was crap.

"He's a merman."

Ella snorted. "Okay. Funny. Is this some sort of weird bit?"

"I'm serious, Ella. He's returned to his home in the sea."

"Den, sweetie. You know I love you, but you don't buy that do you? I mean I've heard some lines, but that takes the cake. He just wanted you to feel better about him ditching you."

I sighed deeply. "It's not a line. He is what I said. I've seen him in his real form and he is the most beautiful being I've ever known. He sang to me underwater. It was magical."

"Wait. Are you being serious right now?"

"Completely."

Ella got up and paced around the small room. "There's no such thing. It's not real."

I pulled out my phone and went to my hidden photos. I held my breath as I put the pin in. When the photo of him in the tub popped up, I nearly choked on emotion as I stared at him. Such a beautiful, serene moment. And it all went to hell after.

I handed the phone over to Ella. She stared at it, mouth agape. "That...that's not real. That's one of those tails people buy to cosplay mermaids."

"It's real. I know every inch of him, with legs or with tail. *That* is who he really is."

She sank back down into the chair. "Holy shit!"

"I know, it's a lot."

"He's a fish!"

"He's not. He is a beautiful person who happens to have a tail and gills sometimes."

"Sure, no big deal."

"When I say I'll never meet another man like him, I mean it." How could anyone compare to Calder? I was ruined for anyone the future might hold. I might find someone I could be happy with, but it would never be the same.

"I don't even know what to say. You fell in love with a merman? An actual, real-life legendary creature?"

"Yeah."

"And now he's gone back to his home in the ocean?"

"Yeah." I rested my head on my hands.

"And you're sure he feels the same way that you do?"

"Without a doubt." As much as it had been terrible to find out he lied to me, I knew he didn't lie about the way he felt, he couldn't. It was written into his every touch and glance.

"Soooo, what are you going to do about it?" Ella asked if it was the simplest question in the world.

"There's nothing I can do. He has...obligations."

'Well, fuck that!"

I scruffed my hand through my hair. "There's. Nothing. I. Can. Do." I repeated slowly. "We're from two different worlds, I have to learn to live with that."

"Like hell you do. WWPED?"

I cocked my head, trying to decipher the acronym."What is that supposed to mean?"

"What Would Prince Eric Do?"

"Prince Eric?"

"Yes. He didn't sit on land and mope about his lost fish girl love, he dove into the sea to go after her."

"But...I can't do that."

"Can't you?"

I stood up as I flashed back to a moment, sitting in a chair covered with an afghan, the scent of mothballs around me. I sat there and promised the old widow that I would follow my heart, wherever and to whomever it might lead. Maybe she hadn't thought it would be a merman, hell...neither did I. But that promise, I meant it, even if I wasn't feeling it yet. I never forgot that moment with Mrs. Chibalski.

Could I really do it? I didn't know where he was, but he'd told me about the islands nearby. That the locals knew of them. Maybe. Maybe I could. But would it make any difference? He was to be wed. I couldn't do anything about that. What if I could simply hold him and kiss him one more time?

"I have to go."

"Yeah, you do."

I hugged Ella. "Thank you."

Coral wove my crown into my hair. She gave me a sad smile as she placed a necklace of shells over my head. *You look very handsome, Calder.*

I dipped my head with a simple, *Thank you, Coral.* I didn't have anything else to offer.

Each second that had passed since returning, loomed heavier and heavier. A day felt like a hundred, while at the same time passing all too quickly. I avoided everyone as much as I could, but I was no longer able to do so. Tonight, everything would change. I wouldn't be my own being anymore. I would belong to Taneesh. Except for my heart. He didn't get to have that.

Marin came into my room, he was adorned in his crown, as was my sister. This was to be a presentation, a show of force and authority. He gave me a wistful look. *Mother says it's time.*

Right. The beginning of the end. My siblings shored up next to me, one on either side.

It's going to be alright. If there's anything I could do, I would. But at least know that we are with you. Marin canted softly. His tone carried a hurt that nearly equaled my own. I wasn't sure if it was empathy or if there was something else bothering him. I had been too blinded by my own whirlpool of despair to give him the attention he needed. I was so fucking selfish. I looped my arms through both of theirs and tried to sound more confident than I felt.

Thank you both. I'm lucky to have you. Let's do this.

We swam together to the large hall where the party was being held. The three of us approached our parents who were seated on their thrones and bowed, honoring them, before taking our places at their sides. Me to my father's left, Marin beside me, and Coral on my mother's side.

Each guest that traveled from different kingdoms was introduced. As much as I despised the fact that they would all be here to lay witness to our engagement, I appreciated that each new being that arrived prolonged the announcement. Until King Katal swam in, his six daughters behind him. He bowed before my father and when his head lifted, my father greeted him with a strong handshake. The princesses took their place behind him as they all waited for their brother's entrance. My heart beat rapidly and my stomach churned.

The steward at the entrance announced Prince Taneesh. He swam in, head held high. He had a deep purple tail, rich bronze skin, and medium-length black hair that floated above his shoulders. Taneesh had a short, full beard that made him appear older than his twenty-seven years. He swam to us, dipping and greeting my parents before his attention turned to me. Taneesh reached his hand out and I shook it, doing my best to force a smile.

His expression resembled my own. A reminder that he was as much a pawn in this as I was. It seemed neither of us wanted this marriage. Strangely, I found that comforting. I didn't miss the way his eyes slid to my brother's quickly before darting back to mine, or the way his vibration changed when he did so. Interesting.

It's a pleasure to see you again, Prince Calder.

As it is you, Prince Taneesh.

He lowered his head before taking his place at his father's side. My father declared the beginning of our meal. They would hold off making an announcement until after everyone had food in their bellies. News was always received better when beings weren't hungry. Of course, it was only difficult news for me. And perhaps Taneesh. While it might be hard for those that lost loved ones in past battles against Indico, this marriage would also bring hope that it wouldn't happen again.

I attempted to be cordial with any that wished to start a conversation with me. Mostly they wanted to know about humans and my time on land. But I couldn't cant about it more than vague responses, claiming the need to reacclimate. It hurt too much to think of anything above because Denver was woven into every part of it. Even the silkiness of fresh fish that I craved while on land, now soured on my tongue. I couldn't enjoy the food I loved. It was tainted with the future that hung over me like a prison sentence.

My father canted a single note, loud and strong, that resonated through the entire hall. All other noise ceased, except for my heart which seemed to beat wildly out of control, making me wonder if everyone in the hall could hear it.

This was it. This was the moment. He was going to make the announcement. Would I leave immediately? Would I be expected to return with Katal and Taneesh, or would I stay until the actual wedding? How long would that be? A million questions fired rapidly through my mind. I should have asked, but I hadn't wanted to talk about it. I suddenly regretted not getting every bit of information I could.

CALDER! My heart stopped completely. That hadn't come from anyone here. A cant that called to me and hit me square in the chest. Denver. And he was in trouble. I pushed up from where I was sitting, not caring that all eyes were on me.

Prince Calder. The stern tone rang out from my mother.

Please excuse me, but I have to go. I swam for the entrance. My father shot across the room, reaching me before I could leave.

In as hushed a tone as was possible when the sea carried our sound, he canted sharply, *What are you doing? You can't leave.*

I'm sorry, but I have to. Someone I care for is in

danger.

That is unfortunate, but your duty is here.

Marin swam over, eyes bouncing between our father and me, assessing how he could help.

I promise I will do whatever you want without complaint if you let me leave now.

Or I could have you detained, My father whispered, making almost no sound at all. *I will not have you disobey me.*

Detain me, fine. But let me do this first. He is...my heartsong. I have to help him. I cut him a look that said I would never forgive him if he didn't let me go.

Marin gasped, his eyes went wide. Even my father seemed shaken by my confession. A heartsong was something taken seriously. They were rare and special, a bond that connected two hearts.

Marin grabbed the king's arm. *It's his heartsong, Father. Let him go.*

My father appeared torn between his roles as father and king. But I could see that shift in his eyes, and king won out, it always would. *I can't.*

I think I have a solution, one that will satisfy everyone, Marin canted with confidence.

Our father stared at him for a moment, aware of the hall full of beings that were watching everything that passed. A slight nod was all I needed before I left. I looked back over my shoulder at Marin with silent thanks as I pumped my fluke up and down as hard as I could, following the invisible tether that pulled me.

I could feel his fear. It filled me. The vibrations of it crawled beneath my skin. *I'm coming, Denver.* I pushed the words out as hard as I could, hoping he would sense it, even if he didn't understand it.

Where was he? Close, so close. What was he doing out here? A shadow cast over me. A big one. I knew the sound and the shape of the beast that made it. A Great White. Wishing I had a spear or a knife, I pushed forward. It was circling something. No, someone. And not just anyone. Denver was in diving gear and I could hear the hiss of the oxygen tank, could hear his rapid, panicked breaths.

"Calder!" He cried out again.

I dug deep into strength I didn't know I had and drove as hard and as fast as I could into the underside of the shark before it could turn towards me. It bellowed when I hit it in that odd voice sharks had and recoiled. Before it had time to recoup, I swam to Calder. He screamed in his face mask when I popped up in front of him before relief flashed in his eyes.

I'm here, love. I'm here.

He reached out and grabbed my shoulder with one hand but scratched at the collar on his suit with the other, his breathing still frantic.

"It...hit my...tank, I think...it knocked...something loose. I can't...seem to...get a...full breath."

I leaned in close, pressing my forehead against his mask. *I've got you, Denver. But I need you to relax. Can you do that for me?*

He seemed to understand what I needed him to do and tried to slow his breathing, but I could hear the difficulty he was having. I had to act fast. I swam around him, examining the tank. I had seen a few abandoned ones over the years, but never thought to study them up close. There were a few different gauges, one that had a line that was leaning to the red. Red was never good. I checked the main hose that connected to the mask, it wasn't sitting right. I finagled it, trying to get it back on tightly, but it was no use. It wasn't going to work.

Denver was shaking, his breathing becoming more erratic. I didn't have time to fix the oxygen tank. I swam back around him to face him. *I can't do it, Denver.* I pointed at his face covering and motioned out. *I'm going to have to take your mask off.*

His eyes went wide as his head moved rapidly from side to side.

Love. It's me. Remember, there is nothing that can harm you in the water when you're with me. I poured as much love, strength, and confidence into my song as I could, hoping he would comprehend it.

Denver lifted his hand and I held it in mine, squeezing his fingers through the gloves. "Okay."

It had three straps cinched tight, one over the top and two that wrapped around the sides of his head. I loosened the straps until I could wiggle it free. Denver grabbed my arm, clenching tightly to me, trying not to give way to the panic that threatened to take over. Once it was off him, I brushed my thumb across his cheek and leaned in. With my mouth covering his, I breathed into him. When I felt him relax and the terror subside, I pulled away.

He was so beautiful. I could get lost in those green eyes. To see him again, really see him, was more than I could have ever hoped for. He was the brine of the sea after a chemical-filled pool. Reviving. Life-giving. Home. Denver smiled, but then his eyes went wide and he shouted, expelling all of the air I had given him. I turned around to see the shark that I hit heading straight for us. I faced Denver once more, giving him the kiss of life until I knew his lungs were as full as they could be.

Don't try to help. Your only job is to hold your breath. I motioned for him to stay there. I pecked a quick kiss on his cheek before facing the very pissed-off shark. Apparently, he wasn't too keen on my sneak attack earlier. I charged him, trying to put as much distance between him and Denver as possible.

I didn't have any weapons or assistance. Normally, if a shark was terrorizing an area where it endangered merfolk, a team of hunters would respond. The goal was always to try to coax or herd a shark to a new feeding ground. But sometimes they were stubborn beasts and we couldn't allow them to stay where it put beings at risk. I was unarmed and alone, but I had something worth fighting for.

I knew its weak points, I only had to avoid the bone-crushing teeth and his powerful tail. He snapped its jaws at me and I dodged and swirled around him. I canted a command for it to stop with all the royal authority I held, but it was far past the point of listening, fueled by anger. It left me no choice, I had to act. I did what I had to do, stunning it, not killing it. To kill it would be a waste with no hunters to collect the body and return the meat to be shared. But it was enough to give me the time I needed to get Denver away.

Swimming back to Denver, I immediately grasped his face and breathed for him again. While I held him, I pushed with my tail at an upward angle. I knew I couldn't take him up too fast or the pressure change would make him sick.

When we paused, I explained it to him. He seemed to grasp what was happening as he wrapped his arms around me, holding on, trusting me. We continued that way for a while. A breath, a swim, a stop, a breath. Hopping our way towards the surface. When we broke it, at last, he gulped in the fresh air. Denver fell against me, smashing his mouth to mine. A real kiss, not merely an exchange. His tongue parted my lips and I met it gratefully. I didn't think I would ever get to feel him in my arms or taste him on my lips again.

"You came for me!" Denver cried out when he pulled back at last.

"Of course, I did. I told you I would hear you no matter what. We're connected, you and I. What are you doing here?"

"I'm sorry, I was trying to be brave and do something heroic. Like crashing into the church to stop the wedding. I wanted to save you. Instead, you had to rescue me. I guess I'm not great at the whole hero thing."

I brushed his silky black hair away from his eyes. "You are my bravest, beautiful boy." He smiled as I used the phrasing his father had. "You faced open water by yourself, and with a shark no less, something I know that terrifies you. And you did that all for me. You are amazing. And you *did* save me. Though, I might have preferred the perfectly-timed interruption not be because you were in danger."

"Interruption?"

"My father was about to announce the engagement when I heard you."

Denver continued to hold me as I swam us to the nearest shore. His hand played in my hair. I missed that. All those little touches. More than words could say. In the ten days we'd been apart, I felt hollow and empty. Having him here with me, I felt whole again.

"What does that mean? Is it over? Would they simply announce it when you get back?"

"I am not entirely sure. There may be some difficult conversations ahead, but I won't lose you again."

I promised my father I would do whatever he

wanted, but now that I had Denver in my arms, I couldn't possibly return to Taneesh.

"I love you, Calder. I just had to find you to tell you that one last time. I hate how things ended. I was hurt and felt betrayed, but I understand why you didn't tell me."

A wave rolled, crashing feet ahead of us. We were nearly there. "Not a minute has passed that you haven't occupied my mind and my heart. I was fooling myself to believe that I could have lived a life without you."

Crash. The power of the wave loosened Denver's grip on me, but I held him tight. I was never letting him go again. When it was shallow enough for him to touch, he walked, slogging his heavy gear. His hand slid down my arm and found mine, our fingers twined together. I called my tail back and walked the beach with him until he flopped down in the sand. Denver unzipped his vest and removed all of his equipment until all that was left was the full suit that covered his body. As soon as he was free, he pushed me until I was laying back in the sand and fell on top of me. His hand lifted the shell necklace on my chest, examining it.

The weight of him on me felt so right. I would have been happier still if he didn't have the rubber suit on. Denver kissed me again. We devoured each other. All the time spent apart thinking we would never have this again consumed us both. I had so many emotions raging through me, I nearly broke under it all. As it was, my eyes burned with tears that fought to fall.

"I can't believe you're here. How did you even find me?" I asked.

"Well, you found me, actually."

"But you were close." Miles away, but in the whole of the world, that was close enough.

"Some internet sleuthing and a lot of luck." Denver grinned.

I shook my head. "No. I don't think it was luck. You may not be mer, but this bond we have goes both ways."

He thought it over for a moment, "I think you might be right. Do you know I sensed you at the festival? Ella thought I was crazy when I told her."

"I know. I felt it the moment you connected with me."

"Unreal," Denver whispered with awe. His eyes flicked up to the top of my head. "Your crown. Wow. I didn't think you could get more beautiful. All that talk of hearing you're a prince, it was still hard to fathom. But you in that crown that seems to have been birthed by the sea, made specifically for you, and with your necklace, you look exactly like what I would imagine a sea prince to be."

Earlier, I hated wearing it, the way it seemed to press down on me with the weight of the future, but now with Denver looking at me the way he did, I wanted to show him that the crown woven into my hair bowed to him. I would give him the whole of my kingdom if it meant I could have him by my side. I kissed him again, our mouths so fused together, there was no him or me, only us.

A splash sounded in the water beyond us. I pushed Denver off and leapt up, ready to take action. When I recognized the signature, I relaxed, though my vision was blurry and I couldn't see her clearly.

"Mother?"

"Mother?" Denver repeated in a surprised tone.

"Son, I wish to speak with you, but I would prefer to do so with a little more decorum."

I looked down, realizing I was naked, half hard. It wasn't unusual to see each other fully, it happened often when you shifted and were left bare. But aroused was not the state I wanted to be in when talking with my mother. Though her appearance was like ice to the heat Denver created. I sat back down on the shore—

not ready or willing to go in the water with her until I knew what she was up to—and commanded my tail. Denver stood behind me, his hands on my shoulders. His touch grounded me, a comforting reminder that he was with me.

"What do you want, mother?"

"No introductions first? Really, I thought I taught you to have better manners."

"Denver, this is Queen Asherah of the Pacificus Kingdom, my mother. This is Denver. The man I love with all that I am and I won't let you take me from him."

My mother tsked her tongue as she closed the distance between us. She sat on the shore where the water kissed the sand and brushed against her tail. "It's a pleasure to meet you, Denver. Though I do wish it were under better circumstances. Calder, you need to return with me."

I scooted myself backward on the sand, shaking my head. "No. I can't"

"I'm sorry I didn't take time to listen to you. I could see that you were distraught when you returned, but I didn't seek to understand why, too focused on the plans being made. There has been a development since you swam off. Son, you need to be a part of it."

"Excuse me, uh...Your Majesty?" Denver stepped out from behind me to stand beside me. He reached his hand down and I held it in mine.

"Yes, Denver?"

"If it helps to know, I love your son very much. He came into my life at a time when I was lost and he helped me find my way. Calder has a beautiful heart and he sees the best in me and supports me. Your son is safe with me. I will never hurt him or your people, your kingdom. I can't offer you anything but my promise. I understand his position and his duties to you, but he also told me that you and the king have a great love. And what we have is great too. More than great. Wouldn't you want that for him?"

My chest swelled with pride at Denver fighting on my behalf. The kind of fighting he did best, with his heart. I kissed the back of his hand.

"I applaud the passionate speech. It does warm a mother's heart to know her son is well-loved. I have always wished for such a thing for all of my children, though we are not always granted what we wish. Not when we have the lives of so many others at stake. It can't all be dreams and heartsongs."

The swelling in my chest popped like a balloon. That didn't sound good. Denver's appeal fell on deaf ears. She would not hear of it. What could I do? If I shifted, we could run. But then how far would we get? It was a small island and there would be nowhere in the ocean that we could hide.

"I know what you're thinking, Son. Relax. As I said, there's been a change in plans. One that I think you will be happy with. Come with me and when the night is done, you can return to your Denver."

"Wait. What are you saying?"

"I, Queen Asherah, solemnly swear that by the time the moon touches the water, you will be free to return to your human companion."

A royal oath? That was a promise that could never be broken. I tilted my head up to Denver, who met me with a worried expression. "It's alright, love. I'll be back. She gave her vow."

He knelt beside me and held my face in his hands. "You better, or I'll come after you, though I'd really rather not encounter that shark again."

I smiled broadly and kissed him. "Wait for me?"

"Always."

CHAPTER 30

DENVER

I sat there on the shore of a foreign island. I used to wonder if I would ever make it out of Bayview Park, if I would be able to see the world. And now, I not only left California but traveled over the seas and under it. Far beyond what I ever imagined I would do.

I'd spent a lot of time watching the water of the bay while Calder swam. I did the same thing now except it wasn't the same at all. The sounds were different, the smells were different. It was a world long from home, and yet, my heart soared with how close I was to Calder. Was it possible that we could leave this place together? At the bay, I never had to wonder, it was him and me and the moonlight. Here, there was so much unknown, even if his mother promised his return. I had a hard time believing this was all real.

It had taken a lot of bartering to convince a fisherman to take me out on a boat and drop me in the water. It was insane. Truly insane. I stupidly thought that if I could swim deep enough, I would find the mer kingdom. I'd gotten comfortable in the water with Calder back home in our isolated bubble, but it made me forget what the ocean was like. That there was no bottom beneath me, no arms holding me, it was just me, alone, in the middle of the black sea. I was no Prince Eric. I was an idiot in scuba gear with no one in sight. I had no exit plan if this went wrong, and it did. Horribly wrong.

But then he came and he saved me, he fought a shark for me. I replayed the whole encounter in my head. It was like a movie I was watching of someone else. It didn't feel real. This wasn't my life. I was a quiet person who ran a small family store and played guitar as a way to speak what I couldn't say. Who somehow had a dream come true and here I was, caught in another one.

Every splash of a fish, swoop of a bird, and crash of a wave, had me looking for red hair breaking the surface. The sun began to sink in the sky and I waited.

Darkness started to choke out the sun's rays. And with no city lights, the moon and the stars were the only illumination. A noise in the water had me jumping. I couldn't see it, but I stood on my feet, just in case.

"Calder, is that you?" I whispered into the night, feeling slightly crazy. It was like that moment in a horror film when the person walks through a dark house and asks *who's there.*

"I'm here, love."

My heart leapt and so did I, running and splashing into the water, following his voice. I felt a brush against my leg and I would have squealed had I not known every wisp or flick of his tail. I fell to my knees and grabbed him, squeezing him to my chest. His arms wrapped around me and he kissed my head.

"What happened? Is everything alright?"

"Everything is wonderful." I felt that pulse of energy that always accompanied his shift.

"So...what does that mean? Are you free of the engagement?"

"I am." He said. I squeaked when he grabbed the back of my legs, scooping me up in his arms. I wrapped my arms around his neck as he carried me ashore like I weighed nothing. I would never grow tired of the way it felt to be in his strong arms. I took him in, noticing the lack of crown, though the necklace remained. I ran my finger over the smooth shells, loving the way it looked on him and how it felt.

"But how? I thought the kings were set on a union."

"They are and they are getting one. When I left to come find you, my brother got to work. He offered to take my place."

"But won't that mean he'll be stuck like you would have been? You don't want that for him."

"No. If he were going to be miserable, no I wouldn't. It would kill me to leave you, but I would hate myself if I thought he would suffer under this arrangement. The prince seemed eager to agree to the change of partners and my brother didn't seem to despair at the idea either. I'm realizing there are things I didn't take the time to notice in Marin. But, I think maybe they'll be okay."

"So, just like that, you're free?" I almost choked on the words. It seemed too good to be true, I needed to hear him confirm it.

"There are some stipulations, ones that I am comfortable with, but yes, love. I'm free."

Calder lowered me to the soft sand and started working the zipper of my wet suit. When the sun had been shining, I wore the top down around my waist, but since it had turned to night, I wore it for warmth. A predatory look gleamed in Calder's unique eyes, one I greatly preferred to the look of an angry shark. With his hands working the rubber suit off of me, I didn't feel the cool night air. I could have been standing in the center of the sun for how hot I felt.

"All I want right now is to touch every inch of your body, knowing that it is mine."

I lifted my ass as he worked the suit down my body, peeling it off my legs. "I'm yours, Calder."

"And I'm yours too, Denver. Forever. Nothing is going to separate us again." He knelt between my legs, pushing them aside, and leaned down over me. His smooth, hard skin on mine. Calder kissed me, our tongues dancing together as he rolled his hips into me. Our hands roamed over each other with desperation, as if it were our first time. Only it wasn't, the map of our bodies was ingrained into our souls. We lay there, naked, on a beach, on an island in the middle of the Pacific Ocean, and explored the memorized terrain. The moon was a witness to our love, both then and now, our cries of release accompanied by the song of the sea.

EPILOGUE

DENVER

I sat on a rock beside the pool, watching him swim gracefully through the salt water. Even a year later, I never grew tired of the sight of him. Somedays I pinched myself, trying to make sure I wasn't dreaming. On other days, I marveled at the beautiful, mundane, everyday life we got to live together.

We returned home soon after that whole shark ordeal. Calder moved in with me and Shadow. He hadn't expected to return to land and the house he'd been renting was lent to new tenants. But after that short time apart, we knew it would be ridiculous to live separately. Shadow was happy with the arrangement too, especially when Calder did as he said and brought him a fresh fish of his own. The horror on Calder's face had been comical at the sight of Shadow attacking the smelt. I kissed him and promised not to let Shadow turn on him.

Calder was tasked with a new role by his parents as part of the arrangement to let him return to land. He'd been given the title of Human Ambassador. He told his parents of the progress he'd seen and the compassionate people that were fighting for a change, while also noting there was still a lot of work to be done. Calder was to return to the sea and report to his parents quarterly, an open line to the human world. No longer cut off and ignorant of what was happening above, trying to counter the misinformation that fed prejudices. He was more than happy with those responsibilities if it meant we could stay together and he could go home without fear. I hoped to be able to go with him someday to see his home but it would take time and some specialized equipment to reach the depths of their kingdom.

Between continuing to pursue his education for the sake of learning how to fight the politicians and corporations, he kept himself busy volunteering. Calder loved working with the marine mammal rescue. Even though they likely had their suspicions about him and what he was able to do, they didn't question it because of the clear, positive impact he made on the animals in their care.

When we returned from that trip to the Pacific, one I wasn't sure I would make it back from, I had several messages waiting for me with gigs lined up. I began playing more regularly until I was given the offer to sign with Legacy & Lore. I was a little overwhelmed when it happened, it was a big mix of emotions. Grief had a way of sneaking up on me at random times. I knew my dad would have been proud of me, I only wished he could have been there to see it. But Calder was. He was always with me.

With his encouragement, I took the offer and handed the keys of Greene Family Hardware to Ella. My dad loved her and between the two of us, she was far more knowledgeable than I was anyway. I knew I could trust her to care for the shop and its customers the way my father would have. I couldn't bring myself to get rid of the "& Son" sign my dad made, but it no longer haunted me. It now lived above my workshop in the garage, hanging proudly. His dream had a home within mine.

When my music started making real money, Calder and I found a house that was set off by itself.

No nosy neighbors to look over our fence or noise flooding Calder's sensitive ears. We had a saltwater pool built with a grotto feature, a cavern set beneath a rocky structure. We'd even had shelves added, where he kept his toys. A little piece of home.

I sat at the edge of the pool, one foot dangling in the water, the other on the cement, my bent knee propping my guitar up. Calder swam over and popped up in front of me, resting his chin on his hands on my knee. He stared up at me, that beautiful, wet, red hair draped around him.

"Play something for me?"

"Hmm...I have a song for you. It's new, so you'll have to let me know what you think."

"I love it already."

I smiled. "That's cheating, you have to hear it first."

"It could be death metal, but if it came from your lips, it would be angels singing."

I couldn't help it, not when he said things like that. I leaned down and kissed him, before sitting up once more. I strummed. Down, down, down, up, down, up. I sang a song about a man who walked out of the sea and into my heart. A man who would forever be the one who held it in his hands. A man I would call my friend, my lover, my soulmate, and if he let me, my husband.

Calder pushed himself higher out of the water until he was eye-level with me, his tail holding him in place. "Do you mean it?"

I set my guitar and hat aside and scooted closer to the edge of the pool. Placing my legs on either side of him, I grabbed his hips—the part I loved—where flesh met scale. "Will you be my husband? It will be your choice this time, no one will force you. I'm perfectly happy with how we are, but..."

Calder wrapped his arms around me and pulled me backwards, a surprised laugh popped out of me as I flopped into the water with him. He kissed me underwater and canted, singing a rhythmic song with one note that pulsed on repeat. I knew enough to feel its meaning. *Yes, yes, yes.*

I sat at the edge of the pool, one foot dangling in the water, the other on the cement, my bent knee propping my guitar up. Calder swam over and popped up in front of me, resting his chin on his hands on my knee.

Thank you for reading *Song of the Sea*—if you enjoyed it, please consider leaving a review.

WANT TO KNOW MORE ABOUT MARIN?

Here's a bonus scene to find out!

MARIN

My blood stirred within me at that quick glance. The same glance I'd caught from him the few times our families had gotten together. I wanted to hate him, to hate my brother, to hate this whole fucked up situation, but I couldn't. Mostly, I just felt sorry for myself.

I was only a year younger than Calder, and yet he was the one who got all the recognition as the eldest. I loved him dearly, I looked up to him, spent half my life wanting to *be* him, but also lived in his shadow. I was always second. Second best, second thought. He was bigger, stronger, and everything my parents hoped he would be. That was...until he flipped out over the announcement of the arranged marriage between him and Taneesh.

Sigh. Taneesh. He matched my brother in stature

and that deep purple tail and long, silky tendrils on his fluke caught my eye more times than I cared to admit. When I heard the news that they were to wed, my heart sank into my belly. *Of course!* It was one more thing Calder would have that I wouldn't. I tried to be supportive, I had no reason to not be. As close as we were, I'd never told my brother that I was attracted to males as well as females. I had only lain with females. But that was because when I thought of being with a male, only one came to mind. And it would never happen.

I missed Calder while he was gone, but a selfish part of me felt relief in his absence. For the first time, I was being trusted with responsibilities that had only been given to him before. I was no longer unseen. I worked harder than ever to prove myself, knowing my time in the forefront would come to an end when Calder returned home. Though if he had to go to Taneesh's kingdom, maybe my parents would know that I would be ready to take his place.

It was a mix of emotions when he returned. I was so happy to have my best friend back. A year was a long time without the closest being in my life. But with his return, I was cast into the background once more. Everything shifted toward the presentation and making the engagement official. Something was off about him though. Calder was forlorn and quiet. He wasn't the same brother that left. As much as I loathed the situation, I didn't like seeing him hurting. The sorrowful vibrations that rolled out of him when he told me he met someone on land. It was clear that he was using every effort to hold himself together.

The night of the party came and we all went through the motions, supportive, encouraging, all while tension flowed in a current around us. Everything would be official. My dream would be over and I would have to let the idea of him go. And Calder, well...he would too.

The greeting between them was half-hearted, the effort on both sides seemed immense. That glance when he looked past Calder over to me. *Fuck!* Was I imagining interest or had it really shone in his nearly black eyes? Did it matter at this point? Before long, he and my brother would be bound together forever. A very public declaration that they were promised to each other.

Each second that passed hung heavily. I scarcely ate more than Calder as he picked at his food. Then something happened and everything changed. Calder shot up and rushed for the door, our father zipping around him to stop him from leaving. I couldn't stay in place, I had to know what was happening and swam over. Each cant between them was hushed, though it carried nonetheless. It wasn't a conversation to be had here in front of the entire kingdom.

He is...my heartsong. I have to help him.

I gasped at the phrase. It wasn't something used lightly. If Calder really found his heartsong, he would be miserable in a life separated from him. That was a bond even greater than vows that would be given for marriage. It was physical and not something you could break.

As much as I blamed Calder for something he had no control over, I couldn't sit by and watch his heart shatter. He was too strong and too big, the brother I worshiped and loved, that it would break me to see him crumble like that.

I grabbed my father's arm. *It's his heartsong, Father. Let him go.*

My father seemed torn between his wishes for his son and his responsibilities to his kingdom. *I can't.*

Everything suddenly fell into place as I realized an answer that could potentially benefit us all. *I think I have a solution,* I canted with confidence.

My father eyed me, the question in his gaze, but

he knew whatever it was could not be discussed with so many ears listening. After a slight nod, Calder left. My mother, ever the level-headed one, announced loudly that our family was going to take a brief recess and encouraged the guests to continue dining and celebrating.

She swam past us, a clear indication for us to follow, even Coral came along. This was to be a family conversation. A lot was riding on the outcome. My nerves were catching up to me. What if it didn't work? What if they disagreed?

We pressed toward the surface, the only truly private place to talk. Once above, my father turned on me with a stern expression.

"What is the meaning of all this? Do you know who this person is that Calder is going after?"

I ground my teeth together. Of course, it was about him! For once, could it just be about me?

"I don't know all the details, but he met someone on land."

"A human?" My mother gasped.

"Not just a human, but you heard him, it's his heartsong."

"Why didn't he tell us?" My father looked far less kingly with the hurt that crossed his eyes.

"Would you have listened if he did?"

They both looked as if they wanted to reply, but didn't. As soon as he returned, everything became focused on the announcement.

"What am I going to tell Katal? We made a vow that I can't go back on. I have to give him a mate for his son." My father's twitching tail churned the water around us.

"I told you...I have a solution."

Both of them stilled and faced me as if seeing me for the first time. Probably were, they could have easily forgotten I was even there with Calder consuming their every thought.

"What can you possibly say to fix this disaster of a situation?"

I rubbed my hand through my hair in exasperation. "I'll do it."

My parents exchanged a look of confusion. "Do what exactly?"

"Marry him. I'll marry Taneesh."

My mother tilted her head, assessing me, while my father gaped at me. He said, "But, Marin, son, you can't marry a male You don't have any interest in them."

"I *can* marry him and I *do* have interest. I just

haven't been as outspoken about it as Calder." What they didn't know is not only *could* I marry him, but it *wanted* to, longed to.

"Are you serious?" My mother asked.

"Completely."

"I don't know about this." My father went back to his tail-swishing, water-churning.

"So you'd rather see Calder in a marriage that would make him miserable and pull him away from his heartsong, possibly causing a rift between you that will never heal, instead of letting me take on the responsibility, one that I am happy to do, by the way, and represent our family?" Fucking ridiculous.

My father grabbed my arm and I half expected a lecture instead, he pulled me into him and wrapped his arms around me. "Thank you, Marin."

When he released me, he faced my mother, whose gaze had softened with affection at the sight of us embracing. "I need to talk to King Katal."

ACKNOWLEDGEMENTS

Besides editing, this is always the hardest part. So much support and encouragement goes into a book that it's a challenge to properly thank everyone who has been there along the way. But I'll try ;)

First of all, biggest thanks goes to my family who have supported me and cheered me on through any writing endeavor, despite the countless hours of me not actively listening while I stared at my computer.

Luke—my Virtual Ass(istant) who also designed the beautiful cover and interior formatting. I don't know where I would be without you. You are an awesome friend (more like family) and I appreciate all of our late night ramblings and how you somehow took all of my crazy and weird ideas and made them into something stunning.

Sheilkuroi—Thank you for the amazing work you do in capturing my characters and bringing them to life.

For my bookish and author friends—Zamma, Joelle, Rye, Mary Ellen, Kota, Kimberly, Ashleigh, Christopher, Natalie, Tricia, Stefka, Lauren, Morgan, my Cruising Crew and my Data Sluts—I love and appreciate all of you and your friendship.

For my ARC and Street Teams—I can confidently say that I have the very best teams, you all rock! Thank you for your time and excitement and for helping me celebrate all the things.

To my amazing readers—Thank you for all the messages, comments, posts, reviews, and for simply enjoying the words I've written. You all keep my passion for writing burning bright, I wouldn't be able to do this without you.

Duckie Mack is the NA/Adult LGBTQ romance pen name for YA LGBTQ author Debbie McQueen. She loves reading and writing stories that show love isn't defined by gender.

She loves adorkable characters, sweet and cute love stories with a little heat, and is a sucker for an HEA.

She lives in Southern California with her family, 2 dogs, and 3 cats, and loves going to pride events to give out free hugs.

Duckie Mack loves to connect with readers, you can email her at authorduckiemack@outlook.com or follow her on social media linktr.ee/authorduckiemack

Other Books

Love Bank Romance Series

All the Stars

Bo Next Door

Love Bites

Keys to My Heart

Standalone

When Awakens the Heart

Chaos Theory

Cruising: An MM Anthology

Duckie also writes as Debbie McQueen

If you love YA Fantasy with a sweet MM romance, a gold-hearted prince, an adorkable dragon shifter, and no hate/negativity for who they love, check out the Dragon King Series

Dragon King Series:

Of Heart and Wings

Bound in Fire

Talons of Love

Scales of Change

Dragon King Legacy Novellas

Breaking the Chains

The Wounds That Bind

SCAN THIS CODE TO LEARN MORE ABOUT DUCKIE MACK ONLINE

Made in the USA
Columbia, SC
06 December 2022